"COME, I WISH TO TALK WITH YOU"

Her eyes widened. "Where?"

"Out here." He propelled her to the balcony and away from the opened French doors.

"Brough, what will people think?"

"I don't care."

"Well I do! I am already caught up in one scandal!"

"It's time we settled this difference between us." He stripped off his coat and put it around her shoulders.

"Now, my dear, may we talk?"

Speechless, she shivered. Snuggling into the garment, she nodded soberly.

Brough looked at her lips so soft and tempting and at the plunging neckline of her delectable dress. He repressed his urge to plunder her mouth very thoroughly and very arousingly. Instead, he brushed his lips against her forehead and drew her gently into his arms ...

Avon Books are available at special quantity discounts for bulk purchases for sales promotions, premiums, fund raising or educational use. Special books, or book excerpts, can also be created to fit specific needs.

For details write or telephone the office of the Director of Special Markets, Avon Books, Dept. FP, 1350 Avenue of the Americas, New York, New York 10019, 1-800-238-0658.

Clarissa

CATHLEEN CLARE

AVON BOOKS ◆ NEW YORK

CLARISSA is an original publication of Avon Books. This work has never before appeared in book form. This work is a novel. Any similarity to actual persons or events is purely coincidental.

AVON BOOKS
A division of
The Hearst Corporation
1350 Avenue of the Americas
New York, New York 10019

Copyright © 1993 by Catherine Toothman
Published by arrangement with the author
Library of Congress Catalog Card Number: 92-97464
ISBN: 0-380-77179-9

First Avon Books Printing: July 1993

AVON TRADEMARK REG. U.S. PAT. OFF. AND IN OTHER COUNTRIES, MARCA REGISTRADA, HECHO EN U.S.A.

Printed in the U. S. A.

RA   10   9   8   7   6   5   4   3   2   1

For my first fans,
Carmeleeta Stewart and Judy Gibbons

1

"JEREMY, HOW COULD you!" Clarissa Dunstan James regarded her younger brother with a mixture of anger and dismay.

"Oh, who would think old Wibberley would take it so seriously? Everybody plays pranks! Only difference is that this one was more elaborate than most." Jeremy Dunstan collapsed into a chair and raised a booted leg to dangle nonchalantly over the arm.

"But a *goose* in the headmaster's *house!*"

"Wasn't easy, I can tell you. We had to do it at night when no one was about. Transporting the thing to the scene was no mean task either. It wouldn't walk like anything normal. Georgie and I had to tie its wings, put it in a bag, and carry it. Then when we let it loose inside, it pecked us and flogged us. It even flew at Georgie and knocked him down! It was a big goose, Clarissa."

His sister suppressed the beginnings of a smile. "How did you get inside?"

"That was simple. We went through a window."

Clarissa slowly shook her head in disbelief. "That was foolish, Jeremy. What if someone had mistaken you for a thief? You could have been shot! And furthermore, I cannot imagine why you

1

would do such a thing when you know how much it strains our finances to keep you in school."

Her brother shrugged his shoulders. "Then so much the better for this. I'm tired of school, Kissy! I don't want to go back. Everyone gets to enjoy London but me, and God knows if we'll ever be able to come again. I just don't see why you and Julia get to have all the fun while I'm stuck with a bunch of musty old books!"

"It is your responsibility to receive a good education. I certainly wish I had a similar opportunity."

He barked with laughter. "Who wants a woman with brains? It's no wonder you haven't caught another husband yet if you go round acting like a bluestocking!"

"I am not looking for another husband," she said severely, "and I am *not* a bluestocking just because I like to keep myself informed."

"But you read such serious stuff, Kissy."

"Fustian, Jeremy! I read the newspaper! And do not call me 'Kissy.' It is a very improper nickname."

He snorted. "We've been calling you that for years."

"That may be, but Julia has managed to stop. Now, do not turn the topic from yourself. I have yet to decide what to do with you. As punishment, I should send you home."

"Kissy . . . Clarissa, you can't! I am sixteen years old and I'm a viscount, for God's sake! You cannot order me about like a child!"

"You *are* a child."

"I am not! Julia's only a year older, and you're trying to catch her a husband."

"It is different with girls." Leaning back, she passed a slim hand across her forehead, feeling the beginnings of a headache throb between her temples. All had been going so well. They were managing on their small hoard of money, and Julia had already attracted an incredible number of admirers. Because of her lack of dowry, the young lady might not make a brilliant match, but surely she would receive at least one good offer. With her little sister married and Jeremy making progress in school, Clarissa would finally have time for herself. Now her brother had ruined her carefully wrought plans.

She gazed thoughtfully at him, wishing that things had been better for them all. It hadn't been easy raising the Dunstan brood. When her mother had died in childbirth, Clarissa had become the young mistress of the house. Her father's death a few years later had firmly established her in that role and had added to it the responsibility of the estate. Poor Jeremy had never really had a man's influence in his life.

In hopes of remedying the Dunstans' situation, Clarissa had accepted the first marriage offer she had received. Captain Mark James, nephew to the vicar, had been kind to her during their short week of marriage. If they'd had more time, they would probably have adjusted well enough to each other and may have been happy together, but he had returned to his regiment and had been killed almost immediately. Clarissa's grief was small. She hadn't known him long enough to form a strong attachment. Unfortunately, probably in the hopes of winning her hand, he had been untruthful about the amount of money he possessed, so she had inherited little from him. With his memory clouded by this falsehood and the demanding necessity to go on as before, there were long periods of time when she even forgot that she had ever been married. When people called her "Mrs. James," she sometimes looked around to see whom it was that they were addressing.

"Kissy?" Jeremy prompted her from her reverie.

"Yes, Jeremy, I'm sorry. My mind is full of so many things of late. And now this . . ."

He had the grace to lower his head and look ashamed. "Please let me stay," Jeremy begged gently. "I can learn a lot right here in London. There are museums and galleries and the opera . . . And perhaps I can be of use to you."

She eyed him warily. He had never cared a fig for anything even mildly educational. Still, she might be able to force him to absorb a small amount of culture, and furthermore, Jeremy under his sister's supervision in London would be preferable to Jeremy running loose in Essex. The boy was uncannily efficient at getting into all sorts of trouble when left to his own devices.

"We cannot afford the opera," she murmured.

"Georgie's family probably has a box that we can use. You see? My contacts might help further your marriage plans for Julia."

"I doubt it. I shall certainly not invite your sister and myself to sit in anyone's opera box! Nor shall I allow you to do it. Who is this 'Georgie' anyway, other than being your partner in crime?"

"His name is Georgie Longwood. Haven't I written about him? He's my very best of friends. You would approve of him, Kissy. He comes from a very good family."

"Who are his parents?"

"They're dead. His brother is the Earl of Abingdon. Do you know him?"

"Good lord, no! I am not acquainted with anyone so grand as that!" she laughed. "I have seen him, though. He was pointed out to me once at a ball."

She had a distinct memory of the handsome, sophisticated earl. He was easily one of the finest-looking men she had ever seen in her life. Moving among the highest circles of the guests present, he had paid little heed to Julia and hadn't even seen Clarissa seated among the chaperons.

"There you have it!" Jeremy cried triumphantly. "I *can* be of use!"

Clarissa shook her head. "You will not badger Lord Abingdon into recognizing us," she adamantly warned, but her mind was twisting with possibilities. With the earl's brother as Jeremy's friend, they just might meet the noble gentleman someday. An acquaintance with him could open more possibilities for Julia. Perhaps even the splendid earl himself? What a prize catch that would be! Julia was very beautiful, and her lack of dowry wouldn't matter to a man as wealthy as Lord Abingdon.

Clarissa made her decision. "You may stay on two conditions. You will mind your manners *and* you will not overspend your allowance. What little bit of money we have must be spent on launching Julia."

"Done! Georgie has plenty of money for what we'll want to do."

"You will not take money from your friend! My goodness, Jeremy, have you no pride?"

"Georgie doesn't care. He often says to me he'd rather foot the whole bill for the both of us than to go along by himself. Damn, I hope he gets to stay in London, too! He has two chances, his brother, Lord Abingdon, and his sister, Lady Westhaven, but he don't like her above half. Too high-nosed and spiteful, he says. She'd probably send him straight to the country. According to Georgie, she cares little for anything but her own consequence."

Clarissa smiled faintly. That was an accurate description of Marie Westhaven, whom Clarissa had met as she was the sponsor of two young ladies in the debutante ranks. The lady's sister-in-law and niece were attractive girls, but they were not the beauties Lady Westhaven puffed them off to be. Julia was much lovelier, and Lady Westhaven knew it. As a result, her thin nose lifted visibly higher in the Dunstans' presence. While she was too conscious of propriety to afford them the cut direct, it was easy to tell that it would have given her the greatest pleasure.

"How is Julia?" her brother asked belatedly.

"She has never been in better looks."

As if to prove the statement, the young lady herself entered the salon. Attired in her beloved petal pink, a color that brought out the roses in her cheeks, and with her bright golden hair framing her face in a riot of curls, Julia Dunstan could be called nothing less than incomparable. The vision was spoiled, however, by the frown with which she greeted her brother.

"What are you doing here? You're supposed to be in school."

"Got expelled." He looked at her mischievously. "So this is the Dunstan entry in the match race? Good enough lines, but can she go the distance?"

Favoring him with a hard look, Julia turned an anxious face to her sister. "Clarissa, surely you are not going to let him stay!"

Clarissa sighed. "Can't you greet each other properly?"

The agitated young lady ignored her statement. "Please do not allow him to remain! He will ruin everything! He has always held me in contempt, and he plays such horrible pranks on me! He should be sent home as punishment!"

"Now, Julia ... Jeremy and I have come to an agreement. He has promised to mind his manners and to be a perfect gentleman. What harm is there in his enjoying a bit of the city?"

The young lady flounced down on the sofa beside Clarissa, her lips forming a practiced pout. "I shall have some rules of my own. First of all, he will not be present when I have callers. Next—"

"Who are you to have rules?" Jeremy cried. "I may only be sixteen years old, but I am the head of this family. I am the Viscount Dunstan, and you are only a silly female!"

"You are not the head of anything," she retorted petulantly. "Clarissa is. You are nothing but a little schoolboy."

"I pity the fool of a man who admires you. I hope that he will see the truth about you before he takes the fatal step."

"Clarissa!" Julia burst into tears.

"Both of you, stop it!" she said firmly, but without raising her voice. "Jeremy, you will not interfere with your sister's gentlemen callers, and, Julia, you will not provoke your brother. Moreover, you will live together in harmony. I have enough on my mind without having to listen to you two brangling with each other! Do I make myself clear?"

"Yes," Jeremy answered grudgingly.

Julia nodded, sniffling miserably into her lace handkerchief and regarding her sister with a tragic, helpless face.

"Well, I certainly shall not introduce her to Lord Abingdon," he said with deadly finality.

"Lord Abingdon?" The young lady lifted curious blue eyes.

"I am his brother's best friend."

"That is enough talk of the earl," Clarissa pronounced with a quelling look at Jeremy. "Let us not raise false hopes. You shall probably never even meet him."

"Oh, I'll meet him, all right," he said with determination. "I'll meet him!"

"Jeremy, there will be no interference in Julia's life."

"I promised, didn't I? I won't interfere! I'll introduce him to you instead. You need a husband, too, and I would delight in seeing you steal him right from under Julia's nose. You're prettier than she is, and a lot more enjoyable to be around!"

She shook her head, rising to her feet. "I have far too much to do to listen to this drivel. Please, Julia, Jeremy, try to get along with each other at least through supper!" With that reminder, she swept from the room.

A number of blocks away from the Dunstans' rented house, Jeremy's friend, Georgie, was standing bravely before his brother, Brougham Longwood, the Earl of Abingdon. "C'mon, Brough, didn't you ever do anything like this?"

"No!" the earl thundered. He glared at his young brother gloweringly, but couldn't help but recall the time that he and his best friend, Brandon Lacey, the Duke of Rackthall, had hired a female of light reputation to waylay the headmaster of their school amidst a crowd of students. The ladybird had spoken quite familiarly with the stiff-necked academician and had clung possessively to his arm, nearly causing a riot. The deed had become legendary, but no one had ever discovered the perpetrators.

Young Georgie winced and eyed his brother sheepishly. "It was just a prank," he muttered.

"Just a prank! You are in school, George, to learn something, not to play pranks!"

"Everybody does it."

"You are not everybody. Now, what am I to do with you? I suppose I'll have to write to the headmaster, or even go there myself, to see if I can get you reinstated. I should turn you over my knee and spank you but good!"

The boy noticed the riding crop lying on his brother's highly polished walnut desk and backed slightly away. "I'm sorry, Brough."

The earl saw the direction of the youth's glance and stifled a grin. He would as soon cut off his own arm as strike his little brother. That was Georgie's trouble. No one had ever properly disciplined him. He had been brought up by servants and allowed to run wild. He wasn't mean, but he was full of mischief, and it was probably too late to do anything about it now. One could only hope that he would outgrow it.

Georgie squared his shoulders and took a deep breath. "Brough?"

"What is it?" he asked irritably, thinking on what kind of influence he could use on the dean.

"I don't want to go back. I'm tired of school. Can't I live here with you?" He gazed hopefully into his brother's hazel eyes. "I can learn a lot from you, and the city itself is educational."

"Great God! I can't raise a young boy!"

"I'm sixteen, remember? I'm not precisely a little boy. Please, Brough, let me stay. At least for a short while? I promise not to be any trouble at all! You'll scarcely know I'm here."

The earl permitted himself a smile. When Georgie wished, he could be very persuasive. Or maybe it was just always so difficult to deny him anything he truly wanted. Perhaps it *would* do the lad good to stay in London for a while. Away from a large flock of boys his own age, he might mature a bit. At least he would be under his and his sister's watchful eyes. His sister! Why hadn't he thought of her?

"Perhaps you could stay with Marie."

"Oh no, sir, please!" Georgie cried. "Not Lady High and Mighty!"

"It would be more suitable."

"Lord, take from me this cup!" the boy wailed dramatically.

"It isn't that bad," Brough laughed. "You would have a womanly influence, and we can still spend time together."

"I don't want a womanly influence. I want you to teach me to be a man! And don't tell me that Sir Jonathan will do that, because he won't suit! He's nothing but a woman in a man's body. Please, Brough!"

"You shouldn't say that about your brother-in-law," the earl chided sternly, though privately agreeing.

"I'm sorry, but that's the way he acts. I don't want to be like Sir Jonathan. I want to be like you! You can show me how."

Brough looked at the earnestly pleading face before him. It was hard not to be flattered by the boy's opinion of him. Perhaps he could teach him some measure of gentlemanly style, manner, and responsibility. He relented. "All right. But there will be a set of rules."

"I'll do anything!" With a vast sigh of relief, Georgie plopped down into a chair. "What are they?"

"I haven't thought of them yet. I didn't anticipate this sort of thing ever happening. But when I do establish them, you will obey them to the letter."

"Agreed!" Georgie looked longingly at the decanter of liquor on the side table. "Shall we have a drink of brandy to seal our bargain?"

"No!"

"Be sporting, Brough. Just this once?"

"No!" Brough ran a hand through his light brown hair. "There will be no brandy! That is the first rule. Do you understand?"

"Yes, sir."

The earl, himself in desperate need of a soothing drink, poured a glass of the spirits and sipped it thoughtfully. "You may have wine with meals and at other times when I permit it."

"Yes, sir. Brough? Do you permit it now? I have had a long trip and then had to face you . . ." He smiled charmingly. "A man should know how to drink."

"All right. Just this once." He rang for a servant. "A glass of Madeira for my brother. One glass only!"

Georgie grinned. "We're going to have a good time together; you'll see. Wait till you meet my friend, Viscount Jeremy Dunstan. You'll like Jeremy. Damn, I hope his sister lets him stay in London, too!"

"You assisted this Dunstan in the goose incident, I believe."

"Oh, it was no more his idea than mine. Jerry and I think alike. I suppose that's why we're best of friends. May I trot over to his house this evening? To see if he's going to be able to stay?"

Brough wondered if Jeremy Dunstan would be the best influence for the wayward George, but he decided that he would not interfere in their friendship. It would be cruel to cut off his brother from his only friend in London. He only hoped that Dunstan's sister would keep a close eye on the boys, but he doubted her efficacy. A woman could have no idea of the kind of mischief that two young lads could embark upon.

"May I, Brough?" Georgie prompted, accepting the glass of wine and sipping it thirstily.

"Not tonight. It's late, George, and we still must have supper. I'll not allow you to thrust yourself upon the Dunstan family at an inopportune time. Tomorrow will be soon enough."

"But Jerry will be wondering . . . and so am I."

"If you're going to stay with me, you will have to obey me. Without debate!" Brough said strongly.

"Yes, sir. Will you be going out tonight?"

The earl eyed him suspiciously. "I was, but I believe I'll stay at home."

"Oh, you needn't do that on my account," Georgie said airily. He leaned forward and regarded his brother intensely. "Were you going to see your mistress?"

"George!"

The young man grinned wickedly. "All unmarried men of your age and status have mistresses, and some of the married ones as well."

"I'm sorry to disappoint you."

"C'mon, Brough, you can tell me."

"That will be enough of that," he said stiffly. "Now, finish your drink. It's time you went up to your room to clean up for supper. You won't dine in your travel dirt."

"Oh, all right." Tossing down the Madeira, Georgie rose and strode across the room, pausing at the door. "Thank you for letting me stay with you. I think we'll get along famously!"

"I hope so, George." The earl shook his head doubtfully. "I really do."

Candlelight flickered in the small dining room, bathing the occupants in a warm glow. Clarissa looked around the table and smiled fondly at her younger brother and sister. How handsome a pair they were, and how closely they resembled each other. Both Julia and Jeremy had inherited their mother's stunning guinea gold hair and her sparkling china blue eyes. With those features, however, all similarity stopped. Jeremy's eyes danced with the mischievousness that was so much a part of his personality, while Julia's revealed the doe-eyed helplessness that she had made a part of hers. Living together in the smaller house with the tension of Julia's Season, it was inevitable that the two would clash. Still, with Jeremy's pursuits with his friend and Julia's occupation with her beaux and parties, Clarissa should be able to keep a modicum of harmony. For her own peace of mind, she would have to.

Julia laid down her fork. "I can't eat another bite, especially with having to bear the sight of his unpleasant table manners."

"What have I done?" Jeremy demanded.

"You wolf your food." She turned to Clarissa. "Besides, it is time that I dress for the rout party. May I be excused? I have no wish for dessert."

"Oh, Julia. I'm so sorry," Clarissa said guiltily. "I entirely forgot that we had an engagement tonight. Let's stay home instead."

"Miss the party?" she asked with shock.

"It will be a sad crush, and this is your brother's first night in town."

"I knew it! Already he is spoiling everything! This is supposed to be my time."

"It is your time. Goodness, we haven't missed an evening out since we came to London! Tonight will be your time as well. I do need to finish fitting and sewing your new ball gown, and I can never seem to find time for sewing things like that during the day."

Julia brightened. "Will it be ready soon?"

"Tomorrow, if I can have this evening to work on it."

"It will be ever so pretty! Yes, Clarissa, I suppose to stay home for once will be preferable to a hot and stuffy rout party."

"Actually," Jeremy mentioned casually, "I had thought of going out myself."

"You?" Julia laughed. "Where would you go? You're just a little boy."

He ignored her and addressed his words to Clarissa. "I thought I might present myself at Abingdon House."

"It's rather late to call, Jeremy," she counseled. "In London one must observe the social niceties."

"Georgie wouldn't care."

"I wasn't thinking about Georgie."

"Do you suppose the earl might actually stay home in the evening?"

"People do not always go out. I wouldn't want anyone to think the Dunstans guilty of a social faux pas."

"Clarissa is right," Julia seconded. "You must follow our lead, Jeremy. You know nothing about such things."

"I don't think the earl would mind either. Georgie says he's a bang-up fellow."

Julia cringed. "Such cant."

"You may visit Georgie tomorrow, Jeremy," Clarissa said crisply. "Tonight we'll all stay at home."

"So I can listen to talk of ball gowns," he grumbled. "What color is it anyway?"

"White," Julia announced knowledgeably. "Young ladies always wear pale-colored ball gowns." Thoughts of the dress eliminated her rancor towards her brother. "Wait till you see it, Jeremy! Clarissa has embroidered the neckline and hem with pink rosebuds. I'll be so pretty! I do hope someone sends me pink rosebuds to wear in my hair."

"They will," he assured her.

She laughed. "How can you be so certain? My beaux do send me flowers often, but I can't just tell a gentleman what kind I'd like him to give me."

"You just did."

"What?"

"I'll buy your pink rosebuds, Ju. You tell me when you want 'em."

"Jeremy!" Her mouth dropped open. "How sweet of you!"

He flushed, returning his attention to his meal. "Family pride," he muttered. "I want my sister to be the prettiest debutante there."

"I'll get the gown immediately so that you may see it! Clarissa, we can begin work as soon as you finish your supper." Julia sprang up from the table and flung her arms around her brother, kissing him soundly on the cheek. "You are a dear!" Hurriedly she skipped from the room.

"That was very kind." Clarissa smiled.

"Hmph! The better she looks, the quicker we're rid of her."

"Is that the real reason?"

"Course it is." He helped himself to seconds and looked up, grinning. "But she *is* pretty, ain't she?"

2

CLARISSA ROSE WITH the sun, despite the fact that she and Julia had been up rather late the night before. Rising early was a habit too ingrained to be uprooted by a taste of London society. Besides that, it gave her the opportunity to assist with the housework before the arrival of the young lady's callers.

The Dunstans had long existed with a skeleton staff, and that had not changed just because they were visiting London. Instead of hiring expensive London servants for the rented house, Clarissa had brought some of their own people from Dunstan Hall. There were Cook and Simmons the butler, both old retainers; the young coachman, who cared for the horses and the rickety carriage, drove the ladies, and doubled as a footman when absolutely necessary; and two maids, who were responsible for cleaning, washing, ironing, helping cook, and assisting their ladies' dressing. Clarissa served as her own housekeeper and pitched in on any chore when needed, which was frequently. Everyone, including the mistress, was overworked, and with the arrival of young Lord Jeremy, there would be more to do.

The servants tried to keep from grumbling.

Cook and Simmons had been loyal to the family for many long years. The younger servants had practically grown up in the service of the Dunstan family. All were familiar with the tight financial situation, but it was a shame that pretty Miss Clarissa (they had never attempted to call her Mrs. James) must do manual labor, especially when Miss Julia lounged in bed for half the morning as though she were a grand lady. They hoped that, in addition to finding a husband for her little sister, their mistress would attract a nice, well-to-do man who wished to marry her. But so far all the gentlemen callers had been for Miss Julia. Miss Clarissa must be hiding herself in the background, for the servants all agreed, she had a much deeper, more arousing beauty than the younger girl.

Her morning toilet completed, Clarissa tripped brightly down the stairs and along the hall to the green baize door that led to the service area. When they had arrived in London she'd given orders that breakfast was not to be served formally in the dining room. Julia took hers from a tray, and to save extra work, Clarissa had her meal in the kitchen at the big scrubbed oak table after the servants had finished. She must remember to inform Jeremy of the procedure.

She entered the kitchen and sniffed the rich smell of hot tea mingled with the aromas of bacon and fresh bread. Cook was at the stove putting the finishing touches on her mistress's repast, while Simmons stood at the window thoughtfully looking out and sipping a cup of the steaming brew. Clarissa paused, appreciating the homeliness of the scene and wishing that their purpose was already accomplished and that she were back at Dunstan Hall.

"Good morning." She smiled cheerfully, sitting down at the table.

"Good morning to you, miss." Cook set her tea and plate before her.

"It has snowed again," Simmons said dourly.

"It won't last much longer. Yesterday I could smell spring in the air!" Hungrily she dipped into her breakfast. "Has someone swept the front stoop?"

"Alice is doing it."

"Good. And Mary?"

"Preparing to wash."

"Then I shall begin my day by tidying the front rooms."

Cook sighed and Simmons scowled. It just wasn't right that the mistress of the house should have to do that. Nor was it right that she should take her breakfast at the kitchen table. It made everyone uncomfortable.

"I know how you feel," Clarissa said softly, "but there is far too much work as it is, and we must keep up appearances for Miss Julia's sake. Besides, I enjoy housework. What on earth would I do if I didn't have work to occupy me?"

Simmons looked as if he were about to comment, but was interrupted by the dining room bell.

"What is that?" Clarissa asked. "Who is in the dining room?"

"I have set a place there for Lord Jeremy." The butler stiffened, waiting for the inevitable response.

"He may eat in here with me. I'll fetch him."

"But, miss, he is the viscount."

"He is also a little boy and he shall eat in here." She left the room and came back with her brother in tow.

"Good morning, Cook, Simmons. Is this a new

arrangement of yours, Kissy?" he inquired good-
naturedly, glancing from her to the embarrassed
servants.

"We have a very small staff, Jeremy. This saves
extra work."

"I don't mind. It's warmer in here, and it
wouldn't be much fun to eat in the dining room
by myself, would it?" He plunged into the large
plate of food that Cook had given him. "Delicious
as usual, Cook. I'm glad you've come to town,
too."

Clarissa finished her breakfast and watched
with dismay as her brother inhaled his food and
began on a second serving. With London prices
being what they were, it was going to be expensive to have Jeremy in the house. His appetite was
enormous.

"I think I'll go over to Georgie's house this
morning to see if he's been allowed to stay."

"It might be more fitting for you to study for a
while first," she reminded him.

"Kissy!"

"I've asked you not to call me that."

"Damn, I'm trying! I can't change my ways
overnight!"

"Don't curse either, young man." She went on
smoothly. "Just because you were expelled and are
to spend some time in London does not mean that
you may neglect your studies. I do not intend to
allow you to fall behind. When the term starts I
wish you to be caught up and ready to begin."

"I'll have to go back?"

"Yes, Jeremy, you will."

He peered at his sister's set expression. "Then
this is just a reprieve."

"If you choose to look at it that way."

The viscount sighed deeply. "Well, perhaps if Georgie stays, he and I can study together."

"I do not believe that would be of any great value."

"Don't you have any sympathy at all?"

"Not where your future is concerned."

"You'd be well advised to see to your own," he muttered.

"That will be enough of that." She stood. "Now I shall be about my business."

Clarissa had begun dusting the salon when Jeremy appeared, schoolbooks in hand.

"This house doesn't have a library," he announced irritably.

"Well, I'm sorry! It was the best I could do under the circumstances."

"I'll wager that Georgie's brother's house has a fine library."

"No doubt. No doubt Lord Abingdon's house has everything, including a wealthy master!" she laughed. "For what money I had available, Jeremy, I was extremely lucky to find something as nice as this." She picked up a delicate china figurine and began to dust it gently.

"Whose house is this?"

"It belongs to an elderly lady who decided, at the last minute, to spend the Season in Italy. She was very particular about whom she rented it to. We passed her inspection."

"Well, I should think so." He gazed around the pleasant room. "I suppose it ain't so bad."

"It is furnished very nicely, and the flowers Julia receives make up for any gaps in decor."

He sat down at a dainty feminine desk and spread out his books. "No flowers for you, Kiss . . . Clarissa?"

"I am Julia's chaperon; I do not receive flowers."

"Then the men in London are fools."

"Study your lessons, Jeremy," she admonished.

He appeared to apply himself for a few moments, then looked up. "Why are you doing maid's work?"

"Because we are shorthanded. Jeremy, study!"

"Yes, ma'am."

She had nearly finished her work downstairs when she heard an arrival in the hall.

"The Honorable Mr. Longwood to see Lord Dunstan," a youthful voice informed Simmons.

So they were to have a visit from Jeremy's young friend. Clarissa hurried to finish, hoping to escape upstairs. Boy or not, she had no desire for a Longwood to see her in her shabby housedress.

"Clarissa?" Jeremy excitedly entered the dining room, followed by a tall, brown-haired youth.

She thrust her dustcloth behind her back.

"Clarissa, this is Georgie. He gets to stay in London, too. What luck!"

"George Longwood, ma'am," the young man drawled. His bow would have been nice enough if he hadn't tried to kiss her hand. In this he was awkward and succeeded only in moistening her fingertips, but he grinned charmingly.

"How do you do." She smiled. "I am Clarissa James."

"So now at last you've met Kissy! Didn't I tell you she was pretty!"

"I have asked you not to call me by that nickname, Jeremy," she said firmly.

"I find it delightful," George Longwood protested, "and yes, Jerry, your sister is indeed a diamond of the first water!"

Clarissa colored. "I thank you for the compliment, Mr. Longwood, but nevertheless, 'Kissy' is not a suitable name for anyone my age, or indeed for anyone beyond the age of ten."

"Oh, don't call him 'Mister'!" Jeremy protested. "Do we have to be so formal?"

"Jerry's right, ma'am. Won't you call me 'Georgie,' as he does?"

"Very well ... Georgie."

"Good! And you may call her 'Clarissa.' ".

"I would be honored, ma'am, if you would permit it." He bowed deeply from the waist.

"Very well," she laughed. "We may as well be on a first-name basis, for I imagine that we'll be seeing each other quite frequently."

"I hope so," Jeremy said, grinning, "since we are the very best of friends. And now, Clarissa, may I go out with Georgie? His brother has lent him his gig and has given us permission to drive about the city. Afterwards he's invited us for luncheon at his club. Then may I spend the night at Georgie's? Lord Abingdon has agreed," he added hopefully.

Clarissa wondered if the earl knew what he was getting into by taking on the responsibility of the two boys all day and all night. Luncheon at his club? What a treat for them! But were Jeremy's clothes good enough for a fashionable men's club? Perhaps if she scrimped even more, she could afford to send him to a tailor. She had never tried to make men's clothes, and if Jeremy was to participate in Longwood society, he must not look like a poor relation.

"All right," she agreed, "but change into proper attire."

"Hooray!" The boys rushed from the room and clattered up the stairs.

When they returned to bid her farewell, Clarissa was impressed by her brother's appearance. He had apparently taken very good care of his

clothes, for they still appeared new and quite stylish. It did not occur to her that he and Georgie
were of the same size.

"Take care, boys; do not get lost in London.
Obey the earl and don't get into trouble!"

"We'll be good," Jeremy promised.

"We won't get lost," Georgie assured her. "I
know my way around London. I've been here before."

She bid them good-bye and returned to her
tasks. At least Jeremy was off her hands for a
while. Lord Abingdon seemed very nice to be willing to entertain the boys all day and night. The
main trouble was that she would have to recipro-
cate, and with her poor means, how was she to
amuse a Longwood? She must think of something.
Perhaps a picnic would be welcome. Jeremy and
his friend might enjoy luncheon al fresco in Rich-
mond Park. Picnic food could be plentiful and yet
inexpensive. But for now she must hurry her work
and be prepared for any morning callers that Julia
might receive. Then there was a ball this evening.
She would do her part with Jeremy, but she must
remember that her little sister was the real reason
that they were in London at all.

"I wonder if he will be here tonight," Julia
mused as their carriage pulled up that evening in
front of the glowing Haversham mansion.

"Who, dear?" Clarissa asked, anxiously straightening a stray curl in the girl's becoming coiffure.

"Lord Abingdon, of course. If he is, Clarissa,
you must introduce yourself and then introduce
me."

"My goodness, I shall do nothing of the sort!"

"Why not? He is Jeremy's host. There is nothing
at all wrong with our meeting him."

"I could not be so forward."

"If it is up to you, we shall never meet him," she whined.

"Not if I have to initiate it myself. Why, Julia, it would be scandalous! You must put all thoughts of my doing so out of your mind."

"He is a prize catch."

"I dislike hearing anyone spoken of in such terms. It makes a person sound like a winning animal at a fair."

"Everyone uses that phrase. Clarissa, you are a stick-in-the-mud." She pouted.

"Oh, I am?" She raised a delicate eyebrow. "You might as well call him a prime 'un."

Julia burst into giggles, restoring her good humor. "He is that! Just think. Wouldn't it be grand if he exhibited an interest in me?"

"Yes it would, but that would not be the case if we put ourselves forward. Forget any such idea. In time perhaps we'll meet him."

"Perhaps," she said thoughtfully, and extended her hand to Gibson, the young coachman, to be assisted from the carriage.

Entering the house and passing through the receiving line, Clarissa relinquished her sister to her group of friends and took her place on the sidelines. Julia was beautiful tonight in the white gown she had made her, her silky blond hair a tumble of curls, ribbons, and rosebuds. She was easily one of the prettiest of the young ladies, and she was popular with many of the girls as well as with the gentlemen. Clarissa was proud of her and thankful that she had been able to arrange this Season for her. If only Julia's temperament were not so difficult at times!

In the shadow of a large potted plant, she watched the first set forming and surveyed the

crowd. The Havershams had attracted the pink of
the ton tonight. It seemed that everyone who was
anyone was in attendance. There were a few new
faces among the guests, but with her quick memory, she recognized most of them even though she
might not have met them formally. Far and away
the most beautiful woman present was the duchess, Allesandra Rackthall, her ebony hair shining
and her neck glittering with emeralds. Clarissa
was not acquainted with her, but knew that she
was the daughter of an impoverished viscount
and that she had married a duke. Julia had been
entranced with the real-life fairy tale and had cast
herself in the same role. Clarissa hoped that her
sister would not be disappointed. Pretty as she
was, Julia did not have the classic, graceful beauty
of such as Her Grace. With her lack of a dowry,
Julia would have to lower her sights.

Clarissa was relieved to see that Lord Abingdon
was not present, and she hoped that he would
stay away. She was uncomfortable with Julia's
suggestion and feared that the flighty girl might
make another attempt at cajoling her into intro-
ducing herself to him. If someone chanced to over-
hear, it would be mortifying. Tomorrow she must
sit the girl down and explain once more the rules
of proper behavior. Julia's society manners were
usually perfect, but in her excitement she might
make a slip.

The dance ended and her sister's escort returned her to Clarissa's side. "My entire card is
filled, except for the waltzes."

"Then you are a success."

"But I have a dilemma! If Lord Abingdon
should arrive and ask me for a dance, I shall have
none left. Couldn't I dance a waltz with him?"

"You could not," Clarissa whispered fervently. "It would be improper!"

"I don't see why." She lifted her nose peevishly. "I shall do it no matter what you say."

"Julia!"

Her escort for the next dance claimed her, and Clarissa was forced to silence. With a coquettish toss of her head, her sister left for the dance floor, leaving Clarissa nearly frantic with concern. This had gone far enough. The young lady had taken leave of her senses. If she persisted, she would have to take her home and lecture her soundly. Above all Clarissa prayed that Lord Abingdon had better things to do with his time than to attend the Haversham ball.

She was not in luck. Several sets later, Lord Abingdon's appearance caused quite a stir. Breathtakingly handsome in his faultless black evening attire, he paused just inside the ballroom door and examined the throng as if searching for someone he knew. He seemed aloof and unapproachable, but Clarissa couldn't keep from admiring him. He was such a fine figure of a man. It was no wonder that Julia threatened to lose her head.

Julia! Quickly she scanned the room, looking for the familiar golden curls. It didn't take long to spot her, for she was dancing quite near to the earl, and apparently, she had seen him, too. Clarissa watched with horror as her sister began to glance flirtatiously over her escort's shoulder.

There was nothing she could do. She couldn't barge onto the dance floor, stop the dance, and drag Julia away. She could only pray that no one would notice.

Luckily, Lord Abingdon seemed not to recognize Julia's foolish behavior. He was looking past her, and apparently he saw who he was looking for and went in the opposite direction.

Clarissa exhaled her pent-up breath. Thank God for small favors! Returning her eyes to her sister, she saw that Julia was irritated and a bit hurt. She felt a moment's pity, which was short-lived, for as soon as the dance had ended, the young lady started off in the earl's direction, her escort trailing behind. Clarissa rose. She must do something now.

Lord Abingdon was standing with none other than the Duke and Duchess of Rackthall and the Marquess and Marchioness of Singleton. Luckily he had his back to Julia, and no one but the duchess noticed Clarissa catching her sister's arm as she made her approach. For a very brief moment the lady's green eyes caught hers and shone with friendly curiosity. It only served to increase Clarissa's shock. She knew! Had she observed Julia all along? Good lord, it could spell their ruin.

"Here I am, Julia. I didn't go for refreshments after all." Taking her sister by surprise, she was neatly able to turn her away without resistance. She smiled at the young lady's escort. "Please excuse us."

It would have become a scene if Julia had jerked away and continued on her errand. The girl knew it. She meekly accompanied her older sister.

"I'm sorry, dear," Clarissa sighed. "I have become so vastly ill with a headache that we must leave."

"Clarissa!"

"I am quite overset. Come, we shall make our farewells."

It was a self-suffering young lady who joined her elder sister in the carriage and started home. "That was the best ball of the Season," she protested irritably.

"You should have thought of that," Clarissa snapped. "I am appalled by your forward behavior."

"I did nothing."

"It was what you were *going* to do. You were going to introduce yourself to Lord Abingdon."

"I was going to inquire after my brother."

"It would do."

"You don't have the headache at all," Julia said querulously.

"No I do not, but I have every right to one. I shall say one more thing and that is all. You know what you did. If you ever again conduct yourself in such a manner, we will go home. I do not mean home to the house in London; I mean home to Dunstan Hall."

Julia knew better than to argue with her sister when she spoke in that firm a tone. Clarissa would do just what she said. Pitifully she lay her head against the meager squabs of the shabby carriage and felt thoroughly sorry for herself.

When Brough saw Allesandra smile past him, he turned to greet whoever was approaching their party. He was surprised to see there was no one. Instead his eye was arrested by the sight of a young lady catching the arm of a younger one, murmuring a few words into her ear, and leading her towards the door. He remembered the little debutante as the chit who'd looked over her partner's shoulder and tried to flirt with him upon his arrival. But it was the older one who now captured his attention. He couldn't place her, and he knew he wouldn't have forgotten ever seeing her previously. She was one of the most strikingly beautiful women he'd ever seen. He turned back to Allesandra.

"Who is that?"

"Who is whom?"

"The lady in the blue silk. You were smiling at her."

"Oh. I caught her eye, so I smiled. I don't know who she is, Brough." She glanced towards the door. "She's very pretty. Do you know who she is, Brandon?" she asked her husband.

"Contrary to your opinion, madam, I am not acquainted with every lovely lady in London."

"Indeed?" she teased.

"Do you know her, Harry?" the Marchioness of Singleton questioned her mate.

"I'll second Brandon's statement, Ellen." He grinned wickedly. "But there was a time when I would have made sure that I became acquainted with her."

"You!" She tapped his arm with her fan.

Allesandra shrugged daintily. "Well, Brough, since the two foremost rakes in England don't know who she is, we'll have to leave it up to you to solve the mystery."

"Rakes!" the duke protested.

"The two of you were just that."

"I'm glad you said 'were.' Harry and I deserve some credit for going through yours and Ellen's taming process."

Brough grinned at his friends' comfortable banter. There was a lot of truth in their teasing. Brandon and Harry had been notorious, particularly in their pursuit of women. Now they were both happily married men in love with their wives. It was strange that those two of their group of friends had gone to the altar first. They'd found their perfect mates in Allesandra and Ellen. He hoped that he would be so lucky.

At times it was difficult not to envy his friends.

They and their ladies had such easy relationships with each other. Each seemed to know what the other wanted or needed and bent to the occasion. They were friends as well as spouses. Their marriages were to be envied.

He looked toward the door, but the lady in blue had vanished. "She's too young to be the chit's mother," he mused.

"Damn, Brough," Brandon interposed. "If you're that interested, ask Lady Haversham."

"Not on your life! I'll do without *that* gossip, thank you."

"Perhaps she'll return," Allesandra suggested.

"He'll still have to ask Lady Haversham for an introduction since none of us know her," Harry remarked.

"I'll see about that when the time comes," Brough said shortly. "Perhaps she doesn't look as attractive up close as she did from a distance." He bowed over Allesandra's hand. "In the meantime, my dear, may I have this dance?"

"I'd be delighted."

Brough escorted his best friend's wife to the dance floor. He glanced at the doorway several times during the set, but the lady in blue did not return. Nor did she appear for the rest of the evening.

3

Bᴜ ᴛʜᴇ ᴛɪᴍᴇ they had reached their London home, Julia had revived her spirits sufficiently enough to confront her sister's displeasure. It wouldn't do for thoughts of returning to Essex to remain in Clarissa's mind. The elder girl was quite capable and just stubborn enough to embark upon such a plan of punishment and to disregard the future. She needed a reminder of how very important it was that they were here, else Julia might find herself wedding a plump old country squire instead of a wealthy and handsome young peer.

Julia fully intended to marry and to marry well. She was weary of their penny pinching, and she hated their shabby country home. Deep in her heart she knew that Clarissa was doing the very best she could, much better than she herself could have managed. *She* could never have stuck to a budget like that, nor could she pitch in and do the amount of work that Clarissa performed. She loved her sister and she respected her. But Clarissa must understand that she, too, had her own ideas on what life should be. She was determined to marry money and a title, and if she must engage in some minor indiscretions to accomplish this, it was what she must do.

Entering the house, she drew Clarissa into the drawing room. "Might we have a cup of tea and some refreshment? It's still early. We missed the supper, you know, and I am famished."

"I am sure that Cook has gone to her room by now. I wouldn't wish to disturb her."

Julia's temper was immediately set on edge. "A servant is a servant. She should be available at any time. I'm certain that Jeremy at Abingdon House could have anything he wished right now, and no one would think a thing of it."

Clarissa sighed. "Julia, I don't know what's come over you. You are familiar with our straightened circumstances. How can you possibly think to compare our establishment with that of Lord Abingdon?"

"Cook should be available! For the same amount of money you could hire a younger cook who would be. And a younger butler, too! Gentlemen ring and ring at the door before Simmons answers."

"May I ask you what would become of them if I hired someone else? Julia, they've been with us forever! And no, I doubt that I could hire a younger cook and butler for the same amount of wages that I pay Cook and Simmons. They work for a mere pittance out of loyalty to this family."

"I'm hungry," she whined. "I scarcely ate anything before going to the ball." Tears gathered in her china blue eyes. "I am frustrated beyond all belief!"

"Would you like to talk about it?"

She nodded unhappily.

Clarissa eyed her warily, unsure of whether Julia was engaging in a fit of dramatics or whether she was truly overset. Sometimes it wasn't easy to tell, and frequently it was a combination of both.

The latter was probably the case tonight. Julia's little scheme of meeting Lord Abingdon had been thwarted, and she had been taken home in disgrace. That in itself was enough to throw her into a performance of martyrdom, let alone if it was accompanied by a threat to return home to Essex.

One never knew, however, for Julia was also capable of being open and forthright. Weary though she might be, Clarissa had never failed to listen to one of her siblings and to give advice when needed. She would hear Julia out.

"Very well then. Let's make our own refreshments."

"Must we have them in the kitchen, Clarissa? Can't we fix a tray and have them in here like civilized people?"

"Certainly, Julia, we shall do just that."

Clarissa left the room, pulling off her gloves as she went. She was surprised to see Simmons lingering in the hall and hoped that he hadn't had his ear to the keyhole. "Please go to bed." She smiled at the old retainer. "Miss Julia and I will be fixing a little bedtime repast before we retire."

"If I might do it for you . . ."

"No, Simmons. I must insist that you go to bed. You have had a long day and you need your rest."

"Thank you, madam."

"You see?" Julia hissed as they entered the kitchen. "He would have done it for us if only you had asked."

"Simmons is a weary old man."

"Perhaps, but if you continue upon your present course, you will be a weary old woman before your time, Clarissa."

Something within her snapped. Clarissa rounded on her sister. "I will have no more of this! I have told you that we are lucky to keep the ser-

vants that we have! Servants do not like to work
for penny-pinching employers. Be grateful and
kind to those who are willing and loyal!" She
plopped down a loaf of bread onto the cutting
board and handed her sister a bread knife. "Get
busy."

Julia hopped. She had gone a bit too far in criticizing the servants and most especially in predict-
ing that her sister would grow old before her time.
That was what had really set Clarissa off. In the
future she would remember that. Obediently she
turned the loaf on its side and began to slice.

While Julia prepared the bread, Clarissa set the
tea water to boil and carved thin slivers of ham
and cheese. Putting the platter onto a tray, she
added a cool crock of fresh butter. Her own appetite rose as she sniffed their meager offerings and
she tried not to think of what delicacies Jeremy
had tasted today.

She had no doubt that Julia was experiencing a
certain jealousy of her brother, but the girl had
many friends and was often entertained in their
homes. Perhaps comparing what they had with
her own home was what had put her on edge.
She hoped that wouldn't happen to Jeremy, for
it was nice that he had someone with whom to
occupy himself. He would be very bored if she
were forced by his dissatisfaction to forbid him
Georgie's company.

Julia placed her sliced bread on the tray and
moved to finish the tea. "This wasn't hard at all.
Alice or Mary could have done it. If Cook is so
old, why can't one of them be available? Also,
why can't Alice stay up to help me undress? Every
time I do so myself, I hear threads popping."

"Must we continue this discussion of servants?
If I had known that this was all you wished to dis-

cuss, I would be in my bed right now. Suffice it to
say, Julia, that all of our servants are overworked.
They need their rest."

"The situation is oversetting to me."

"I'm sorry, but there is nothing I can do about it
outside of helping you myself. I'll be glad to assist
you out of your gown, Julia. I certainly don't wish
it to be torn." She picked up the tray and made
her way to the drawing room, with her sister trailing behind. She set it down on the low tea table
before the hearth, noting that Simmons had built
up the fire before he had retired.

Poor Simmons! He disliked their situation as
much as Julia, or maybe even more. He disap-
proved of his mistress engaging in housework,
and he despised the fact that she and now the
young viscount took their breakfast in the kitchen.
It wasn't proper, but there was no remedy to the
problem. If they were to keep up appearances in
London society, they must engage in these little secrets.

Town life was becoming very tiring for Clarissa.
With housework in the morning, sewing new
things for Julia, and chaperoning the young lady
to the myriad of events, including many late night
affairs, she was feeling her energy flag. The girl's
prophecy of her becoming a weary old woman before her time was frightening. Surely her fatigue
wasn't beginning to show.

She watched her sister daintily pour the tea.
Julia was such a pretty girl. Surely she would
make a good match to someone with enough
wealth to make her comfortable. She had not the
constitution nor the stubborn pride to manage the
kind of difficulties that Clarissa herself faced on a
daily basis. She had been a sickly child and she

had become a delicate young woman. Her strength would give out under such a regimen.

Julia served her and waited until they had fixed their sandwiches before she opened conversation. She drew a deep breath. "Clarissa, I do not believe that you acted fairly at the ball. What harm is there in catching Lord Abingdon's attention?"

"Nothing at all if it is done properly, but you were being forward about it."

"I was merely putting myself in his way."

"Thrusting yourself, more like. You were chasing him."

"Perhaps that is how it looked to you, but I assure you that no one else would have noted it."

Clarissa remembered the look in the Duchess of Rackthall's sparkling green eyes and shook her head. "That isn't true. I think that Her Grace noticed. Oh, Julia, it looked as though you were attempting to join their group!"

The young lady shrugged. "That is only your opinion."

"We were lucky Lord Abingdon had his back to you. If he had seen you, Lord knows what would have happened next."

"I would have curtsied nicely and thanked him for his hospitality to my brother."

"That is ridiculous!" Clarissa snapped. "Lord Abingdon would have seen right through it. He is not like one of your admirers. He is a polished older man, who has probably suffered countless little girls throwing themselves at his head."

"He would have been polite."

"No doubt he would, and then he and his friends would have gone away and laughed about it."

Julia's anger flared, darkening her lovely blue eyes. "Well then, what am I to do?"

"About what?"

"About obtaining an introduction to him. *You* refuse to introduce me, so—"

"How can I introduce you?" Clarissa cried with frustration. "I haven't been introduced to him myself! Believe me, if I had, I would introduce you to him just as quickly as possible. But there is nothing I can do!"

"You and Jeremy could go calling on him," she said smugly.

"Me? Go calling on a bachelor! Have you taken leave of your senses?"

Julia gritted her teeth. Why did her sister refuse to go along with even the simplest of ploys? Since Jeremy would be spending time in George's company, it seemed only reasonable that his guardian should wish to meet those with whom he associated. Clarissa was being completely unreasonable. It was almost as if she wished to foil Julia's plans.

"I fail to see why you can't," she said unyieldingly.

"My reputation would be in shreds if I did such a forward thing!"

"What difference does that make to an old maid?" Julia challenged.

Hurt stabbed Clarissa's breast. For the first time in her life she ached to slap her sister's impertinent face. What was happening to Julia? Despite her tendency to the dramatic, she had always been so sweet and kind. Had her frustrations with their genteel poverty completely overset her mind?

"You could do that for me," the girl went on relentlessly. "After all, since you care so much for Jeremy, shouldn't you wish to make the acquaintance of the people with whom he associates? It seems altogether proper."

"No, Julia," Clarissa stated. "I won't do what

you ask. Have patience. Jeremy and Georgie are good friends. In time we shall probably meet Lord Abingdon."

"I haven't got time! The Season is well under way already."

"So?"

"I intend to marry Lord Abingdon," she announced, "and I need time to bring him up to scratch."

If Clarissa had not been so exasperated, she would have laughed. As it was, there was a long moment before she could trust herself to speak at all. "I don't think that will happen," she said as gently as she could. "He doesn't even notice you."

"Am I not an Incomparable?"

"Yes, dear, you are, but don't waste your time grasping for the moon. You have many fine young gentlemen who admire you. Look among them for a match."

Julia waved an airy hand of dismissal. "They are children."

"Not all of them."

"Well . . ."

"I must caution you that we cannot afford a second Season," Clarissa reminded her. "Do you wish to return to Dunstan Hall without any definite possibilities?"

"Nooo . . ."

"Then mind what I am saying." She rose. "I'm going up to bed, Julia. If you recall, my mornings come very early. You'll tidy up the food?"

"If I must," Julia murmured irritably.

"Thank you."

"I *will* wed a wealthy, handsome peer," Clarissa heard her sister vow as she closed the door behind her. "Just you wait and see."

* * *

Brough Abingdon arrived home late. With the exception of the Mystery Lady, the Haversham ball had little in the way of unmarried and interesting females. As usual, he had spent the evening with his friends and danced with their wives. He had asked few others to take the floor with him. The only laughable note had come from the silly little girl who had made a juvenile attempt to flirt with him. He should have obtained an introduction and asked her to dance with him. From the way she had stared at him with those big moon-calf eyes, it would have been the highlight of her Season. More important, he might have met the beauty who had left the ball with her.

Brough thought of how her rich brown hair with its threading of gold had glistened in the candlelight. He remembered her slim but well-endowed body, with the blue silk of her gown gliding softly over her curves as she walked. She had seemed to move with the controlled grace of a tigress. He would watch for her reappearance. The next time he would not let opportunity escape him. He would obtain an introduction.

He glanced at his timepiece. It was late, but not so late that two excited sixteen-year-old boys would have retired. He decided to check up on them.

"Where are the young men?" he asked the footman in the hall.

"In the library, my lord. Playing chess."

"Thank you." He strolled down the hall and opened the door, peering at an empty room. "Not here, Palmer."

"Sir?" The servant stared at him with bewilderment. He hurried after the earl and looked into the room. "They were here earlier, my lord."

Brough glanced at the half-played game of chess. "Perhaps they grew tired and went to bed."

"No, sir," the footman declared emphatically. "They did not leave this room. I've been in the hall all evening."

The earl raised an eyebrow.

"I have indeed, sir. I didn't leave it for an instant, and I've been wide-awake."

"Hm." As he sauntered around the room, his eyes fell on a partially opened window held up by a small stick. "So! Those little scapegraces! They've flown the damn coop."

"My lord?"

"Look here."

The footman observed nervously. "I'm sorry, Lord Abingdon. I had no idea that—"

"It isn't your fault, Palmer. I didn't hire you to be a baby-sitter. But I am going to teach those two a lesson, and you can help me if you would."

"Of course, my lord."

Brough went to his desk and removed one exquisite pearl-handled dueling pistol. Loading it with powder alone and no ball, he laid it on his shining walnut desk. "I want you to lock up and put out all the lights. Then go outside and hide nearby. When they come through that window I'm going to pretend that they're robbers and shoot at them. If they try to run, you grab them."

"Both of them, sir?" he asked incredulously.

"I'm going to let both of them get in before I shoot, but I might have an escapee. If so, just toss him back in the window."

"I understand, my lord."

"Good! Then let's hurry."

Brough poured himself a drink of brandy, blew out the candles, and settled himself in a chair facing the window. He grinned in anticipation. This would be a frightening lesson that the pair would long remember. He wasn't surprised to find that he would have to take strong measures to control them. There was too much mischief in their eyes to leave any doubts about that. He only hoped that they would quickly learn that disobedience wasn't worth the effort.

He hadn't long to wait. Within the hour, he heard furtive sounds in the bushes outside.

"There's no light, Georgie," the young viscount whispered.

"Dammit, candles don't last forever!"

"But those were new."

"The servants probably thought we went to bed and put them out. Are you coming, Jerry?"

"What if your brother's back?"

"Not this early. Brough's a 'man about town.' He won't be home until the wee hours."

"But all the lights are out."

"He may not be coming home at all. He's probably spending the night with his mistress."

Brough grimaced. Why was George so obsessed with that?

"Come on then. Let's hurry! I'm freezing. Boost me up and then I'll pull you."

The window scraped upward. A head appeared in the moonlight, then a body scrambled across the sill and dropped to the floor. The earl nearly laughed out loud as his little brother turned to help his friend.

As soon as Jeremy's feet touched the carpet, Brough leaped from his chair. "Robbers!" he shouted, firing.

There was a wild scuffle. Jeremy tried to dive back outside, but the sash fell, pinning him at the waist. George flopped onto the floor. "No! Don't shoot! It's me, Brough! It's Georgie!"

Laughing, Brough went to the fireplace, lit tapers, and exposed the two. His brother cowered against the wall while his friend kicked his legs helplessly, his backside turned up temptingly. "If this were you, George, you'd feel my crop. I've a notion to do it anyway. Would his sister approve?"

"Probably," the youth replied honestly.

Doubting that any woman would condone corporal punishment, the earl raised the window to release his captive, and the grinning Palmer unceremoniously pushed him inside. He looked down at the two boys sprawled at his feet. "Well, what do you two have to say for yourselves?"

They stared fearfully at him. "Nothing, Brough." Georgie shrugged. "We're guilty, I suppose." Simultaneously they stood, turned, and bent over.

"What, may I ask, are you doing?"

"Aren't you going to whip us?"

"Good God, no! But I hope you've learned a lesson here tonight."

The two faced him. "Yes, sir. We certainly have."

"Brough?" Jeremy begged with the familiarity gained over a superb luncheon at White's. "Please don't tell Kissy."

"Who is Kissy?"

"My sister."

He stifled a laugh. What a name for a proper lady! He wondered if this Kissy was as kissable as her name suggested. "I won't tell her this time, but if it happens again, I shall."

"It won't! Thank you, sir."

"Now you may tell me where you've been."

They exchanged anxious looks. George squared his shoulders. "Nowhere really, sir. We only walked the streets to see what the city was like after dark."

"London can be a dangerous place at night. Do I detect the scent of blue ruin?"

"We only had one glass," his brother confessed.

"You have better heads than I would have credited. George, haven't we discussed this before?"

"Yes, sir."

"Must I post a guard on you?"

"No, sir. We'll follow the rules from now on, I promise!"

"Very well. Go on to bed, and in the morning you will behave like gentlemen."

They gratefully departed, and he heard their voices drifting up the stairs. "See, Jerry, he's not bad even if he is getting on in years."

Getting on? He had the impulse to grab George and thrash him anyway.

"Kissy would have been worse."

Shaking his head, Brough leaned back in his chair to finish his brandy. What had he gotten himself into? They may have learned a lesson tonight. At least they had been badly frightened. But he wondered how long it would be before something else would happen. The boys were high-spirited, inquisitive, and impulsive. How were he and this Kissy person to keep up with those two? Most especially, how was he to do it? The burden would fall on him, for what woman could keep up with two mischievous, fast-growing young males? He wondered if he hadn't made a great mistake in allowing George to remain in London. Instead of coping only with him, he would have to take on his friend as well. It was certain that both of them would walk right over Miss Kissy.

Clarissa, despite her weariness and her irritation with Julia, remembered just as she sank into bed that she had agreed to assist her sister with her undressing. With a sigh, she got up again and drew on her wrapper. She certainly didn't want Julia to rip out her meticulous sewing.

Padding down the hall, she tapped on Julia's door and opened it. The scene within removed any anger or disgruntlement. The girl was having a difficult time removing her gown. Clarissa had cut and fit the garment to such perfection that it clung to her like a second skin. Removing it would be a struggle, especially for one with particularly juvenile impatience.

"Here, let me help you."

"Thank you," Julia said flatly. "You see? I can scarcely manage. I need Alice."

"We have been over that before, and I do not intend to do so again, especially when we have so simple a solution," Clarissa warned. "I'm up as late as you are, and I can help you remove your gown."

"But what about my hair?"

"You can dress your own hair for bed. Do not expect me to play lady's maid, for I won't. My goodness, Julia, don't be so helpless!"

"I am practicing to be a lady. It is expected of me, especially if I am to wed properly."

"Ladies make do with what they have. If the day comes when you are fortunate enough to have your own dresser, I am sure that you will know how to go on."

"But—"

"Julia! Enough of it tonight!"

Over and over and over. Once the girl latched on to a topic, she worried it like a dog with a bone, and this was one subject that would probably continue to rise until she was diverted by something else. Picking up the night rail that Alice had laid out, she slipped it over Julia's fair curls and kissed her sister's forehead.

"Good night, dear."

"Good night, Clarissa. I was just thinking ... perhaps Alice could nap during the evening while we are gone. Then she would be ready to serve me at night and do her day work as well."

"Good night," Clarissa said with grim finality, and fled to her room, leaving her sister to ponder the situation of too few servants and too much work.

4

JEREMY WAS AMAZED and delighted at the variety of food offered at Lord Abingdon's breakfast buffet. There was bacon, ham, and kidney pie, both scrambled and hard-boiled eggs, fruit, muffins, and thick, crusty slices of white toast and butter. What probably seemed commonplace to Georgie and his brother was a paradise to him. He heaped his plate high, guiltily wishing that he lived with Brough.

Food was not the only reason that he envied Georgie. He coveted his brother. The earl was a good sport. He had chastised them for their misbehavior the night before in a rakish sort of way. It wasn't at all like Kissy would have done. She would have devised something horrible that would have mortified them, seriously disturbed their consciences, and would have lasted a whole lot longer. Brough understood young men; Kissy did not.

Although he cared deeply for his sister, Jeremy missed the influence of a man in his life. He could scarcely remember his father, a shadowy figure who had largely ignored him. It hadn't seemed to matter until lately, when he turned sixteen. Of course, there were men at school, but they didn't count. He didn't want someone to show him how to be an academician. He wanted someone to show him how to be a real man. Someone just like Brough.

He dug into his meal, happily finding that it tasted as good as it looked. It suddenly occurred to him that he could never invite Georgie to spend the night at his house. Not with Kissy's morning arrangements. It was one thing to be poor. Georgie understood that. It was quite another thing to take your breakfast at the kitchen table with one's sister clad in a housedress, preparing to clean and dust. He must talk with Kissy. Surely she didn't have to scrimp that much.

"Tell me about your sister, Jeremy," Brough said pleasantly.

The viscount started. It was as though his lordship had read his mind.

"She's a widow," was all he could think of to say.

"Indeed."

"It wasn't much of a marriage," Jeremy explained. "He died in little more than a week." Noting a strange expression on his host's face, he added, "It wasn't Kissy's fault. Captain James was killed in the war."

"How unfortunate."

"Oh, I don't think she cared that much. I didn't either. I didn't like him."

"Why not?"

"He always wanted her all to himself."

"That *is* strange," Brough agreed, biting back a smile.

"I thought so. I don't think he liked Julia and me either." Jeremy applied himself to his breakfast. He didn't want to talk about Kissy. He felt traitorous enough wishing that he lived with

Brough. It made him feel worse to discuss her behind her back. She had always tried her best to make a good home for them.

"I believe that when a man is on his honeymoon, he wants his bride to himself," the earl remarked.

"But they didn't go on a honeymoon. Captain James didn't have the time for it, and Kissy wouldn't have wanted to leave us."

"A honeymoon is more a time than a place." Brough laughed. "I don't know why I'm making statements like that. That's a subject I know nothing about!"

Jeremy looked at him, his blue eyes thoughtful. "You're probably right about it just the same . . . all that romantic nonsense and so on. But shouldn't Captain James have realized that in marrying Kissy, he was marrying all of us? She's almost like our mother."

"Yes, he should have realized. Perhaps he just didn't have the chance."

"Maybe."

Brough drained his cup. "It is time for me to leave. I have a great deal of business to attend. What are you boys going to do today?"

"May we drive around the city again?" Georgie asked.

"If you will remember that you are young gentlemen."

"We will!"

"All right then, but if you are not to be here for luncheon, tell the housekeeper."

Georgie nodded. "Have a good day, Brough."

"Thank you for letting me stay," said his friend with a grin.

"Anytime, Jeremy."

When his brother had departed, Georgie turned

excitedly to his friend. "I have an idea of what we can do. Let's take his high-perch phaeton!"

"His phaeton! Would he allow it?"

"He said we could drive. He didn't say what we could drive!"

"I don't know ..." Jeremy hadn't liked being in trouble with Lord Abingdon, and he didn't want to chance losing his welcome in this luxurious house. Aside from the value of the earl's friendship, he had never slept on a bed so soft, nor eaten food so good. If Brough got angry enough, he might put a period to all of it.

"He'll never know. We'll have it out and back before he ever gets home."

"I've never driven a high-perch phaeton, Georgie. Have you?"

"Well ... no ..."

"I think it's a lot different than driving anything else. For one thing, Brough's is a four-horse phaeton."

"Look, Jerry, if it's too difficult, we'll turn right around and come back. Damn, nothing can happen to us at a walk!"

"I've always wanted to ride in a high-perch phaeton."

"Then let's do it!"

The boys waited until the earl was safely gone and strolled casually to the stables behind the house. "The phaeton," Georgie ordered in the voice of one who has long been the master.

The groom hesitated. "His lordship gave no orders ..."

"My brother," the young man emphasized, "has allowed me the use of his stable."

"Yes, sir."

Jeremy felt a sense of foreboding. "Perhaps we

had better ask him first," he whispered to his friend. "It is probably his finest team."

"Then it stands to reason that they will be that much easier to drive!"

Jeremy nodded. "That makes sense."

An impressive team of grays danced from the stable, shaking their heads and jangling their harness in the cool air. The two boys eyed them with awe. They were the finest horses that either one of them had ever seen.

"They're a bit feisty, Master George," the groom warned. "His lordship ain't had 'em out in a while."

"So it stands to reason that the exercise will help them," Georgie said briskly with a confidence he was fast losing. "Come, Jerry, let's be off!"

"Take care of them," the servant warned. "They're his lordship's pride and joy."

They took their places in the vehicle and started from the mews. Jeremy watched his friend shuffling the eight straps of leather in his hands. "Georgie, don't you remember how to hold the reins?"

"I'm trying to. I've never driven four-in-hand. Why don't you take two of them while I try to remember?"

Jeremy had driven nothing but the one-horse gig at Dunstan Hall, so he decided that he should put one set of reins in each hand. Still it didn't seem to work. His horses pulled at the bit, bent sideways, and refused to go along smoothly with Georgie's. "Let's go back."

Georgie was having his own troubles. One of his grays was threatening to rear. "We can't go back so soon and face that groom. I'd rather turn up my toes and die. Let's go round the block where he can't see us and halt them. After a suitable interval, we'll return."

But that didn't work either. The high-strung horses refused to stand still. "We were better off with them walking," young Longwood said. "I think I've figured it out. Let me have your reins."

Jeremy happily relinquished them, watching his friend lace them through his fingers. "That . . . looks like it might be right."

"Let us see." He carefully moved the horses forward. "Good! It works! They're walking ever so much better. Let us walk them to the park, then we'll turn around and go back."

By the time they had reached the park, Georgie was full of confidence. "I've got the hang of it, Jerry. Let's try a short trot."

"If you think so. This is fun."

The grays quickly obeyed, moving in unison down the pathway. "If anyone our age sees us, they'll be impressed," Georgie bragged. "Look how well they're going. Oh, Jerry, they've got mouths like feathers! These are the finest horses in the world. Let's spring 'em!"

"No!" Jeremy cried, but even if his friend had heeded it, it would have been too late.

The horses responded with such blistering speed that the boys were thrown backwards. "Help me, Jerry!" Georgie shouted, trying to gain control of the flying animals. Both boys hauled on the reins, but as it was, the thoroughbreds stopped on their own. Rounding a turn, the near leader bobbled and drew up, bunching the others abruptly. Nodding his head, he lifted a foreleg.

"Dear God," Georgie breathed, "he's lamed himself."

"No," Jeremy said direly. "*We* have lamed him."

They looked at each other, terror written on both faces.

"Let us look, Jeremy. Perhaps we are lucky and it's just a stone."

It was not. The gelding's knee was swelling rapidly. The beautiful gray turned pain-filled eyes upon them and held his leg aloft.

"What are we going to do? Brough will kill us!" Georgie said with horror. "At least he'll kill me. You can get away from him."

"I wouldn't allow you to take the blame alone! We're friends and we're in this together." Jeremy looked at the slender leg and considered. "Kissy can help. She has all kinds of remedies for this type of thing, unless . . . unless it's broken!"

"It can't be broken. It just can't be!"

"Let's lead them to my house," Jeremy said grimly. "Kissy will tell us one way or another."

"Should we walk him that far?"

"What choice do we have?"

"You're right." Georgie's hands trembled on the reins. "What if some of Brough's friends come by and recognize us? They'll tell him . . . My God! We'll have to tell him sometime."

"Maybe we can get Kissy to do that, too. She's a lady, so he can't be mean to her."

"No, but he'll come after us later."

Jeremy's shoulders sagged. "It can't be helped."

"No. At the very best, he'll send me to the country. At worst . . ." He drew a deep breath. "I'll just have to stand up and take it like a man."

Miserably they tugged at the reins and began leading the horses very, very slowly from the park.

Clarissa was sitting with her sewing in her bedroom window seat when a movement in the yard below caught her eye. Jeremy, Georgie, a highly fashionable, high-perch phaeton, and a beautiful team of four perfectly matched grays proceeded painfully toward the stable, the near leader limping badly. She knew instinctively what had happened.

Laying Julia's new dress aside, she threw on her shawl and ran down the stairs and out the door. "What—"

The parade drew up. "Kissy," Jeremy begged mournfully, "please help us."

"What has happened?" she cried. "These horses . . . they are . . ."

"My brother's," Georgie said tragically.

"And you took them out without his permission."

"Well . . . it wasn't exactly that, but . . ."

"I hope you both are very, very ashamed of yourselves," she said softly, "because Lord Abingdon will be extremely hurt by this."

"More like he'll be extremely angry."

"Then I hope he thrashes you both within an inch of your lives!"

"Kissy," Jeremy pleaded, "we don't care what happens to us. We'll take our punishment. Can you help the horse?"

"Why didn't you take him to his own stable? I'm sure Lord Abingdon has very knowledgeable grooms."

"Well . . ." her young brother murmured cautiously, "we thought you might help us with Brough as well."

"I shall not do that. You will take all the responsibility for your actions! But this horse will not be made to suffer any further. Unhitch him."

"Us?"

"Yes, you, Georgie! And you, Jeremy!" She bent

to examine the leg. "I don't believe it's broken, but if this horse could cry, he certainly would."

"Please, Kissy, don't make us feel any worse."

"You should feel worse. You should feel just as awful as I can make you feel!"

Mournfully they released the gray and gave over the reins to Clarissa, watching her lead him slowly into the stable.

"What shall we do with the others?"

"Unhook them for now and bring them in. You can take them home later." She let the gray stand in the aisleway while she filled an empty box stall with straw.

The boys followed after her. "Where is Gibson, Kissy?" Jeremy asked.

"He has driven your sister on a visit to one of her friends."

"That's about right. Just when we need him, the Prune has to command his presence!"

"You two are big, strong boys. Georgie, you may fill those stalls with straw. Jeremy, fetch me a cloth and a pailful of the coldest water you can find." She stroked the horse's sleek neck. "There now," she crooned. "We'll have you feeling more comfortably in no time."

They obeyed her, then flopped down in the sweet-smelling straw. "What now, Kissy?"

"Get up! You two are going to soak this horse's knee with cold water. While you are doing that, I shall make you a list of ingredients for a poultice, then you'll be off to the market to fetch them. While this horse is injured, the two of you will care for him, feed him, water him, groom him, and clean his stall. You'll prepare the poultice yourselves and treat his injury. Unless, of course, Lord Abingdon has other ideas."

"What will Gibson be doing all this time?" Jeremy asked.

"Gibson has his own duties. He will not assume the extra ones that you yourselves have created. Get busy!" With that, she left the building.

It took Clarissa only a short time to find the receipt for the poultice and to note down the ingredients, but she would have been even quicker if the image of Lord Abingdon had not invaded her mind. She could picture the remorseful boys standing before the cool, sophisticated aristocrat, and began to feel sorry for them. What could she do to help pave the way? After all, they were very young and they had the thoughtlessness of youth. Surely he must understand that. But those thoughts were not helping the poor horse. She pushed it all from her mind and hurried back to the stable.

Gibson had returned after leaving his young mistress at her friend's house to go back for her later. Knowing instinctively that these must be Abingdon animals, and wondering why young Lord Dunstan and his aristocratic friend were performing physical labor, he suspiciously hadn't volunteered to help the two culprits he found in his stable. Instead, he leaned against the wall, lost in appreciation of the earl's wonderful horses. If only he could be in charge of fine horses such as these! Abruptly he saw his mistress coming and came to attention.

"Hello Gibson. I assume you have noticed that a punishment is going on here."

"Yes, ma'am." He didn't comment, but he anticipated the boys facing a great deal of lordly rage.

"I thought we should use our regular poultice?"

"Yes, ma'am. That should turn the trick."

"Boys!"

Glad to leave their chore, they hurried to her.

"Here is the list. I do hope that you have money, for I shan't give you any."

They nodded.

"Well then, buy these things and hurry back. Time is essential if we do not wish Lord Abingdon's horse to go through life with an over-sized knee."

They looked at her with large eyes. "Kissy . . . about Brough. What shall we—"

"I'm thinking on it. Now, go!"

They breathed a collective sigh of relief and scurried from the barn. With the horse's treatment under way, she had turned her mind to think about them and their further dilemma. Everything would be all right. Kissy would come up with something.

Clarissa knelt by the fine-limbed gray. "Gibson, if you will fetch me another pail of the coldest water, I will continue here."

He complied, but when he returned he silently took the cloth from her hand and began to do the job himself.

"Really, Gibson, this is not part of your duties."

"You'll want to show the boys about the poultice, ma'am."

"Thank you." She stood, stroked the gelding's silky black nose, and strode toward the house.

"You must keep stirring. The thicker the mixture becomes, the more you must stir or it will stick to the pot and burn," Clarissa instructed the two boys at the coal stove, paying little heed to the door knocker echoing through the house.

"It's him!" Jeremy cried.

"It can't be." Georgie shook his head. "He

doesn't know where you live. And it's too early for him to be home anyway."

Simmons appeared at the doorway, his face strained. "Miss Clarissa?"

"I am not at home," she directed briskly. "Stir, Georgie. You must not let it stick to the bottom!"

"I beg your pardon, miss," the butler interrupted, "but you *must* be at home." He glanced with pity at the young viscount and his friend. "You see, it is Lord Abingdon."

Two spoons clattered to the floor. The blood drained from two faces. Two young men bore all the signs of fleeing out the back door.

"Stir!" Clarissa commanded, wiping her hands on her apron and wondering what on earth she was going to say to the earl. She flung her hands to her hair. La, she must look like a kitchen wench!

"We are dead," Georgie said morbidly.

"Oh, good grief! He can't be that bad!" She squared her small shoulders. "Simmons, have we any brandy? Gentlemen like brandy, don't they?"

"Yes, miss, they do, but we have none."

"Then wine. Anything! Just bring some fortifying refreshment." She took a deep breath. "I should send the two of you in there and stay out of this myself."

"Kissy, you can't!" Jeremy cried. "You have to help us. Please!"

"I've told you not to call me that!"

"I'm sorry. Please help us, Clarissa!"

She sighed with disgust. "I'll try. More's the pity, I don't know why! But I will, although you don't deserve it, you know."

"We'll be good forevermore!"

"Hmph."

"What are you going to say?" Jeremy trembled.

"I don't know. I'll think of something." She started from the kitchen.

"Miss Clarissa?"

"Yes, Simmons?"

"Your apron, miss."

"Oh, dear lord!" She ripped it off, threw it aside, and started for the salon.

The earl was still standing when she breezed into the room. He bowed and kissed her hand elegantly, his lips barely brushing her skin. "Madam, I am Brougham Abingdon. And you are ..." He registered brief shock, then grinned engagingly. "I'm sorry. The name my sources have given me is Kissy."

She flushed. "Those boys! My name is Mrs. Clarissa James. Won't you sit down, my lord?"

"Thank you, Mrs. James. I have been anxious to meet you." He hesitated. "I believe that we have some problems in common."

"Yes, my lord, we do." She sat down beside the fire, and he took the seat across from her. It seemed inordinately hot. Earlier the cool spring day had seemed chill enough to light the fireplaces, but now she felt as if she might roast. She hoped that her guest was not too terribly uncomfortable.

The earl looked at her intently. "I believe I have seen you somewhere before. Did you attend the Haversham ball?"

"Yes." She felt herself blushing. How could he have recognized her? His back had been turned to them. Surely he couldn't have witnessed Julia's unhappy display.

"Right now I am looking for two horse thieves. Have you any knowledge of their whereabouts?"

"I do."

"Good! If you will inform me ..."

She looked into his eyes, noting that they were hazel with little flecks of gold. They weren't intimidating eyes, so why did she feel overawed? It was because of him as a whole. Brougham Abingdon was too handsome for comfort. He made her feel tongue-tied and provincial.

"Mrs. James?"

"Oh yes, they are in the kitchen."

"The kitchen?"

Simmons fortuitously entered the salon at that moment with the tray of refreshments. Setting it on the small table between them, he magnificently poured two glasses of wine. "Will that be all, madam?"

"Yes, thank you." She nodded as he bowed and left them, wishing she could cling to his coattails as she had when she was a little girl.

Lord Abingdon smiled. "I must confess that my curiosity is out of all boundaries. What is my brother, of all people, doing in your kitchen?"

She drew up her courage. "The young men are being punished."

"Excellent! For what?"

"I wish you would drink your wine, my lord," she blurted. "It is ever so good."

He laughed, tipped the glass, and drained it. "Now that I am fortified, Mrs. James, will you tell me what those scamps have been up to? Somehow I feel that it is something I am going to dislike intensely."

Clarissa felt her chin quiver. "You had best have another," she said miserably.

He nodded to her to pour. "My phaeton is broken up."

"No, sir."

"Then it is my horses."

"One of them, my lord. The near leader."

"It's Gypsy! I could throttle those boys! This time they will really be punished!"

"I fully agree." She looked at him with relief, glad that the telling was over. But then her eyes narrowed as she asked, "This time? Have they done something else?"

"Oh, only a minor infraction. Tell me what happened to Gypsy."

"A sprained knee, my lord. That is what the boys are doing in the kitchen. Preparing a poultice."

"That is their punishment?"

"Only a part of it. They are to take complete care of the horse until he is well. They must feed, water, and groom him, care for his injury, and keep his stall spotless. I intend to see that much of their time is occupied doing these chores. Unless you have another idea, my lord?"

He gazed at her with admiration. "I think you are wonderful."

Clarissa nearly choked on her wine. "Sir?"

"If I had done something like this when I was a boy, I would rather have taken a thrashing and been done with it. This will continue on and on. Each day they will be reminded of their misdeed."

"Exactly so. And that is not all. They will apologize to you, my lord."

"Will that be so hard?" he asked thoughtfully.

"In this case, yes."

"Then let us be about it. Will you show me to the kitchen, Mrs. James?"

"The . . . kitchen?"

"Yes."

"Surely, my lord, you do not wish to go to the kitchen!"

"If my brother can go there, why not I?" He grinned.

Clarissa laughed uncertainly. "Very well."

When the two young men saw who followed Clarissa into the kitchen, they both stood to attention and then immediately and alarmingly burst into tears.

"Good God," the earl murmured, "I'm not that frightening."

"Stop this at once!" Clarissa snapped. "That horse cannot cry, and so you shall not. Stop it, I say!"

Sniveling, they wiped their eyes on their sleeves.

"I'm sorry, Brough," Georgie began. "It's all my fault. Jeremy didn't want to."

"But I didn't stop you!"

"Enough." Lord Abingdon walked forward and put his arms across their shoulders. "Have you learned a lesson?"

"I'll never take anyone's horse without asking specifically!"

"Nor I!"

"Well then. Mrs. James has lined out your punishment. When the horse is able to be moved to my mews, I shall oversee it. You two are going to be very busy."

"Yes, sir."

He gave them a little shake. "Now, if your poultice is ready, let us go to see Gypsy."

After they closed the back door behind them, Clarissa collapsed at the table. What a horrible day it had been! But she had met the earl, and he was easy, not nearly so intimidating as he had seemed at first. She sighed with relief. It could have been a very difficult encounter. Indeed she herself had made it much more difficult than it might have been.

"An earl!" Cook marveled. "In my kitchen! Why, he's not so high and mighty!"

"Oh yes he is," Simmons contradicted. "He's so grand, he can go anywhere he pleases and no one will forget who he is."

Clarissa was simply glad that the worst was over. Now they could merely concentrate on making Gypsy well. She thought of how the earl had put his arms across the boys' shoulders. Someday he would be a good father, kind and understanding, knowing the proper time for punishment and the proper time for reassurance. The boys knew that he wasn't happy with their deed, but they also knew that he was willing to forgive them.

She was still at the table and was somehow not surprised when they returned through the kitchen. "What do you think, my lord?"

He frowned a little. "It's very soon to tell, but the boys have assured me that they will do their best. Also I believe that some lessons in the phaeton are in order." He turned to Georgie and Jeremy. "You see, you need only ask. You don't have to go behind my back."

There was a bustle in the hall, and the kitchen door was flung open. Julia sailed in with a flourish and stopped dead in her tracks. Her mouth forming a pink O, she took one look at the earl and swooned.

5

BROUGH TURNED THE gig in to the narrow alley, which passed very close to the Dunstans' rented house, and drove up to the small mews. Gibson hastily materialized from within the stable and took the horse's reins while the earl alighted. He pressed a coin into the groom's hand.

Gibson's eyes grew wide. "Oh no, m'lord. Miss Clarissa wouldn't allow it."

"It is my custom," Brough said firmly. "Furthermore, my horse has caused extra work for you. I must insist."

"I thank you, my lord." He pocketed the money. Miss Clarissa would probably never know. Besides, the earl was far more formidable than she. If he were ever forced to leave the service of the Dunstans, he wanted Lord Abingdon to remember him. Even a lowly position in that gentleman's stable would be far more preferable to being the head groom in some others.

"How is my horse?"

"Somewhat better, sir. A bit of the swelling has gone down. The young gentlemen are mucking out his box now."

Brough was surprised. Yesterday they had had good intentions. This morning George had risen and left before breakfast, presumably to assist in the care of Gypsy. He could picture the boys helping with the feeding and caring for the injury, but to muck out a stall? His brother? He must have underestimated the determination of Mrs. Clarissa James.

He entered the stable and paused to breathe in the sweet smells of hay, well-cared-for horseflesh, and liniments. He was certain that Gibson had no boy to help him. The man did it all on his own, yet the place had been spotless both yesterday afternoon and this morning. The stalls were clean, the aisle and yard swept, horses groomed, and polished harnesses hanging neatly. Even the earl's own stable was not always in such perfect order by the middle of the morning. Mrs. James must inspire conscientious hard work as well as loyalty among her staff.

"It is almost your turn, Jerry."

"My back hurts."

"So does mine."

Brough walked forward and peered through the iron bars into the box stall. A manure sack was spread in the middle, with the young viscount beside it, rubbing the muscles in the small of his back. George was at work nearby, forking away soiled bedding. The earl grinned at their expressions of distaste. Jeremy caught sight of him.

"Good morning, Brough."

"Good morning, boys. How is it going?" He stepped around the corner and entered the stall.

Georgie happily took the opportunity to stop and lean on his fork. "All right, I suppose, but Gibson can clean *two* stalls in half the time it takes us to do this one."

"Experience." He fondled the gray's nose and

glanced down at the gelding's bandaged knee. "How does his leg look?"

"Gibson says it's better. It does look less swollen."

"I see you've got your poultice at work, so I'll take your word for it."

His brother nodded, then smiled brightly. "Would you like to help, Brough?"

"Certainly not! What would my valet say?" he laughed. "No, I believe that I shall pay a brief call on Mrs. James if she is at home."

"She is," Jeremy said with disgust. "She is chaperoning the Prune and her admirers. If the men in London had half sense, they'd be admiring Kissy. She should put herself forward instead of taking a backseat to Julia all the time. Kissy's worth ten of her!"

"I daresay." Brough bid the boys good-bye, left the stable, and strolled around to the front of the house to make his entrance.

During the harried events of the day before, he'd had little time to make further analyzation of the appearance of Mrs. James, and still less to assess that of her fainting sister. A few discreet inquiries at White's, however, had revealed that Miss Julia Dunstan was considered an Incomparable and that she was very popular among the younger set. No one remembered ever seeing her elder sister. Apparently Mrs. James kept herself so completely in the background that no one had even noticed her presence.

The elderly butler let him in, took his hat and topcoat, and escorted him to the salon, throwing open the door with a flourish. "Lord Abingdon."

Brough saw at once why Miss Julia Dunstan was hailed as Incomparable. She was very pretty in an innocent, schoolgirlish way. Her hair was a bright, shining blond, her complexion creamy and unflawed, and her mouth graced by pert dimples. Her eyes were a brilliant blue, and right now they were turned on him with an expression that was a childish attempt at seductiveness. He could have laughed.

"Good morning, Lord Abingdon," she said breathlessly, worriedly looking around her circle of admirers for a place for him to sit.

"Good morning, Miss Dunstan." His eyes flicked around the room and finally rested on Mrs. James sitting on a love seat in a corner very much out of the way. "Mrs. James."

"Good morning, my lord," she replied in a voice soft and mellow.

He made his way across the room and sat down beside her. "I have visited our young men."

Clarissa laughed outright. "Are they still at work?"

"Yes. I fear they are not the speediest of stable-boys."

"They will learn." She looked down, continuing her sewing. "The horse is much better today."

"You saw him?"

"Oh yes."

He gazed at her bent head. Clarissa Dunstan James had the most entrancing hair he had ever seen. Not blond like that of her brother and sister, it was a thick, rich brown that gleamed with brilliant golden highlights as though it had been sprinkled with gold dust. Even though it was done in a demure knot at the nape of her neck and covered with a matronly little lace cap, its beauty could not be hidden. He had the greatest impulse to pull the hairpins out and let it tumble down her back.

She glanced at him and smiled, displaying dimples like her sister's. He knew at once that his impression at the ball was correct. Clarissa James was a stunning Beauty. If she were dressed fashionably, she would drive men to distraction.

He couldn't help looking at her fully developed breasts. Though well concealed in her modest dress, their luscious fullness could not be denied. Nor could the sensual curve of her hip. Her brother was right. The men of London were blind.

"Lord Abingdon?"

"Yes?" he asked a little breathlessly.

"I find it uncomfortable to have you staring at me so," she said pleasantly.

Though the room had become overwhelmingly warm, the heat seemed to center in his cheeks. "I must apologize, ma'am. Your beauty has caused me to forget my manners."

"Oh my goodness!" Clarissa laughed. "If you wish to look at a pretty lady, you should sit in the other end of the room! But perhaps there are no chairs available."

"I didn't notice," he confessed. Didn't she realize how beautiful she was? "I wanted to talk with you."

"I'm glad, for I wished to talk with you also."

"About the boys?"

"Yes." She set aside her embroidery and turned to him, her knees nearly touching his. "Since we have permitted them to stay away from school until the end of the term, I believe that we should not allow them to forget entirely about their schoolwork. I have already caused Jeremy to spend some time each day with his books, but it is hard to keep him at it when Georgie doesn't do it, too."

"I see." Brough frowned, wondering how he was going to fit the time for tutoring his brother into his busy schedule. Having Georgie live with him was becoming increasingly complicated. Possibly he could hire a tutor.

"Perhaps I have overstepped," Clarissa murmured. "Please think nothing of it."

"No, it is a good idea. I was merely trying to find a way to fit it into my schedule."

"Oh, do not concern yourself with that, my lord. Georgie can study with Jeremy, and I will help them. It might make their work more interesting if they may do it together. I do not mind at all."

"It strikes me that you are already very busy, Mrs. James. I was considering a tutor for them."

"I cannot . . ." She looked at him with large, candid eyes. "My lord, I cannot afford it."

He knew instinctively that she would not allow him to pay for it. There was no point at all in insisting on it. It would embarrass her even more than her admission of lack of wealth.

"Lord Abingdon, I understand completely that you would prefer a professional tutor for Georgie. Do not let my idea that the boys work together stand in the way."

"Mrs. James, I would be happy for your assistance, and when I get the chance to help, I'll be pleased to oblige."

"Thank you, sir!" She smiled her sunny smile.

"But if it becomes too much for you . . ."

"Oh no, it will not! I have lots of time."

Brough spent another half hour with the lady, discussing their high-spirited brothers, and then took his leave. He was extremely pleased that he had made her acquaintance. Her unexpected knowledge on how to deal with youths seemed so much greater than his own that it was hard to believe that she herself could not be much older than they were. Her assistance and advice was going to make it a lot easier to live with George.

* * *

Flattered by Lord Abingdon's perusal of her, Clarissa took greater pains in dressing for the Huntsfords' ball that evening. She wore her newest dress, one that, in a lapse of consideration for Julia, she had made for herself before they arrived in London. It was a deep emerald satin with a creamy overskirt. On the bodice she had affixed seed pearls cut from an old dress she had found in the attic. With it she wore her mother's pearls and earrings.

Seeing her mistress taking an interest in her appearance, Alice decided to do something more with her hair. Without asking permission, she arranged the rich tresses in an elaborate Grecian knot, softened with delicate, wispy curls to frame her lovely oval face. When she was finished she knew that she had never seen Miss Clarissa look more striking.

Julia knew it, too, and was unhappy. It wasn't fair that she must make her entrance beside her attractive sister. She was the reason for being in London, not Clarissa, who was a widow and should be dressed like one. What had gotten into her? Surely she wouldn't put her own self forward at the ball.

She did not. After greeting their hosts, Clarissa retired to her usual spot in the background. Now that she was here, she felt foolish for going to so much trouble with her appearance. This and every other night belonged to Julia. She had wasted money making this dress for herself, and it was cut too low in the bodice to be made to fit her sister's youthful figure. But what was done was done, and she might as well forget about it. Didn't everyone succumb to a dream now and then?

"I would very much like to have the supper dance . . . and the last waltz."

Clarissa startled, looking over her shoulder. "Lord Abingdon!"

"I saw your sister, but I had the devil of a time finding you. What are you doing way back here?" He came around her, bowed, and lightly kissed her hand. "May I sit down?"

"Of . . . of course."

He seated himself in the little gilt chair beside her. "You look ravishing tonight, Mrs. James."

Heat rose in her cheeks. "Thank you, my lord, but Julia—"

"Julia is pretty for the child she is. Let her play the games with the other children."

She wondered what kind of games he was referring to. He was certainly playing games with her senses. Few men could be as handsome as Lord Abingdon in evening dress, his brilliant diamond stickpin sparkling with every breath. *Two* dances? The supper dance *and* the last waltz? It was beyond belief.

"It is unfortunate that society will not allow me more than two dances. I would like very much to rescue you from this dark hole. Allow me at least to escort you to a more favorable location."

Clarissa smiled. "Thank you, my lord, but I am quite contented here."

He raised a quizzical eyebrow and stood, bowing again. "Very well then, Mrs. James. Until later?"

She nodded and watched his departure, her heart pounding. It could only be because of their common interest in their brothers that he paid her any attention whatsoever. The sophisticated and very eligible Lord Abingdon could not be interested in her for herself. She had been wed to another man, no matter how brief the time. No one would choose a widow when he could have his choice of all the young beauties on the Marriage Mart. She couldn't hold a candle to Incomparables like Julia. No, he simply wanted to cement their relationship for the sake of the boys.

Remembering Julia, she looked anxiously around the room for her lively sister. As was to be expected, the young lady was dancing, but her eyes were fastened on the earl as he moved through the crowd to join his group of friends. At least she had been introduced to him, so she wouldn't make a cake of herself in that respect. Still she bore watching. One never knew what the girl might do next. She hoped that Julia would remember her warning.

Luckily the evening passed uneventfully, and soon Lord Abingdon was bowing over her hand. Clarissa rose, feeling as though all eyes in the room were upon her, but apart from a few curious glances, the guests carried on as before. Her sister, however, had noticed, and a tiny frown briefly knitted her brow before she returned her attention to her escort.

It had been a long time since Clarissa had danced, but the steps quickly came back to her. The earl was accomplished at the art and was easy to follow. Soon she was moving as effortlessly and as gracefully as she had done in the county assemblies.

His lordship was delighted. "You dance beautifully, Mrs. James. You are depriving many by hiding in the corner."

She laughed. "You forget, my lord, that this is not my Season. It is Julia's. I must play the role of chaperon."

"Of course, but you should not allow your role to become detrimental to your own enjoyment."

"I do not." She curtsied, ending the dance, and took his arm. "I am having a very good time."

Being on the opposite side of the ballroom, they were among the last to enter the room set aside for the supper. When they entered, a great many people were already occupying the tables. Julia, seated by the door, beckoned to them.

"Lord Abingdon, Clarissa, you must sit with us! I have saved a place." Though her invitation included her sister, the young lady's warm smile was entirely directed at the earl.

Clarissa glanced up at him.

"If you do not mind," he murmured, "I would prefer to sit with my friends."

She nodded. "Thank you, Julia, but Lord Abingdon has made other arrangements."

"Oh well!" The girl tossed her blond curls. "Another time perhaps."

Clarissa knew that Julia was unhappy, but there was little she could do about it. The earl was not interested in the young lady's charms. He hadn't danced with her and he wasn't interested in sharing her company for supper. Julia was probably too young for him. She hoped that her sister would take his polite disinterest in stride.

She soon forgot about Julia's dilemma when she realized that Lord Abingdon was leading her to the table of none other than the grand Duke and Duchess of Rackthall and the Marquess and Marchioness of Singleton. So these elegant people were his special friends? It was beyond belief that she, Clarissa Dunstan James, would be sharing supper with the cream of tonnish society. How proud her mother would have been! It was too bad that there were only Julia and Jeremy to share the excitement.

The men rose as Lord Abingdon performed the introductions and seated her next to Lord Singleton. "Shall we fetch the ladies' suppers?"

Clarissa felt a sense of panic as the earl and his friends left her alone with the beautiful duchess and the tall, pretty marchioness. What could she talk about? She had nothing in common with these two fabulously wealthy, sophisticated peeresses.

The duchess broke the ice. "Brough has told us a great deal about your efforts to deal with those mischievous young men, Mrs. James." She smiled. "It seems that you have your hands full!"

"Yes indeed," Clarissa laughed, relieved that Her Grace had chosen a topic that was easy for her to discuss. "But surely they have learned their lesson at last! They aren't bad boys. They are merely high-spirited."

"How is the horse?"

"Greatly improved, ma'am. I believe that he shall be as good as new."

She nodded. "Brough is proud of that team. Tell me, how on earth did you devise such a punishment?"

"I have always tried to suit the punishment to the transgression. Somehow it makes the lesson stick a little better."

"I shall remember that when my son, Brannie, is older."

"Have you no children of your own, Mrs. James?" Lady Singleton asked.

"No, though I almost feel as if Julia and Jeremy were my children. My mother died when they were very young, you see, so I have practically raised them."

"You yourself must have been very young for that role," she said kindly.

"Yes, but I hope . . . I hope I have done well."

Lord Abingdon set her plate before her and removed two glasses of champagne from the tray of a passing waiter. "Done well at what, Mrs. James?"

Raising my brother and sister, my lord." She smiled. "I hope I have done well."

"You have done magnificently. In fact, you have done more and are doing more than should be expected."

"There is no one else," Clarissa murmured.

"I'm sure that Brough is glad for your assistance with George, Mrs. James." The Duke of Rackthall grinned, joining his wife. "He can't handle him! Harry, do you remember when that little scamp put a snake in Brough's bed?"

The Marquess of Singleton laughed. "What about the box of spiders he loosed in Marie's room?"

"He's not that bad anymore," Lord Abingdon protested, "but I am glad of Mrs. James's assistance."

Snakes? Spiders? Clarissa looked at him with wide brown eyes. Surely there were no snakes to be had in London, but spiders were a different matter. The old cellars and attics were probably full of them. If Jeremy and Georgie played that trick on her, she would thrash them both within an inch of their lives.

"Now see what you have done," the Duchess Allesandra admonished, tapping her husband's wrist with her fan. "You have frightened Mrs. James."

The earl squeezed Clarissa's hand and brought it to his lips. "I think you need not worry. The boys like you too well to make you the victim of such a prank."

"I hope so," she said doubtfully.

Clarissa began the second half of the evening with a rise in popularity. In addition to dancing with the Duke of Rackthall and the Marquess of Singleton, she received requests from other men as well. When the time came for her waltz with Lord Abingdon, she was amazed at how quickly and enjoyably the hours had passed. Instead of sitting alone, half-bored, she'd had a pleasant evening and could scarcely believe that it was almost over. She knew that her success was due to the show of interest by Lord Abingdon and his friends, but she couldn't help feeling a bit pleased with herself.

When the orchestra began the last dance, Lord Abingdon took her in his arms and swept her expertly across the floor to the lilting tempo of the violins. Closing her eyes, she concentrated solely on the music. It was so very romantic, and he was the perfect partner. No one could ask for a more wonderful way to end an evening. Any lady who had ever waltzed with the earl must be very jealous of her at this moment.

"I hope that you have enjoyed your evening," he said when the dance had finished.

"I have. Very much," she said softly. "Thank you."

"I should rather thank you." He tucked her hand through his arm. "The pleasure has been mine. You waltz divinely."

"You are easy to dance with, my lord." She glanced around the room for Julia and saw her standing on the sidelines, impatiently tapping her foot. "I must collect my sister."

"I shall see you to your carriage." He escorted

her to the young lady and gallantly offered Julia his other arm.

Unsmilingly she accepted it. "I should have waltzed also," she said petulantly. "I was invited."

"You are too young," Clarissa said flatly. "We have discussed this before."

"The patronesses at Almack's—" Lord Abingdon began.

"That makes no difference," Julia interrupted. "We have no vouchers for Almack's because we are nobody." She paused, looking up at him. "You could get them for us."

"Julia!" Clarissa cried. "My lord, you must ignore her. She has an unfortunate habit of speaking before she thinks."

"I suppose that I could ask Allesandra to obtain them," he said slowly.

"Please do not! I could not presume so upon the duchess. Lord Abingdon, you must promise me to forget this nonsense!"

"But you should participate in all that London has to offer." He smiled and left them to fetch their wraps.

The minute he was gone, Clarissa rounded on her sister. "I cannot believe that you could be so forward!"

Julia shrugged delicately. "Perhaps something at least will come from this wretched evening. And speaking of forward, you should see to your own conduct. You hung on him like a leech, and how late you were returning from supper!"

"I could scarcely leap up alone and leave them all sitting there."

"You are an embarrassment with your social climbing," Julia said with a pout. "I only hope not everyone noticed."

"We shall talk of this later." Clarissa forced a

smile as Lord Abingdon returned with their cloaks.

It seemed an eternity of false gaiety until he had seen them safely into their carriage and trotting briskly through the darkened streets. Clarissa's evening was ruined by her sister's outburst. She had *not* behaved badly and she had *not* pushed herself forward. Julia's accusations were wrong. No doubt the young lady was consumed with jealousy. After all, she had experienced what Julia would have dreamed of, the supper and the dances with the highest-ranking peers. No wonder the girl was angry. They were in London because of her, not for the entertainment of her elder, widowed sister. Clarissa reminded herself of that and was determined that in the future she would stay in the background, where she belonged.

6

THE NEXT AFTERNOON, by the time Clarissa had finished assisting Jeremy and Georgie in their studies, Julia's callers had begun to arrive. In the morning the young lady had gone for a shopping excursion with her best friend, Mary Grantham. Thus it was late afternoon before Clarissa had an opportunity to speak with her younger sister about the troublesome evening before.

She found the girl at the pianoforte, her slender fingers drifting idly across the keys in no real melody. "Julia? A word with you please?"

"What is it?" her sister asked coldly. "Am I to receive a scold? Am I to be banished to the country?"

"No," Clarissa said patiently, "although you were rather bold in asking Lord Abingdon for the vouchers."

"I don't care. He owes us something. After all, his horrible little brother spends as much time here as he does at home."

"I believe that if you thought about it, you must agree that Jeremy spends an equal amount of time at Lord Abingdon's house. The earl owes us nothing. Indeed it is probably the opposite. Lord Abingdon provides a carriage and horses for the boys. Jeremy often spends the night at his house, and more and more frequently he takes his meals there."

"So? You help Georgie with his schoolwork and you helped with the lame horse."

Clarissa smiled. "That is very little indeed. Besides, I am not a professional tutor. I know Lord Abingdon would have preferred to hire a qualified person to instruct his brother, but we thought it would be wise to keep the boys together."

"They could have had the same tutor."

"We cannot afford that. The earl was kind enough to suggest engaging one, but I could not accept. We couldn't have paid for our share."

Her sister's hands fell hard onto the keyboard in a resounding chord. "You told him that? You let him know that we were poor as church mice?" She looked up with flashing blue eyes. "Now tell me how I shall find a husband. No one will marry me!"

"Oh, Julia," Clarissa said shortly, "anyone with two good eyes can see that we are not well-to-do. You cannot pretend to be something you are not. The truth is so obvious! And you *will* find a husband. There are plenty of fine men who will not care whether or not you have a great fortune. You have youth and prettiness. You are vivacious, and when you wish, you have pleasing manners. Some men require nothing more. My goodness, you are considered to be an Incomparable! You will succeed."

"I want a rich husband, one with a title. I want to be 'Lady Julia'!"

"That would be very agreeable, but do not neglect wedding someone you care for and who will care for you."

"You didn't."

"It was a mistake!" she cried. "I'm sorry I did it! I thought it would be best for all of us, but it was not. I don't want you to make the same error."

Julia shrugged. "I won't. I'll make sure he has money. Is there anything else you wish to talk with me about?"

"This isn't easy," Clarissa sighed, "but I think you are being very childish about my dancing last night. I did not put myself forward. Indeed Lord Abingdon made a special effort to seek me out."

"Why?"

"I don't know. Perhaps he wished to talk about the boys."

"Did you?"

"Not particularly . . . I don't remember! The subject came up once or twice . . ."

"I suppose that you told him that my dancing card was full?"

"He did not ask, Julia, and I did not mention it."

Her sister flung herself up from the piano stool and went to the window, standing with her back to the room. "Don't place yourself in my way, Clarissa. I am the one who is supposed to find a husband. You had your chance. If your marriage was a mistake, it is one you must live with. You are used goods now."

Clarissa thought of her short, pitiful marriage to Captain Mark James. Parts of it had been very distasteful. She'd had to steel herself to keep from shuddering at his touch. Marriage shouldn't be that way. Recalling the easy affection she had witnessed between the duke and duchess and the marquess and marchioness, she definitely knew it wasn't that way for everyone. She shouldn't have married Mark. She hadn't known him well enough. She hadn't loved him, hadn't really cared for him in the way a wife should care for her husband. It had merely seemed the wisest thing to do at the time. In truth she had wed him as a means to receive assistance with the responsibility that seemed to grow heavier every day. Well, she wouldn't do that again. She'd learned her lesson.

But used goods? She was still young. Perhaps someday she would find a man she really wished to marry, a man who would be very much like Brougham Abingdon. Wealthy or not, titled or not, it didn't matter so long as he was kind and thoughtful and affectionate.

Still Julia was right. It was the girl's turn. She was the sole reason they had come to London. If Clarissa's success diminished that of her younger sister, she would be only too happy to remain in the shadows. After all, no unmarried man whom she had danced with was eligible for her. They were far too grand and too noble to bother with an impoverished, countrified widow.

"Julia," she said quietly, "I wouldn't dream of placing myself in your way. You are the reason we have come to London. I do want you to be a success and to find the perfect gentleman."

"Good!" The girl turned on her heel to face her sister. "Then you will have no objections about staying home tonight. I have been invited to attend the Renfrews' ball in the company of the Granthams. I'm sure that you will agree that Lady Grantham is a perfectly suitable chaperon."

Clarissa did not, for she had observed the lady exhibiting a lack of common sense on several different occasions, but she held her tongue. Just this once she would trust to fate. Her sister, who was probably still calculating the possibility of vouchers to Almack's, would no doubt be on her best behavior.

"I imagine that you will be happy to spend a quiet evening at home," her sister continued.

"Perhaps I will cut that green silk and begin your new afternoon ensemble."

"Make it into something for yourself. I will no longer wear homemade fashions. Today I ordered a dress from Mary's modiste."

"You did what!"

"I will not be outshone by the others. I am the only young lady whose dresses are not made by a fashionable dressmaker."

The blood drained from Clarissa's face. "Julia, we cannot afford it! We haven't the money!"

"We shall manage," she said airily. "We always do."

"We can't! Listen, Julia, we can scarcely afford the bills as it is. I don't know how we are going to pay for that dress! How could you do this?"

"I want pretty things like Mary has." Her enormous blue eyes filled with tears. "It isn't fair! If I am to catch a rich and titled husband, I must look the part!"

"Do not dwell on that, or you may be disappointed. As I have told you, think on marrying someone who will love you and make you comfortable. It isn't necessary that he be titled or wealthy."

"Then who will support this family?"

Clarissa sank to the sofa. "My dear, I have never expected that of you. When you are happily settled, we shall go on as before. I want you to be happy, Julia. I will not allow you to marry a man for no other reasons than his title and his wealth."

"Well, I want to be wealthy. I'm tired of being poor. And I shall marry whomever I please. It doesn't matter whether I care for him or not! You are tyrannical, Clarissa. I shall stand for it no longer!" Angrily she hurried out of the room, slamming the door behind her.

Clarissa felt a familiar pain building between her temples. What was happening to them? First Jeremy had been expelled from school and had already been involved in destructive mischief. Now the formerly obedient Julia was kicking over the traces in a premature attempt to be independent. There would be a large bill from a dressmaker's shop, and their money supply was dwindling rapidly. What was she to do?

Her head felt as though it was going to burst. Pressing her fingertips to her forehead, she left the salon and slowly climbed the stairs to her own room. Taking a light dose of laudanum, she stretched out on the bed and waited for the ache to subside.

She would have to cheapen up on their already simple meals. Perhaps she would send one of the maids back to the country and double up on the work herself. Furthermore, Julia could clean her own room. That would teach her neatness and would also drive home the lesson of spending without consideration for the size of one's purse. She could eliminate the washing woman, and she and Julia could do the work. If all that failed, they must simply leave London earlier than they had intended.

Perhaps the whole idea of coming here had been a foolish one, but she was responsible for seeing that her little sister was married to someone who would care for her. Julia had not formed a *tendre* for any of the young local men. She had to have this chance.

Oh, why had Father squandered the family fortune? Had he cared so little for his children? Fighting back tears, Clarissa fell into a troubled, painful doze.

George Longwood leaned back in his brother's chair and put his feet upon the glossy walnut desk, kicking aside some of the earl's papers in the process. Thoughtfully he uncorked the decanter of brandy, took a slow swig, and offered the bottle to his friend. "Sorry I can't give you a glass to drink from, Jerry. Mustn't leave any evidence, you know!"

The viscount drank a satisfying sip and handed it back. "No problem at all so long as we aren't caught."

"When we're finished, we'll add water. He'll never know that any is missing." He studied his shining Hessians. "Now, let us consider our most important business. My sister has done me ill, and I intend to pay her back. I hope that you will join me in this endeavor."

"What has Lady Westhaven done?"

"She's trying to talk Brough into sending me home to Longwood Hall. She says that by allowing me to remain in London, I am being rewarded instead of punished for my perfidy at school."

"What did he say?"

"Nothing. He listened, though. He listened very attentively. I can't help but think he was considering the matter."

"Surely he won't follow her advice!"

"I don't know. You can never tell about Brough. Nor can you underestimate my beast of a sister. If she is persistent, Brough may give in merely to shut her up."

"He can't!" Jeremy cried, visualizing his life in London without his friend.

"Exactly! So I thought we would provide a distraction, something that will take Marie's mind off this subject and will pay her back as well. Naturally I've come up with an excellent idea, and if you knew Marie, you would know why this will be the perfect prank."

"Explain."

"Does that mean you're in it with me?"

"Of course! So long as we won't get caught."

"We won't. We can't," Georgie said smugly. "This is what we'll do. We'll invite a large number of people to a rout at Marie's house. Only there won't be a party! Can you picture her face when all those guests begin to arrive?"

"What if she's out?"

"She won't be. She's always late leaving for any engagement. Besides, what difference will it make if she's out? The damage will have been done! It just won't be as much fun for us, that's all."

"You intend to be there?" Jeremy asked incredibly. "She'll see us and put two and two together."

"We'll hide. There's a cloakroom just off Marie's vestibule. At the dinner hour, we'll sneak in the servants' entrance and hide in there behind the coats. We'll hear every word. Then late at night, we'll slip away."

"It seems like a long evening," he said doubtfully.

"Mark my words, it'll be worth it. Are you game, Jerry?"

The viscount nodded. "If you say so."

"Good! Then that's what we'll do. Now let us get down to the details. How many people shall we invite? One hundred? Two hundred?"

"Let us just begin to write and see how long it takes us." He could already see that this elaborate prank was going to cost them many hours in writing the invitations, and he was beginning to won-

der if it was worth it. Georgie, however, appeared
to think that it was. Nothing, it seemed, could be
more devastating to Lady Marie Westhaven than
to be descended upon by a multitude of uninvited
guests to a most fictitious party.

"I have already obtained a sufficient quantity of
Marie's stationery," young Longwood announced,
patting a package beside him.

Jeremy looked at him with awe. "You think of
everything."

"Certainly. There must be no flaws." He withdrew two quills from his brother's desk drawer
and opened the inkstand. "Shall we start? Don't
forget, Jerry, use your best handwriting!"

Julia did not regret her sister's absence at the
dinner table, nor did she feel responsible for bringing on Clarissa's migraine. She had said what
needed to be said, and that was that. Clarissa was
entirely too overbearing and dictatorial, and it was
time that it was called to her attention.

With the help of Alice, she dressed for the Renfrew ball. Attired in a pretty petal pink gown, she
studied herself in the mirror and was once again
glad that her sister was indisposed. With a lofty
flourish, she ripped off the concealing lace tuck at
the bosom.

"Miss Julia . . ." the maid protested.

"I don't need it. The dress covers me well
enough," she said firmly.

"But Miss Clarissa would surely not approve."

"My sister would agree. After all, I am here to
find a husband, and things haven't been going
well lately. I must appear more sophisticated.
Now, hurry with my hair, Alice; I don't wish to be
late." She watched critically while the maid plied
the curling tongs through her bouncy curls.

"There! It is exactly how I want to appear!" she cried excitedly. "Don't you think I look older and more worldly?"

"Miss Julia, perhaps you should step into Miss Clarissa's room so that she may see you before you leave."

"Goodness, Alice, I wouldn't dream of it! My sister has one of her terrible headaches. It would be cruel to disturb her. No, she has seen me in this dress many times before."

"But, miss . . ."

"I do believe I hear the carriage. I mustn't be late. Good evening, Alice."

"But Miss Julia . . ."

She hopped lightly to her feet and tripped gaily down the stairs, heady with the feeling of independence. Poor Clarissa! It was just as well that she had accepted this invitation from the Granthams. Her sister's migraine would have forced them to stay home tonight. Besides, Lady Grantham was much more fun to be with. She was pretty and high-spirited and did not tend to keep her daughter under her strictest gaze every moment. The ball would be much more enjoyable without Clarissa.

Greeting her chaperon, she sat down beside Mary on the soft plush seat of the Grantham carriage. Even the trip to and from the Renfrew establishment would be much more pleasant. The coach was new and comfortable, not at all like the ancient Dunstan conveyance.

Chattering merrily of her own First Season, Lady Grantham kept the young ladies in stitches all the way to their destination. Once through the receiving line, she admonished them to mind their manners, to refrain from waltzing, and to avoid dark corners unless the gentleman was very rich or very noble. Then, with the tip of her fan, she released them to seek her own pleasures.

For the first time Julia wondered if Lady Grantham was not quite The Thing. She seemed respected and respectable. Mary's manners were charming. But the woman was quite obviously more intent on her own entertainment than in watching over the two girls. Clarissa would have never left her to her own devices. As wonderful as it was to be on her own, she must take care. There would be no one to remind her of any tiny improprieties.

Julia quickly became wrapped up with her friends and with filling her dance card and soon forgot all about her sister's absence. Surrounded by admirers, Julia was in her element. She had even attracted young Vincent Arlen, the eldest son of a duke. In his mid-twenties, Lord Arlen was considered a matrimonial prize. While he lacked the good looks and the cool sophistication of Lord Abingdon, he was not a conquest to be overlooked.

The evening was well under way when she caught her first glimpse of the Earl of Abingdon. Standing alone and looking over the crowd as seemed to be his custom on arrival, he was distressingly handsome in his perfectly tailored dark evening attire, a diamond stickpin glittering from his snowy cravat. Julia smiled. She had held back two dances in expectation of his presence. Tonight, without the interference of Clarissa, she would dance with him.

It wasn't necessary to attempt to attract his attention or even to approach him. Lord Abingdon was looking for her. After the dance, he came directly to her side, his presence causing her escort, the young son of a baronet, to withdraw hastily.

"Miss Julia." He bowed. "You are looking quite pretty tonight."

"Thank you, my lord." She curtsied, her pulse throbbing with excitement. "You are looking very handsome," she blurted.

He smiled indulgently. "I have been watching for your sister."

Julia's heart fell. Clarissa had interfered without her even being here. It wasn't fair!

"Clarissa isn't here tonight, Lord Abingdon. She dislikes any social occasion, particularly balls. She never enjoys herself. So when Lady Grantham offered to chaperon me, she was only too glad to stay at home."

"I see," he said quietly. "I had thought . . . Well, never mind. Will you convey my best wishes to Mrs. James?"

"Yes, my lord."

"Then I bid you good evening."

He hadn't asked her to dance! Briefly stunned, she took a deep breath and hurried after him. "Lord Abingdon?"

He paused. "Yes, Miss Julia?"

"I have dances available." She looked up at him with what she hoped were entrancing blue eyes.

The earl was too well controlled and too much the gentleman to let the shock register on his face, but he was speechless for a moment.

Julia, realizing her forwardness, blushed. "I only meant . . ." she stammered.

He bowed curtly. "I shall be honored to dance with you, young lady, provided that I may do so as soon as possible. I intend to leave early."

"Thank you, sir," she said humbly. "After the next one?"

"Very well." He nodded and departed, seeking out his own friends.

Julia spent the rest of the ball in misery. Dancing with Lord Abingdon wasn't even any fun. He was

perfectly polite, but his friends had grinned knowingly, making her wonder if he hadn't told them
the whole of it. What she had done was mortifying. He wasn't interested in her. He was only being a gentleman in acceding to her bold demand.
And she certainly hadn't been a lady!

What was worse, she was a traitor to her sister.
Clarissa had very much enjoyed Lord Abingdon's
attention at the last ball, and Julia had as much as
told him that she had detested it. Why had she
been so jealous of her sister's good time?

She thought of how despicable she had been toward Clarissa earlier in the day. It was she who
had caused the terrible headache. Her sister was
doing the very best she could with their limited
means, and she, too, deserved some enjoyment
from their sojourn in London. Perhaps it wasn't
too late to cancel the dressmaker's order. At any
rate, she would try doubly hard to be pleasing to
her elder sister. She would help with the work and
she would be sweet and kind. Somehow she
would make it all up to her.

At least the evening was not a complete failure.
The marquess, Vincent Arlen, had seemed very attracted to her. If he came up to scratch, she would
see to it that her family need never suffer hardship
again. She would give them money to repair and
redecorate the old home; she would take Clarissa
to a stylish modiste and buy her an entire new
wardrobe; she would even send Jeremy to Weston.
How they would praise her after that!

She closed her eyes and pictured it all. Lady
Arlen, the marchioness. Someday a duchess! It
was a fairy-tale scenario, and she was perfect for
the role. How foolish she had been to think of
wasting herself on a mere earl!

7

CLARISSA'S NIGHT WAS no more soothing than her afternoon had been. She had awakened late in the evening with only a dull remembrance of the debilitating headache and had drunk some broth that Cook had prepared. After that slim repast, she had gone back to bed and slept badly, tossing and turning till morning.

Unwilling to face the day ahead and the problems with Julia, she took her time rising. It was at least an hour later than usual when she finally descended to the front hall. At the foot of the stairs, she could scarcely believe the scene before her eyes. Through the open door of the salon, she could see Julia, attired in her oldest dress and an apron that must belong to one of the maids, busily, though somewhat dangerously, wielding a feather duster with fevered determination.

"Julia?" she asked in wonderment.

"Oh, Clarissa. You're up!" The young lady paused in her endeavors. "I would have brought up your breakfast to you, but I decided that you needed every moment of sleep you could get."

"What are you doing?"

"Cleaning," she said brightly. "Now, sit right down and I shall serve you."

Watching her suspiciously, Clarissa seated herself while Julia, in a flurry, brought her a footstool.

"While I work, you may breakfast in here and we will chat." Hurriedly she left the room and returned with a tray bearing tea and toast. "Cook said that this is all you would want for breakfast on the morning after a headache."

"Cook is right." She watched while her younger sister awkwardly set the tray on the table beside her and poured the brew. "What is going on here?"

"Going on?" Julia asked innocently. "Nothing." The young lady swatted so powerfully at a china figurine that the force nearly sent it tumbling.

"Please be careful!" Clarissa cried. "I would hate to have to pay for these things."

"Hm, no matter how perfectly awful they are, I suppose they would cost a great deal. Doesn't everything?" Her shoulders slumped. "I have sent Gibson to the dressmaker's to ask if the order can be canceled. I was wrong in ordering the gown. It was too expensive."

Clarissa sighed, sipping the strong hot tea and hoping against hope that it would not be too late.

"I still want you to have the green silk. You have precious few pretty dresses, and I have so many. Also, to be honest, the color does not suit me at all. It's much too dark for a debutante."

"But, Julia, you loved that fabric!"

"Nevertheless, I insist," she said with the air of a martyr. "You will be so pretty in it. Oh, I do hope the dressmaker will comply! What will we do if she won't?"

"I shall think of something," Clarissa said soothingly. "Come now, Julia, everyone makes a mistake once in a while. Wise people learn from them. Dear me, it isn't the end of the world!"

"Perhaps not, but . . . but that isn't all." Twisting the duster in her hands, Julia burst into tears. She flew across the room and threw herself to the floor at her sister's feet. "I was so cruel to you! I said such horrible things! It was I who caused your headache!"

"Now, now, it is over and done with. Let us think no more of it." She stroked the girl's saucy blond curls.

"I have repaid your kindness with poison!" Julia cried dramatically. "I shall never be worthy of forgiveness!"

Clarissa smiled, catching the inside of her lip between her teeth to keep from laughing. "Surely not that. Our purpose for being here must certainly cause tensions to be high. A slip in temper is not to be wondered at. Perhaps I have been a bit too severe with you."

"Oh no! If you had witnessed last night . . ."

Smile fading, Clarissa drew a deep breath. "What did you do?" she asked, attempting to keep her voice pleasantly level.

"At the ball last night, I . . . I threw myself at Lord Abingdon. I even asked him to dance with me."

"Julia!"

"I did," she wailed, burying her face in her sister's lap. "I don't think he liked it very much."

"Of course he wouldn't like it! What did he do?"

"He danced with me. He is too much of a gentleman to refuse, but I'm sure he told his friends. Otherwise they would not have been so amused." She lifted her head, her eyes searching her elder sister's. "I do hope that no one else realized. Surely he would not tell everyone, would he?"

Clarissa shook her head, more from helplessness

than from denial. "Lord Abingdon seems to be a perfect gentleman. We must assume that he made no more comment than that which was necessary."

"Actually he was looking for you, Clarissa. He wasn't interested in me at all. I think he liked you, but I have ruined that as well."

"He asked for me?" Her heart seemed to flutter and then quicken its pace.

Julia nodded miserably. "He was wondering where you were, and I said that you had stayed at home. I told him . . . I told him that you hated social events. I . . . I even intimated that you had had a miserable time at the last ball and were glad to stay away from this one."

"I see." An ache spread through her chest. How happy she had been that evening! Lord Abingdon had been the perfect partner in the dances and at the supper. Even though he was merely being kind, he had made her feel pretty and desirable. Now indeed, Julia had probably ruined any chance of her ever again enjoying his company at any social gathering. No man's vanity could withstand such a slur. How could she even look him in the face again?

"I was jealous of you," her little sister admitted. "He is everything I ever dreamed of. But no more! I have learned my lesson."

"Well then," Clarissa said briskly, squaring her shoulders, "if that is so, we must consider that all is not lost."

"You do not hate me?"

"Of course not!" She hugged Julia's slender shoulders.

"Perhaps if I told Lord Abingdon that I was wrong, that you had truly enjoyed yourself beyond belief . . ."

"No! For goodness' sake, Julia, think how forward that would make us seem. The least said in this case, the better. Leave it alone. You would only succeed in making us both appear foolish. He was merely being kind to me anyway. To bring up the subject again would make it look as though I wished to encourage his attentions."

"But don't you?"

"There is no future in it," she said firmly. "I am a widow, poor as a church mouse. Lord Abingdon is an earl and very wealthy. On top of that he has to be the most handsome man in London! His interest in me has only to do with Jeremy and Georgie."

"Are you so sure? You are very pretty for your age, Clarissa, and we *are* the daughters of a viscount. You should try to snare him." Shed of her guilt, Julia brightened. "You will not believe whose attentions I have attracted! Vincent, Lord Arlen, a rich marquess! Last evening he was very frequently at my side, and I will assure you that I behaved very properly towards him."

"I'm glad of that."

"Would it not be wonderful if I became a marchioness?"

"If you loved each other, it would indeed."

"That doesn't matter!" She bounced with excitement. "Besides, I believe that I could love him very easily. He is handsome, wealthy, and he has a title. Just think, when his father dies, he will become a duke. Certainly I could love him!"

"Please do not get your hopes up."

"I shall not, but do not be surprised to see me bring him up to scratch."

Clarissa tried to lift her own mood as she watched her sister's spirits rise, but her thoughts kept drifting back to Lord Abingdon. What could he think of her now? How would he act when

they saw each other again? They would certainly
cross each other's paths. The boys' friendship
would bring them together, but that was all. The
only thing they had in common was their mischievous brothers' relationship. They would meet once
more, and when they did, she must take care to
conduct herself as usual. She must never let him
know how unhappy Julia's remark to him had
made her.

She pushed the earl from her mind. What she
should be thinking of was Julia's preoccupation
with marrying a wealthy peer. She must find some
way to teach the girl that it was the man himself
who mattered, not his money nor his title. It
would be difficult to do while moving in a social
circle whose members placed little regard on marital love and fidelity. Clarissa knew, however, that
she was right. Hadn't her own travesty of a marriage proved it? Somehow she must make Julia see
the truth of the matter. Love and honesty and
friendship were what really mattered most. That
was what made true happiness between a man
and a woman. It hadn't happened for her. For Julia
it must.

By the time the ladies had finished their housework, the front entry hall had filled with flowers
from Julia's admirers. Glancing at the cards,
Clarissa recognized most of the names, but as
usual, there were a few new beaux to add to the
list. Most prominent among them was Lord Arlen.

The marquess had sent an enormous bouquet of
full-blown pink roses, which Julia reverently arranged in their best vase and placed lovingly in a
place of honor on the piano in the salon. After
standing back to admire her handiwork, she

leaned forward to sniff the fragrance. Dreamily she turned to Clarissa.

"Do you suppose he'll call today?"

Clarissa hoped that he would. She was becoming very curious about the young man who had dominated their conversation, and was anxious to meet him. Perhaps she would sit a bit closer to Julia today so that she could hear all that transpired.

"Maybe I should wear one of his roses in my hair."

Clarissa nearly choked. "No, Julia. I don't think that would be the thing at all. It would make you sadly overdressed."

"I suppose so, but I do wish to attract his attention."

"I think you already have done so," she laughed. "Just look at all those roses!"

"But how will I show him that I favor him?"

"Simply be yourself. Be sweet and kind and mannerly."

"That would show him nothing."

"It will show him that you are a proper young lady. For Heaven's sake, Julia, you scarcely know the young man! Give it time."

"He is the one I want."

"Then do as I say. If he is looking for a marchioness, he is seeking a young lady who is above reproach. You must behave perfectly."

"I know that," she said, her voice edged with a tiny irritation. "Still, there must be some way that I can draw him on. I know! I can pay him more attention than I do the others. I shall hang on his every word! Don't men like to be thought interesting and highly intelligent?"

Clarissa couldn't help smiling. "Yes, I suppose they do. But you must take care not to ignore your

other beaux. Above all, you must not be unman-
nerly."

"I shall be cautious." She looked at the clock on
the mantel. "Oh dear, see what time it is! I must
freshen up. La, Clarissa, I shall be on pins and nee-
dles to see if he comes!" She hugged her sister and
started towards the stairs. "Please hurry with your
own toilette. Callers should be arriving soon."

As Clarissa followed her, she was hailed on the
steps by Gibson.

"Miss Clarissa, I was sent on an errand by Miss
Julia and . . ." He blushed with embarrassment.

"Yes. I know all about it." She gripped the hand-
rail and prayed for good fortune. "What was the
outcome?"

"That was a nasty woman, that dressmaker. She
said the material was already cut, so it was too
late to stop. If Miss Julia won't pay, she's going to
send Bow Street Runners and mean bill collectors,
and she'll tell all her customers that Miss Julia is a
cheat. Said she'd ruin Miss Julia and you too,
ma'am."

Clarissa exhaled audibly. "Well, I shall have to
come up with the money then. Thank you for trying, Gibson."

The groom guiltily thought of the gratuities the
earl had given him each time he came by to check
on his horse. "I've got some money saved back,
Miss Clarissa. You can have it."

She shook her head. "I couldn't take your sav-
ings, Gibson, but it was kind of you to offer."

"We could call it a loan, ma'am."

"Thank you. But I shall come up with something. I always do!"

"Yes, ma'am. Just remember, if you ever need it,
it's there."

"I do appreciate it. I don't know what I'd do

without the loyalty of you and the others. You've all stood by me through some very hard times. Perhaps someday things will be better and I can repay you for everything you've done for me."

He dropped his gaze to the floor. "Dunstan Hall is our home, too, and the Dunstans are our family, Miss Clarissa. We don't need any repayment."

She swallowed with difficulty. Once again she was reminded how much she was depended upon, and how many *she* depended upon. It wasn't just Julia and Jeremy. It was the whole population of the estate.

Quickly, before she burst into tears, she ran up the steps to her room and began dressing in the proper attire to receive guests. It was well that she hurried, for just as she entered the salon, the knocker fell on the front door. Among the first of the gentlemen callers was Lord Arlen, who bowed low over her hand when Julia made the introductions.

"How do you do, Miss James?" he said in cultured accents.

"Very well. And you, Lord Arlen?"

"Tolerably." He shifted his eyes to Julia. "Much more tolerably now."

Clarissa stifled a groan as her sister dimpled at his flattery.

"Please sit down, my lord." Julia daintily patted the seat beside her. "I wish to thank you for the lovely bouquet. How could you ever know that roses are my favorite flowers?"

"But they must be." He languidly flipped up the tails of his blue coat of Bath superfine and seated himself. "You remind me of a rose. Your delicate beauty, your sweetness . . ."

The girl blushed becomingly and unfurled her fan, fluttering it coyly.

Other admirers began to arrive. Julia greeted each pleasantly, but kept her attention on every word Lord Arlen murmured. Clarissa caught the eye of Sir Howard Milsom, one of her sister's older and most loyal beaux, who stood leaning negligently on the mantel and watching the scene with barely disguised amusement. Grinning at her, he shrugged and rolled his eyes. Smiling back, Clarissa could not but agree with his unspoken sentiments.

Lord Arlen was a fribble. He was an immature young dandy puffed up with his own consequence. He was hardly the man for Julia. If she was to wed at this age, she needed an older man who was settled and who could control her childish impulses, a man who could indulge her fancies and yet keep her in line. A man like Sir Howard. He was perfect! Why hadn't she recognized that long before? Above all, why hadn't Sir Howard offered for Julia before Lord Arlen had come along? Clarissa would have welcomed his suit, and Julia would probably have agreed. Now it was hopeless. Julia wouldn't even entertain the thought so long as she was so very smitten with the young marquess.

Clarissa smiled again at the baronet and echoed his gesture with a slight shrug to her own shoulders. That would let him know that she, at least, agreed with his view of Lord Arlen. It would give him hope and might keep him within Julia's circle. But somehow she felt it wasn't necessary. It seemed as though Sir Howard was enjoying himself to the utmost.

Her thoughts were deflected as Simmons entered the room and came to her side.

"Miss Clarissa, Lord Abingdon is in the stable.

Gibson isn't there, having gone to purchase oats. I thought you'd want to know."

Her heart tripled its beat. "Oh dear, I wonder if he needs anything in particular."

"I wouldn't know, madam."

"Perhaps I should see." The room seemed suddenly to have become very warm and stuffy. A fine trace of perspiration moistened her lip. Moths seemed to flutter in her stomach.

She had known that she must face Lord Abingdon sometime. She didn't know it would be this soon. She took a deep breath. "How can I leave Julia?" she whispered half to herself.

"I shall leave the door to the salon open and shall remain just outside within view," the butler intoned.

"Oh dear." She stood, her knees weak. "Yes, I had best be hospitable."

"Yes indeed, Miss Clarissa." The butler smiled. This was exactly what he and Cook had planned when they espied the earl's arrival.

Brough was slightly surprised to see the Dunstan stable empty of the faithful Gibson when the line of saddle horses, phaetons, and curricles in front of the house testified that the ladies were at home. The man must have been away on an errand or he would have been present, polishing harnesses and hardware that didn't need cleaning or grooming horses that already shone. Gypsy's coat had never looked better before his stay in Gibson's care. The earl wished his conscience were not so good. If he was like most of his peers, he would offer the groom an exorbitant salary and steal him from the Dunstans.

He let himself into Gypsy's fragrant box stall, stroked the gelding's shoulder, and knelt to examine his knee. There was no wrap on the animal's leg now, and the injury seemed to be healing satisfactorily. Clarissa's poultice had been successful. The horse barely favored it. It was time to take him home.

Brough was almost sorry. He had enjoyed his visits to the immaculate little stable and his conversations with Gibson. His own employees were too much in awe of him to chat casually about horses. Also Clarissa's cook usually put in an appearance with a plate of her delicious sugar biscuits and a pitcher of lemonade. He wondered if Mrs. James knew what treasures she had in her employ. They made him want to release his London-bred servants and bring to town the old retainers from his country seat. There were none so comfortable to be around as people who had served one's family for generations and who had grown up on the estate.

He watched Gypsy's ears as he massaged the knee. Only a slight flicker indicated any discomfort. Yes, he must take him home.

"Good morning, Lord Abingdon." Her rich voice washed over him.

"Mrs. James." He stood, smiling. Damn, why did she wear that lace cap? Her hair had been so beautiful at the ball.

She stepped into the stall and bent to examine Gypsy's leg. "His knee is much better, don't you think?"

"I believe he'll be fit in no time." He watched her slender fingers knead the animal's joint. "You know a great deal about horses' injuries, don't you?"

She laughed. "Old wives' remedies."

Somehow the statement disturbed him. "You certainly aren't old, madam, and you are not a wife."

"No, my lord," she said stiffly, "I suppose I am neither."

He had irritated her, and for the life of him, he didn't understand why. She *wasn't* old and she *wasn't* a wife. She was a lovely young widow who should be thinking of finding another husband. My God, she shouldn't bury herself, pining away for that Captain James, whoever he was. He hadn't been good enough for her in the first place.

She straightened. "It was a figure of speech."

"What?"

" 'Old wives' remedies.' It was a figure of speech."

"Yes, of course." He felt foolish.

"Like 'old wives' tales.' "

Brough grinned. "I know. I'm wooden-headed sometimes."

Eyes sparkling, she tilted her head. "My lord, I can scarcely believe that."

He was entranced. Abandoning her little tiffish mood and looking at him like that, she was breathtaking. She must get over her dislike of balls and social activities. The lady could have London at her feet. Men would swarm to her like bees to honey. Damn that matronly lace cap!

"It's true, Mrs. James," he said soberly. "My friend Brandon's wife often comments on the thickness of a man's skull. I fear I've fallen victim to her tongue more than once."

"You're roasting me."

"Never! Allesandra is very good at putting people in their place."

"The duchess is so sweet."

"She's also a manipulator."

"Lord Abingdon!" she cried with shock.

"But everyone loves her dearly."

"They should." She returned her attention to the

horse. Gypsy curved his neck around her while Clarissa scratched his pointy ears. "Oh, you are a love," she crooned. "Lord Abingdon, he is such a wonderful horse. The whole team is fine. I imagine that they are magnificent when put through their paces."

"Would you like riding behind them, Mrs. James?" he blurted. "It won't be long before Gypsy is fit for some easy work in the park. Would you like to accompany me?"

She looked over her shoulder with surprise.

"I would enjoy it," he urged. "With your old wives' remedies and tales, you might give me a few pointers."

Clarissa laughed. "I doubt that! You are probably a member of the four-in-hand."

He shrugged in smiling assent.

"Well then, I would be delighted, but I don't wish to be a burden."

"You could never be that."

"My lord, you flatter me."

Brough shook his head. "Don't you realize . . ." He halted his ready lecture on her making the most of her charms. It would probably anger her.

"In the meantime I'll be taking Gypsy home. He's fit enough to walk the distance. I don't wish to take advantage of your hospitality."

"It has been no trouble whatsoever." She lowered her eyes. "Lord Abingdon, about last night . . . about Julia. She is sometimes rather impetuous . . ."

"She's very young."

"And immature?"

"I didn't say that, Mrs. James."

"No," she said carefully, "but you meant it. Perhaps I should have waited until next year to bring Julia to town."

"She'll be all right. As you say, she is somewhat impetuous, but she will learn."

"If she does not disgrace herself first. I hope she has learned from last night. She seems to have done so."

Clarissa looked so concerned that he wished he could take her in his arms and comfort her. She was too young herself to fill the role thrust upon her by her parents' early demise. In their previous meetings she had struck him as being strong and so capable. Today she seemed delicately vulnerable.

"Mrs. James, no one will know of Miss Julia's little faux pas."

She sighed deeply. "I can't thank you enough. It would ruin her if people knew of her boldness."

"How did you know?"

"Julia told me herself. She was quite overset at her own behavior."

"So you see? She is learning."

"Yes, but I must never again allow her to attend a social engagement without being present myself." She started from the stall. "Even now I have allowed her to be alone too long with her suitors, despite delegating Simmons to keep an eye on things."

He leaped at the chance to encourage her. "I quite agree. You should always be present, Mrs. James. I believe that you can enjoy yourself and still keep a close eye on Miss Julia."

Clarissa smiled enigmatically, bid him good day, and glided from the stable.

Brough watched her cross the yard and enter the house through the back door. Suddenly he realized that Cook hadn't brought him his usual treat. With the exception of Simmons, whom Clarissa had mentioned, the lady's servants must be on holiday today.

8

CLARISSA'S DAYS CONTINUED on, much as they had before Julia's little exhibition. The girl seemed to have returned to her normal sweet self and offered her sister no cause for panic. Indeed she seemed quite lighthearted and cheerful, a state of mind induced no doubt by the attentive courtship of Lord Arlen. Clarissa had not changed her opinion of the young marquess, but she was forced to view his pursuit with favor. Anyone who could make Julia so happy must not be considered unacceptable.

Jeremy, too, was behaving himself. He and Georgie applied themselves to their books without complaint, then spent the rest of their days at Lord Abingdon's house or driving about London seeing the sights. Clarissa knew that they had actually visited the Tower of London and Week's Mechanical Museum, because they described them in such detail. Perhaps they had learned their lesson as well and were turning over a new leaf.

The only disappointment in her life was that she hadn't seen Lord Abingdon since their meeting in the stable. He hadn't been present at any of the social events that she and Julia had attended. He was in town, however, for Jeremy often mentioned

him. He must have better things to do with his
time. It was true that the latest entertainments had
been deadly dull. A socially experienced gentleman like the earl would know in advance which
parties were to be avoided. It was foolish that she
kept glancing at the door upon any new arrival.

Clarissa had been greatly satisfied with her last
interview with him. The stable lent an informality
which had made everything easier. He seemed to
bear no ill will towards herself or Julia. He had
put her at her ease and reassured her that no one
would hear of Julia's little mistake. The incident
was over and done with.

If only she didn't long to see him so! It was ut-
ter foolishness and she must set it aside. Now that
Gypsy had been returned to Lord Abingdon's stable, her only link with him was their fellow chap-
eronage of the boys. With everything proceeding
smoothly there, he had no real cause to seek her
out.

Determined to put him from her mind, she went
in search of Julia. They would go shopping. She
needed some trim for the walking ensemble she
was finishing for the girl, and she just might see
some fabric cheap enough to make one for herself.
Afterwards they could stop for an ice at Gunter's.
That would be just the thing to drive the misty
dreams from her head.

She found her sister in her room, trying on the
gown that had arrived just this morning from the
expensive modiste.

"Oh, Clarissa," the young lady wailed. "It's not
one whit better than those you have made for me
yourself."

Clarissa carefully looked over the frothy confec-
tion and mentally disagreed. The dress was exquisite. It was the palest of petal pink, so lightly

tinted that she wondered how a fabric could be dyed with such delicacy. The little puffed sleeves, Clarissa's bugaboo, were set in perfectly, with nary a puckered stitch. The neckline was just the right depth for a girl of Julia's tender years, so that the gown could stand on its own without the distractive addition of protective tucks of lace. There was no doubt that Madame was very gifted and that she had been inspired by her young client's loveliness. It was such a pity that they could not afford to have the woman make all of Julia's clothes. Well, she had this one at least. Clarissa had to admit that it was worth the cheap cuts of meat that they had been forced to dine upon.

"Julia," she said softly, "I have never seen you look so beautiful."

"But I am mortified! This dress shall always serve to remind me how horribly selfish I was."

"Now, we have put all that behind us. I want you to enjoy the gown, and I know I shall enjoy seeing you in it! You must save it for a very special occasion."

"The Singletons' ball, I think." Having received her sister's approval, Julia preened before the mirror. "Do you think Lord Arlen will be impressed?"

"If he has eyes in his head," Clarissa laughed, "and do not forget your other beaux, like Sir Howard. They'll be enchanted as well."

"Hmph. Who cares about Sir Howard? He is too old. Why, he must be as old as Lord Abingdon."

"Oh, not quite that old," Clarissa said laughingly. "And if he were, what, pray, is wrong with that?"

"Older men are not romantic."

It was on the tip of Clarissa's tongue to argue that neither Sir Howard nor the earl were "old men," but she let the comment pass. Julia was happy, and there was no sense at all in threatening it. There was time enough to put Sir Howard forward if Lord Arlen failed to come up to scratch.

"I thought you might like to go shopping."

Julia's eyes lit up. "Can we afford it?"

"Only for a few small items, I'm afraid, but we can look at everything else and then go for an ice at Gunter's."

"I shall be ready in minutes!"

Clarissa assisted her out of the gown. "I'll direct Gibson to put the horses to and send Alice to help you dress."

"Thank you, Clarissa," she gushed. "I love looking in the shops and planning what I'll purchase when I am Vincent's marchioness."

" 'Vincent'? Surely you don't call him by his first name?"

Julia winked saucily. "Only to myself."

Her sister shook her head. "You gave me a start."

"You worry too much, Clarissa. Never fear, I shall continue to behave with all propriety. Isn't it foolish, though, that everyone must be so formal?"

"There are important reasons for it." To avoid further discussion, Clarissa quickly left the room. Julia! She realized she had been lulled into complacency by the young lady's perfect and proper behavior. She must remember to stay on her guard.

After giving the orders to Simmons, she went to her own chamber and dressed herself, hoping that she looked passably well in her old tawny-gold walking dress. The color wasn't particularly fashionable, but she had always thought that it brought out the flecks of amber in her eyes. Goodness, why was she concerned about that? Shopkeepers didn't care how their customers looked so long as they had money in their reticules. She quickly finished her toilette and waited for her sister in the entrance hall.

It wasn't long before the young lady joined her, for Julia could indeed ready herself in minutes when she particularly wished to do so. Looking like a breath of spring in her apple green walking costume, the girl shone with anticipation. "Clarissa, I desperately need ribbon to match this color. Can we afford it?"

She nodded assent, suddenly wondering why she had made Julia yet another walking dress. The girl really didn't need it, as much as she herself did. Ah well. At least she had the green silk that her sister had presented her. She could have a new ball gown from it if she ever found time to sew for herself.

"Let us be on our way." Leaving the house, she gave Gibson the directions and settled herself beside her sister in the old carriage.

"We should easily be able to find a matching ribbon," Julia chattered. "Apple green is a very stylish color."

Clarissa listened with only half an ear as the young lady expounded upon current fashions. The enjoyment seemed to have gone out of the day for Clarissa. Next to her sister, she felt positively dowdy. It wasn't fair that Julia had all the pretty new things.

She jerked herself up, astounded that she should have had such a thought. It was for Julia's sake that they were here in the first place. If it weren't for her, she would be home in the country, thinking about the spring planting instead of modish attire. What was wrong with her? Why was she suddenly feeling so dissatisfied? The tawny-gold was certainly good enough for Essex. Clarissa lifted her chin. And damn, it was good enough for London, too!

Burlington Arcade was a marvelous development in shopping. With its high, vaulted ceilings, hanging lanterns, and the myriad of shops all assembled under one roof, it was a purchaser's paradise. It was an orderly one as well. Its mixed patronage of nobility, gentry, and ordinary Londoners was watched over carefully by stern uniformed beadles. Pickpockets were swiftly and severely dealt with, and there was no running, pushing, cursing, nor spitting. It provided a welcome relief from the boisterousness of the city streets.

They quickly found the apple green ribbon and the trim for the new walking dress they had set out to look for, then wandered through the other shops perusing all the fabulous merchandise. Clarissa paused to finger a bolt of peach muslin. The color would be perfect for her, and the price was right.

"Clarissa." Julia tugged at her arm. "Did you see the pink cashmere shawl I was looking at? I have no proper wrap to wear with my new ballgown, and it would be exactly the thing. It isn't expensive either." She eyed the fabric. "I don't need another dress right now, and I don't think I'd look well in peach."

Clarissa smoothed the muslin one last time and turned away. "Very well," she said softly. "Show it to me."

As usual, Julia's sense of style was unquestionable. The shawl was perfect, and it was so inexpensive that she wondered if the shopkeeper hadn't made a mistake. "We'll have it," she smiled, "and you must let me wear it sometime."

Julia giggled and hugged her, knowing that Clarissa, with her vivid coloring, would never be caught dead in pink. "You are the best of all sisters!"

"Remember that the next time you set out to cause me a headache." She counted out her precious coins, seeing with dismay that few remained in her reticule. She would have to dip once more into her precious hoard.

"Mrs. James, Miss Julia."

Clarissa whirled to look into the smiling eyes of Lord Abingdon.

"Out shopping, are you?"

"Yes, my lord," Julia bubbled. "Just look at my pretty new shawl! I shall wear it to the Singletons' ball. Won't it be absolutely perfect?"

"Julia!" Clarissa admonished. "Lord Abingdon is not interested in ladies' attire."

"On the contrary, ma'am, I enjoy viewing a well-dressed lady, such as you are yourself today. The color becomes you."

Clarissa flushed. He knew as well as she did that her dress was old and unfashionable. Why must he pretend otherwise?

"We're going to Gunter's for an ice," Julia fluttered.

"Indeed? Perhaps I may join you?" His response was to Julia, but his gaze had never left Clarissa.

"If you please," she murmured politely.

"I would be delighted." He took up their purchases and escorted them out of the arcade and onto the street.

Gibson, seeing the earl, sprang to sharpest attention and snapped open the carriage door so smartly that he nearly dislodged it from its ancient hinges.

"Gunter's," the earl commanded, handing the ladies inside and stepping in after them.

Clarissa's distress increased as Lord Abingdon positioned himself on the lumpy seat across from them. Good Heavens, was he seated in the place where the spring had broken free of its webbing? What would he think? The old vehicle was dilapidated and it smelled musty. Dear lord! How could she be caught in such a twist?

He didn't seem to mind. At least he continued to exchange pleasantries all the way to Gunter's. Perhaps he was just too much a gentleman to show displeasure at a spring jabbing his bottom, or maybe he was lucky enough to have seated himself to the left of it. At any rate, she was thankful when they arrived at the busy confectioner's.

Julia was immediately accosted by a simpering group of her girlfriends. She begged to sit with them, so Clarissa was left alone with Lord Abingdon. Miraculously he got them a table and placed their order.

"They seem so young," he mused. "It's hard to imagine that each one of them will probably be a matron by year's end."

"I believe they're worse when they're all together and not under the particular attentions of a gentleman, when they can all act the proper lady."

Her ideas were born out by the next arrival at Gunter's. Lord Arlen strolled up to the young ladies' table, bowed to all, and drew up a chair next to Julia's. The girls immediately assumed a sophisticated demeanor.

"Arlen," the earl observed.

"Yes." Frowning slightly, Clarissa sampled her orange ice.

"Is something wrong?"

"With the ice? No, it's delicious." She smiled, savoring the rich citrine flavor, and cast her eyes toward her sister. "Lord Arlen's attentions have been quite marked."

Lord Abingdon followed her gaze. "Please do not think me discourteous, Mrs. James, but I cannot like it."

"No?"

He took a deep breath. "I don't wish to force my opinion."

"I would very much like to hear it, Lord Abingdon," she said swiftly. "You are much more knowledgeable about members of the *ton* than I am."

"All right ... Arlen is rather a wastrel, but his family, of course, does sit on a sizable fortune. They stand his nonsense. Oh, he'll probably grow up and change his ways, but he'll marry for money, Mrs. James. He'll wed a lady with a large dowry. That family always does."

"I see." Her eyes sought his. "I understand."

"I don't wish to ..."

"No, my lord, I'm glad you've spoken plainly. You are well enough acquainted with this family to guess that Julia's dowry must be minuscule, and you are right. I thank you for telling me this."

He covered her hand with his. "I wouldn't want you or Julia to be hurt."

Sensing a presence behind them, Clarissa turned to see her sister. "Yes?"

"Oh ... nothing." Julia tossed her head and smiled. "It was merely an invitation from Mary. I'll talk to you about it later." She returned to her friends.

With regret, Clarissa withdrew her hand from Lord Abingdon's comforting clasp. Now what would she do? She trusted the earl's assessment of the situation. She must steer Julia clear of the young marquess. It was going to be very difficult.

Piqued, Julia sat down with a flounce. So Arlen and his family wanted money? Well, money was what they would think they were getting. She quickly found her opportunity.

"Will your sister permit you to go?" Mary asked, turning to her.

"No," she said resentfully, "my sister will *not* allow me to go shopping with you. Clarissa is so tightfisted. Just look at where we live and the clothing I am forced to wear! It is 'everything for Jeremy'! She'll probably even withhold my dowry and give it to him!"

"Julia, I didn't realize!"

"She can't do that," Lord Arlen stated.

"Oh yes she can. We have a great deal of money, but she controls it. It's my money, too! It was left me by my aunt."

"Legally she cannot withhold it. Not when you are married, Miss Julia."

Julia turned hopeless blue eyes on the marquess and sniffled into her handkerchief. "Do you think so? Do you really think so?"

He smiled confidently. "I know so. I am sure of it."

Singleton House glowed with light. As they stepped from the carriage, Clarissa gave a final look of approval to her lovely sister. In her new dress with the pink shawl, Julia could not have appeared more ravishing. She would attract more than her share of beaux tonight. Hopefully one of them would supplant Lord Arlen.

"You must be sure to share all of your charms among your beaux tonight," Clarissa advised. "I know that you like Lord Arlen a great deal, but he is not the only young man in London. You must give the others a chance. You may find that you like someone else best."

"I shall be *la belle*," Julia laughed.

"Very good, for tonight you shall indeed be an Incomparable. I've never seen you in better looks."

Singleton House was everything that Clarissa had expected it to be. Both grand and tasteful, it embraced the best of what wealth and sophistication had to offer. But even though it was sumptuously decorated for the ball, she could sense that it was a home as well. There was an indescribable warmth among the servants and the atmosphere itself. Somehow it was obvious that the master and his lady loved each other.

As they passed through the receiving line, the dark, handsome marquess bent his head to her ear. "You will save me a dance, Mrs. James?"

"I would be honored."

"What is this?" the marchioness teased. "Should I be jealous?"

Clarissa didn't miss the look of fondness that passed between her host and hostess. "I think not," she laughed, curtsying.

Lady Singleton took her hand. "I'm so happy you could come."

"I'm happy to be here. You have a lovely home, Lady Singleton."

"Thank you." She dimpled. "I'm glad you called it a home and not just a house, for that is how I want it to be." She leaned closer. "Please call me 'Ellen' instead of Lady Singleton. The title makes me feel like a ship in full sail."

"I would be honored . . . Ellen. Of course, you must call me 'Clarissa.' "

"I shall be happy to do so. Brough has told us so

much of you, and I did enjoy our supper at the ball."

"Ellen," her husband interrupted gently, "you are holding things up."

"Oh dear, I am indeed." She shrugged. "Well, if that is the only disaster that befalls me this evening, I shall consider it all a success."

A success? How could anything the marchioness touched be anything less? She was perfectly charming.

Clarissa directed Julia to the ballroom, where the girl was immediately mobbed by her waiting beaux, among whom, of course, was Lord Arlen. There was nothing she could do about that. He would have his allowable two dances, but that was all. Other gentlemen would occupy the rest of Julia's evening, and perhaps one of them would make an impression. And she herself would dance one set at least, even though it was with a married man who was head over heels in love with his wife.

"The supper dance and the final waltz?"

"Lord Abingdon!"

"Well?" He bowed over her hand.

"I'd be delighted." She caught her breath. How handsome he was in his elegant black evening attire! In this room full of beautiful men, he had to be the most outstanding of them all.

He nipped two glasses of champagne off the tray of a passing waiter and escorted her to a chair. "Shall we sit together and watch the antics of the ingenues?"

"So long as the *ton* does not count it as a dance. I refuse to miss the opportunity to waltz with you, my lord. You do it so well."

"As do you, Mrs. James." He seated her and presented her with her drink. "The *ton* may think what it likes. I am a friend of the Dunstan family."

"You are indeed." Clarissa's eyes turned toward the middle of the room and she watched Julia tilt her head towards Lord Arlen and flash her eyes coyly at him. "I have tried to caution her."

"You didn't tell her what I said?"

"I couldn't. You don't know Julia, my lord. I must use other means to get around her."

"Are you sure that's best?"

Clarissa nodded. "She can be very stubborn, and she does fancy herself in love with him."

"Is she?"

"She is in love with wealth and title. I want something better for her."

He chuckled. "Money and title are the basis for many marriages, Mrs. James."

"I am not naive, my lord," she flashed. "I am only too aware of that."

"My apologies, ma'am. I didn't wish to irritate."

"I married for what I thought was money. I shouldn't have done that. It was dishonest. I don't want Julia to do the same."

Immediately she realized that the conversation was growing too personal, and changed the subject. Lord Abingdon visited politely for a few more moments and then went on his way. Clarissa felt deflated. Why had she snapped at him like that? He was only trying to be helpful. Dear Lord, Julia and her problems were entirely oversetting her. She wished that they could leave London and go home for a few days. In Essex she could put herself back onto an even keel. But there was no money for travel. Money! Why did everything always lead back to that?

The evening seemed to plod. She danced her set with Lord Singleton, then glanced around the crowded room for Julia. Where was the girl? A quick survey told her that Lord Arlen was also ab-

sent. Clarissa's heart began to pound. She noticed
the open doors to the balcony and hurried toward
them. Surely Julia could not have allowed him to
take her out there alone!

The cool air was welcome after the heat of the
ballroom, but the sight she saw was not. In the far
corner stood Julia and Arlen, arms around each
other. As she watched with horror, the marquess
bent his head to kiss her. Clarissa's anger flared.
How dare he compromise the girl! She started forward.

"No."

Hands caught her shoulders and whirled her
around. She looked up to see the smoldering eyes
of Lord Abingdon fastened on a point behind her.
She tried to pull away.

"Not now."

"But . . ."

He propelled her across the balcony to the opposite side and down the stairs into the garden.

"Lord Abingdon, I must—"

"Arlen saw me. The scene is over. Let's not
make another one."

Her knees had turned to water. She leaned
against him. "I must take Julia home immediately."

"Walk with me first, Mrs. James. Let your temper cool."

She realized the good sense in that. In her present state of mind, she would storm into the ballroom, scold Julia soundly, and make a bigger
scene than the one she had already witnessed. She
took his arm.

"You are right, my lord."

He led her down a brick path lighted by softly
glowing Chinese lanterns. Clarissa was glad at
least that Arlen hadn't taken Julia to the garden.
The shimmering illumination, the muffled strains

of the orchestra, and the sprinkling of stars over-
head were very romantical.

She was powerfully conscious of the man beside
her. When she had leaned against him, she had
ached for him to hold her. Lord, she was no better
than Julia. If Lord Abingdon wished, he could take
her in his arms and kiss her senseless. She would
not stop him. Instead she would toss all her
proper upbringing out the window and kiss him
back. It would not matter that there was no future
in it. She shivered.

"Are you cold?"

"A little."

"Good. That means that your temper is cool-
ing." He took off his coat and draped it over her
shoulders.

She breathed deeply of the essence of spicy Impe-
rial water and of his male scent. "What shall I do?"

"Nothing now. Continue on through the ball as
though nothing has happened. Arlen knows he
was caught. He'll try nothing more tonight. But tomorrow you must talk seriously with Julia."

"I dread it."

"I understand, but you must do it. Better now
than later."

"I suppose so."

"May I make another suggestion?"

"Please do."

"Stay at home for the next few days and don't
receive callers. You need time away from all of
this. Put it about that Julia is indisposed."

"Yes, that's a good idea."

"And now, if you are collected, we should return
to the ball or we'll start a scandal all our own."

Clarissa smiled. "I hardly think that."

"Don't be too sure," he murmured.

9

JULIA WAS VERY quiet on the way home from the Singleton ball, which gave Clarissa reason to believe that Lord Arlen had informed her that they had been seen. In the morning she was sure of it, for the girl kept to her room far beyond her usual hour of rising. After informing Simmons that they would not be at home to visitors, she climbed the stairs and knocked on the door.

"Come in," Julia called lightly.

Clarissa entered, closing the door behind her. "I hadn't seen you this morning, so I came to check. Are you ill?"

"Oh, only a trifling headache."

"How unusual! You seldom have headaches, Julia. Perhaps a draught of laudanum would help."

"None of that, Clarissa. I don't wish to be put to sleep. As it is, I've scarcely time to dress before my callers arrive."

"Don't worry about that. I've instructed Simmons that you are indisposed."

"What!"

"You will receive no callers, Julia, not for several days. During that time you may reflect upon your outrageous behavior of last night."

"You can't do this to me!"

"Oh yes I can." Clarissa stood firmly in front of the door. "I'll do it if I have to lock you in."

"You cannot hold me prisoner!" Julia began to pace up and down the room. "I have done nothing wrong!"

"You have disgraced yourself."

"There is no disgrace in kissing a man to whom one is almost betrothed."

"Almost betrothed?"

"Yes!"

"I don't think it will happen."

Julia whirled at her, her dressing gown skirt swishing and her golden curls bouncing angrily. "Then you are wrong!"

Clarissa took a deep breath. "Julia, please calm yourself. You must listen to me. This isn't easy, but—"

"Why should I listen to you? Your behavior last night was not in the best of taste either. The amount of time you spent alone with Lord Abingdon? La, anything could have happened! But," she sneered, "you are such an old maid that we must guess that it didn't."

"I am *not* an old maid!"

Julia made a mock curtsy. "You are right. You are a widow. You've been with one man. Another would make little difference."

Clarissa drew back her hand. Before she could stop herself, she struck her sister hard across the cheek. The girl cried out and fled across the room, throwing herself on her bed and pressing the injured flesh against the pillow.

"Oh, Julia. Oh I'm so sorry." Clarissa slumped against the doorframe and tried to shut out the sobs. "That was horrible of me." She watched the girl shake with weeping and moved numbly forward. "Please forgive me."

"Kissy, I'm sorry! I didn't mean what I said. *I* was horrible!" Julia flung herself into her arms.

Clarissa held her close until the tears subsided. "Dear Heavens, I've never in my life struck either you or Jeremy."

"It's my fault! I shouldn't have said what I did. What is happening? I know that nothing shameful would happen between you and Lord Abingdon. I only wanted to hurt you!"

"Shhh ... it's over now," she soothed, "but I will insist on our having a few days privacy. The strain is growing too much. We need time alone."

Julia nodded soberly.

"We'll sew, and we'll think of other things to do."

"All right."

Clarissa kissed her sister's reddened cheek. Lord Abingdon would have been very disappointed in her performance. She had handled things so badly. Now she couldn't, she just *couldn't*, tell Julia about Lord Arlen. Not after what had happened. She would have to wait.

Brough settled himself into a soft winged chair before the flickering fireplace, poured himself a glass of brandy, and opened a book. It seemed so very quiet in the house with the boys spending the evening at Jeremy's. Recently they had been constantly underfoot, and unfortunately their favorite room in the house was his library. He didn't mind spending time with them, but once in a while, like tonight, he wanted to sit at home in peace. He wondered if Mrs. James ever tired of the two.

Mrs. James. Somehow he didn't like calling her that. It didn't suit her. She was too young to be a widow. When he called her "Mrs. James" he felt like looking around the corner to see if a husband was lurking nearby.

Poor lady. How had she fared in her interview with her little sister? The tension was becoming too much for the both of them. Clarissa was too young to shoulder the kind of responsibility she was called upon to bear. Damn, she was scarcely more than a girl herself, despite her marital status. To make matters worse, young Julia was jealous of her, and well she should be. The girl's pale, delicate looks were entirely eclipsed by her elder sister's striking beauty.

Clarissa was a man's woman, one whom he could be proud to have on his arm and one who could, no doubt, provide a great deal of pleasure in private. He had known it instinctively. He suspected that Brandon and Harry would agree now that they'd meet her. Once again he wondered why she seemed so oblivious to her own desirability. Didn't the lady ever look in the mirror?

Closing his eyes, he remembered how she had felt in his arms the night before. Soft, vulnerable, she had needed his protection. Good God! What was he thinking of? He wasn't ready to take that step! He doubted that she was either. Her main considerations were Julia and Jeremy, not her own future. She looked on him as a friend and fellow guardian. Nothing more.

His thoughts were interrupted by a noisy commotion in the hall. Doors slammed, feet echoed on the marble entry. Over it all resounded his sister's strident, demanding voice.

"Where is he?" Marie shouted like an alewife. "He will not hide from me!"

The door burst open, banging against the wall and rattling the candle sconces. Grasping George and Jeremy by the collars of their coats, his sister propelled the two forward. With an amazing display of strength, she shoved them toward her brother.

"I have had enough, Brough, I have finally had enough! You are going to send him back to school, where he belongs. If they will not take him, which would not surprise me, you will send him to the Hall. No longer shall he remain in London!"

Brough's hazel eyes flicked from the angry Lady Westhaven to the two recalcitrants, both looking anything but repentant with those faint grins upon their faces. "What has happened?"

"They have humiliated me before the *ton!* I shall never recover my social standing after this. I am mortified beyond belief!" Pushing back a loose strand of brown hair, she collapsed into a chair and passed a faint hand across her forehead. "Give me some of that brandy, Brough. I am fading."

"Brandy, Marie? Not sherry? This must be serious indeed for you to forget your ladylike demeanor."

"Do not tease me!" she snapped. "This night's work will reflect upon you as well."

"You'd best tell me what has happened." He served her and returned to his seat. "I assume that George and Jeremy have played a prank at your expense."

"It is far worse than a prank." She tossed down a swallow of the liquor with a dashing flair that would have done credit to a Corinthian, then wrinkled up her nose. "This is disgusting stuff! Have you become such a pinchpenny that you would serve watered-down brandy?"

"What?" He tasted his own drink and set his jaw, studying the boys. "I'm sorry, Marie. It is a surprise to me as well. I shall ring for another bottle."

"Don't bother! I do not wish to be interrupted by servants. Not when I'm telling you of how these boys have ruined my reputation."

"What has happened?" he asked wearily.

"Unbeknownst to me, they sent out party invitations in my name. Scores and scores of guests arrived."

Georgie snickered and received a quelling frown from his brother.

"Naturally I was surprised; no, I was appalled! Of course, I was unprepared to entertain. People thought ... thought it was *I* who formulated the joke! Some of them even became angry because they had turned down other invitations. I have become a laughingstock and a person to be despised!"

"What did Jonathan do?"

"Jonathan? Ha! He just stood there with his mouth open! Who cares what Jonathan did? What I am interested in is what *you* are going to do, Brough. This cannot continue. You must set your foot down."

The earl shifted his gaze to Jeremy and George. "Well?"

Jeremy lowered his eyes, but George continued to look evenly at his brother. "C'mon, Brough. What was the harm in it? It was a well-planned, well-executed prank. At least give us credit for devising it. Marie has no sense of humor."

"Do you see me laughing?"

"You would if she weren't here," he mumbled, finally looking down.

"No I would not. I am becoming tired of your mischief."

"Turn him over your knee," Lady Westhaven

urged. "Pound his bottom black and blue! You are wasting your words, for he will not listen. He is a spoiled, mean-tempered child. Spank him."

Brough stood. "Go home, Marie. I will handle this."

"You will not. You will merely rap his knuckles. I want to see him pay for his transgression!"

"Madam, if I spank his bottom, I will have him drop his breeches," he said briskly. "Now, do you wish to witness that?"

Lady Westhaven's cheeks turned a deep rose.

"Go home, Marie," he repeated.

She leaped to her feet and started towards the door. Clasping the doorknob, she paused. "I shall expect a full report of the punishment. Furthermore, I shall also anticipate seeing him leave London." Defiantly she stalked from the room.

"Palmer!" Brough called through the open door. "Bring me my riding crop! And a bottle of brandy," he added.

Georgie blanched. "Brough! You can't!"

"Oh, I most certainly can." He took his place behind his desk. "Why shouldn't I?"

"It'll hurt!"

"You should have thought of that before you entered into this ridiculous scheme. Why did you do it anyway?"

"Because of Marie. She's always criticizing me, always trying to have me sent away. She deserved it!"

"How did she catch you?"

"We hid in the cloakroom. I guess we laughed too hard and she heard us."

Brough sighed with exasperation. "What am I going to do with you two? Jeremy, what is your sister going to say about this?"

Before the youth could reply, the footman entered the room. "Your crop, my lord, and the brandy."

"Thank you, Palmer. George?" He rose and came around the desk.

His brother's eyes widened. "Are you ... are you really ...? Please, Brough, I shall apologize to Marie and endeavor to behave properly. I won't do it again, I promise!"

"Bend over."

Gritting his teeth, his brother obeyed.

The earl cut a stinging blow across the seat of the tight breeches. He heard George's sharp intake of breath and felt miserable. He was glad he hadn't made the boy lower his unmentionables. It could have caused a welt. Restraining himself to keep from gathering his brother in his arms, he laid down the whip.

"I hope that you will remember to mind your manners."

"Yes, sir." He swallowed, his eyes shining with unshed tears.

His friend manfully squared his shoulders and bent over.

"What are you doing, Jeremy?"

"I am equally guilty, sir. I deserve the same."

"Stand up. I would never strike someone else's child. No, I shall take you to your sister."

"Yes, sir." He straightened, hanging his head. "I'm sorry for what we did."

"I hope you are both very sorry. Boys, you can't keep this up! It seems as though you are no sooner out of one scrape than you're into another. I'm not going to send you away, George. Not this time. But if this mischief continues, I will have no other choice. I am a busy man. I have no time for foolishness."

"Thank you, Brough. We'll do better."

"You may now tell me about my brandy."

"We drank it," Georgie admitted, "while we were writing the invitations. We added water so that you wouldn't notice its disappearance."

"It doesn't work that way."

"No, sir. We won't do that again either."

"Very well," he said coolly. "Now go to bed. I'm taking Jeremy home myself."

"Kissy will be furious!" the young viscount cried with sudden horror.

"Probably so," Brough said wickedly. "I am looking forward to the punishment she will devise for the both of you."

"I've already been punished," Georgie complained, rubbing his backside.

"A little more will only underline the first. Good night, little brother. I will see you at breakfast to describe the horrors of what is to become of you."

Clarissa was glad to have the time of respite before going out again. With her sister retiring early and Jeremy spending the night at Georgie's, she dismissed the servants and settled down for a quiet evening alone in the salon with only her sewing to concentrate on. Taking advantage of Julia's repentant mood, she had decided to sew for herself. Dreamily she had poured over the fashion plates of *La Belle Assemblie* until she had selected a style, then cut the pretty green silk to suit. Tonight, safe from interruption, she could make a good start on the construction. She would be at her best in this ball gown. The color was perfect for her. Even if no one noticed her among the dowagers, she would know that she looked as well as she could.

A knock on the door, echoing hollowly through the front entry, startled her. Who could be calling at this hour? It would be no proper person, not this late. She determined to ignore it.

The knocker fell again. Oh, why had she sent Simmons to bed? The unwanted visitor was going to be persistent. Clarissa laid aside her sewing and crept out of the room to the door as the rap sounded once more.

"Who's there?" she asked in what she hoped was a firm voice.

"Brough Abingdon."

"My lord!" Her hands went quickly to her hair. What could he want at this time of night? Unless Jeremy . . . She slid back the bolt and opened the door. On the stoop stood the very elegant gentleman in a many-caped outer coat, and beside him, a sheepishly deflated Jeremy. "Trouble," she said flatly.

"I'm afraid so," said the earl.

"Please come in." Whatever had happened must be serious indeed for his lordship to have brought Jeremy home himself.

Seeing her shoulders sink, Brough wished he had let the matter rest until tomorrow. He could have spared her a good night's rest before facing her with this new disaster. He had been selfish. He'd wanted her opinion and support before facing Marie again in the morning.

In the absence of Simmons, Clarissa herself removed Lord Abingdon's coat from his broad shoulders and hung it away in the cloakroom, her hand lingering briefly on the soft wool. Well, at least the topic was not Julia. But Jeremy! How could he get into mischief again?

"Please come to the salon, my lord." She led the way on reluctant feet. "Will you join me in a glass of sherry?" She shot Jeremy a sharp look. "I believe I shall be needing a lift."

"Thank you." What she needed was a stiff glass of brandy, Brough thought, and not of the watered-down variety either. Once more he cursed himself for disturbing her evening. His eye fell on the cut-out panels of silk. She'd been sewing a dress for herself or for her sister. He earnestly hoped it was for Clarissa. That shade of green would be devastating on her. But did she have to do her own sewing? He knew that the family was hard-pressed, but surely not so financially tight as that.

Clarissa handed him the wine and sat down, studying Jeremy. "Well, young man, what is it now?"

He looked uncomfortably at Lord Abingdon. "It was a prank, Kissy, on Lady Westhaven."

She closed her eyes. If they could have chosen from all the residents of London a person to play a trick on, they couldn't have picked a worse one than that. Marie Westhaven would be so irate that she would probably even scheme to throw a cog in the wheels of Julia's progress, just for revenge.

Brough described the evening's events while Clarissa sat in shocked silence.

"She deserved it!" Jeremy stated with a sudden show of self-defense. "She acts all high and mighty and better than everyone else."

"Jeremy!" Clarissa cried. "You are speaking of Lord Abingdon's sister!"

"He knows how she is, don't you, Brough?"

"Be still!" She looked helplessly at the earl. "I am so sorry. He has never been disrespectful. Jeremy, you will apologize at once."

"I'm sorry, Brough. It's just that—"

"Enough said, Jeremy." He rose. "I should have put this off until tomorrow. Tempers are too sharp-set for discussion this late at night. I shall come by in the morning, Mrs. James, and we will decide what to do with the two boys."

"Of course," she murmured, accompanying him to the door and fetching his coat. "I am so sorry. I don't know what got into Jeremy."

Brough looked into her tragic face and couldn't help reaching out gently to touch her cheek. "Perhaps the boys are becoming as tired of being in trouble as we are of dealing with it."

"Then why—"

"In the morning."

She shut the door behind him, the nerves in her cheek quivering wildly. She laid a trembling hand on it and turned, spying Jeremy slinking up the stairs.

"Oh no you don't! You'll go right back into the salon, young man, and you will explain yourself to me. Lord Abingdon may be willing to wait until morning. I am not!"

10

Although it had been very late when Clarissa retired, she had not fallen into a sound sleep, but had spent yet another night in a fitful doze, tossing and turning. When she awoke she was exhausted enough to wonder how she was ever to get through the day ahead. At least there were no social plans. The impending interview with Lord Abingdon would be all that she could bear.

What horrid thoughts could the earl have of her? Despite his little caress at the door, his opinion of her and the whole Dunstan family must be very low indeed. First his horse had been injured, then Julia had behaved so badly towards him, and now Jeremy had rudely insulted the lord's sister, to say nothing of all the little tangles in between. There was a Dunstan at hand in all of his troubles. He probably wished he had never laid eyes on them. What was worse, his bad opinion could hurt Julia's success at making a match. Clarissa couldn't afford to take a chance on that. So far the earl had been the soul of patience, but it couldn't last. Lord Abingdon was a man, and men had notoriously short tempers when it came to the disruption of their comfort. The root of the problem must be eliminated. Therefore she had forbidden

Jeremy to associate with Georgie, and she was seriously considering sending him home to Essex.

Surprisingly her brother hadn't protested, argued, nor begged for reprieve. He seemed to know that he had pushed her beyond her limit. But neither, however, had he been apologetic or contrite. He had done what he had done, and that was that. He was prepared to answer to the consequences.

Clarissa sighed. Perhaps he was growing up at last. If Jeremy was willing to accept the responsibility for his own actions, his stay in London had had some value at least. Still, she reminded herself, she could take no chances. He must be sent home. Her decision would probably please the earl. With Jeremy leaving, he could, with a clear conscience, send Georgie home as well and regain his peace and quiet.

Not knowing when Lord Abingdon would arrive, she left her housedress hanging and slipped into a simple, hopefully becoming, lavender gown. She took greater pains with her hair, arranging it in a loose knot at the nape of her neck with a few wispy tendrils framing her face. She left off her little matronly lace cap. This would probably be the last time he would come to call, and she wanted to look her best.

Treading wearily downstairs, she made her way to the kitchen, greeting Cook and helping herself to a cup of tea.

"You don't look so well this morning, Miss Clarissa. Headache again?"

"I wish it were. I wish I could take a strong dose of laudanum and sleep through the entire day."

The cook *tsk-tsk*ed in the licensed manner of an old retainer.

"I know." Clarissa nodded. "That isn't the answer to my dilemma."

"Is it Lord Jeremy and Miss Julia again?"

"It's Jeremy today. Tomorrow it will probably be Julia. Then Jeremy again. At least they seem to take turns in oversetting me, but why oh why must they complicate everything? Life, even here in London, would be so simple if they would only use their heads."

"They're high-spirited, Miss Clarissa, and they're young. They leap before they look." She set a plate of ham, scrambled eggs, and toast before her mistress. "They'll come round in time."

"Time is what I lack." She stared at the food before her. "Cook, I'm sorry. I don't think I can eat a bite. Save this for Jeremy. No matter what disaster occurs, his appetite is always gargantuan."

"You'd better eat, Miss Clarissa. You're growing too thin."

It was true. Her gowns had been fitting slightly looser, but this was no time to begin to remedy the situation. She took a piece of toast, but pushed the rest aside. "I can't do it. Please keep this warm for Jeremy."

Cook shook her head as she removed the plate. "It won't do."

"If I can just get through this morning, I promise to do better at luncheon. I appreciate your concern, Cook, but I just can't eat right now. Lord Abingdon is coming to discuss Jeremy's latest mischief, and I am all to pieces."

The older woman chuckled. "That handsome lord would do that to a woman. Per'aps you should thank Lord Jeremy for giving you the opportunity to shine. The more the earl is with you, Miss Clarissa, the sooner he'll see what a treasure you are."

"I'm sure that nothing like that is on the earl's mind, and it is certainly not on mine. In fact, I am considering sending Jeremy home to Essex as punishment for his misdeeds and as a means to provide myself with a little peace."

"Begging your pardon, Miss Clarissa, but you don't need peace. You need a man to lean on."

"I can manage," she said stubbornly.

"There's too much on you. That's why you have those headaches. Mark my words, if you married Lord Abingdon, they'd stop in an instant."

"Marrying me will never cross his mind. I am not fine enough for him. Besides, I am used goods."

Cook's anger flared. "Whoever told you that?"

"No matter," she murmured morosely. "It's true."

"It is not! Any man, even a duke, would be lucky to win you for a wife."

"Thank you, dear friend." Clarissa stood and hugged Cook briefly. "You are so kind to me."

"Hm!" Her rosy cheeks took on an even deeper hue. "I've served the Dunstans all my life and want nothing but the best to happen. And the best would be if you married Lord Abingdon. That's what I say. That's what all of us think."

"It won't happen," she said softly. "He wouldn't want to take on all our problems. The best that can happen is that Julia will find a nice young man to wed. Then I can concentrate wholly on Jeremy."

"What about yourself?"

"I just want them happy and settled. That's all I care about." She grimaced. "Now I'd best go to the salon and consider what I am going to say to the earl. I doubt that he'll be in the best of moods."

* * *

Two wretched hours of dread passed before the door knocker fell. Having sent Jeremy to his room to study and Julia to hers to finish stitching a simple hem, Clarissa received Lord Abingdon alone and without the threat of interruption. At his entrance, she stood and made her curtsy.

He responded with an elegant bow. "Why so grim, Mrs. James? You look as though you are facing the Inquisition." He grinned.

"I almost feel as though I am. Will you have refreshment, my lord?"

"A cup of tea would be just the thing."

She rang for Simmons and gave the order, returning to her chair and sitting down nervously on its edge. Her hands were trembling. Embarrassed, she folded them, clenching them together in a manner to still their movement.

He drew up a chair opposite. "Have you spoken with Jeremy?"

"I have. My lord, I am mortified by what he has done. I hope you will accept my apologies, and I intend to write the same to Lady Westhaven. I am sure she, too, must be completely mortified. I believe that both boys should apologize to her publicly in the newspaper. That way the unfortunate guests will know what happened and will hold her innocent."

"That might help to get Marie off my back. What she really wants, however, is for me to banish George to the country."

"I have come to the conclusion that that would be the best course for me to follow with Jeremy."

He frowned.

"You disagree, my lord?"

"Isn't that merely setting the problem aside, madam, and not confronting it?" he asked gently.

It was, she acknowledged to herself, but how

much more of this could she bear? How could she explain to him how the house was often in a turmoil, how her headaches were increasing in frequency, and how Julia's chances were being jeopardized? This Season in London had to be successful. There could be no other. That was something that Lord Abingdon, with his vast wealth and position, wouldn't understand.

Simmons entered with the tea tray and set it on a low table between them. Clarissa saw that Cook had outdone herself. Not only were there tea and biscuits, she had also provided tarts and petit fours and small sandwiches on silver plates. The kitchen had been busily preparing for Lord Abingdon's call.

Thinking fondly of the servants and their misguided hopes, she filled his cup. To her horror, the china rattled. "Cream and sugar, my lord?" Even her voice sounded different. Instead of its soft, rich timbre, it seemed high-pitched and shallow.

"One lump of sugar please." He leaned forward, studying her with those expressive hazel eyes. "Mrs. James, you are overset. You and I are thrown into this situation together. Between us, we will find a solution. Two heads are better than one, you know."

"I am just so mortified," she said frankly.

"Would you prefer that I come back at another time?"

"Oh no!" She couldn't face this confrontation again. "Let us settle it now."

"Very well." He sat back to sip his tea. "I did think seriously of sending George home. How often has he promised me that he would stay out of trouble? I believed him each time. I don't like the feeling of not being able to believe my own brother."

"I don't think that they deliberately set out to make false statements."

"No, I don't either. That is why I am determined to find the key to teaching George to think before he acts."

"Probably the key is nothing more than growing up."

"Most likely you are right."

Clarissa began to relax. He was going to be sane and sensible about the matter. He was not going to shout, nor deliver her and her brood a thundering setdown. Once again the earl was proving his forbearance and willingness to understand. In fact, he was showing much more tolerance than she felt toward the boys. What a wonderful man he was! What a wonderful husband and father he would be! His chosen lady would be very, very lucky.

She plunged ahead. "If I thought I could benefit Jeremy, I wouldn't send him home, but I foresee nothing but a continual series of scrapes. I do not have the time nor the patience to deal with it just now."

"Crying craven, Clarissa?"

She gritted her teeth. His words and their underlying accusation incensed her so that she barely took notice of his use of her first name. "You forget, Lord Abingdon, that I am also responsible for Julia," she said archly, "and her Season is the only reason that we are in London at all."

"Yes, of course. I beg pardon." He helped himself to one of Cook's delicious chess tarts. "You must do what you feel is right, considering all the circumstances."

Clarissa looked at him uncomfortably. Why did she feel as though she had disappointed him? Didn't she have to do what was the easiest for her?

"Lord Abingdon, I care very much for my family, but there are occasions that I must make choices. This is Julia's time. She must make the most of it, for I cannot afford another. I won't allow Jeremy's pranks to threaten her success. Please try to understand. I have appreciated your help with everything, but I cannot go on like this."

"Won't you give me one more chance?"

Gazing into his earnest eyes, Clarissa found herself melting. How could she refuse him? How could anyone refuse him anything?

As if realizing his advantage, he pressed on. "George and Jeremy need a man in their lives. It's not easy to be sixteen years old. I remember it well. One isn't a boy and isn't yet a man. It's an in-between state, like being a strip of land between two armies, with each one fighting for it. One moment you've slipped to one side, the next moment to the other. Perhaps it is the same way for a female?"

"I don't know."

He raised an eyebrow.

Clarissa shook her head. "When I was sixteen I was helping manage an estate and being a mother to Jeremy and Julia. I had a very short childhood." She laughed, trying to make light of it. "So I must rely on what you say, my lord."

He briefly fell silent. "I'm sorry."

It was the wrong thing to say. Clarissa's irritation returned. How dare he express pity for her? She was not an object for his altruism!

"I do not wish anyone to feel sorry for me, my lord. What happened, happened. I do not have the time nor the inclination to sit around feeling sorry for myself, so I certainly do not wish others to do so."

"Please accept my apology, ma'am. I seem to do

nothing but offend you this morning. It is not my intention."

Once again her anger melted in the face of his sincerity. "I know," she murmured. "I'm being rather touchy today. Forgive my ill temper."

"Of course, so long as you'll forgive me."

"You are forgiven." She smiled. "More tea, my lord?"

"Thank you."

Clarissa leaned forward to fill his cup. "You mentioned another chance at straightening out those boys. Have you a plan?"

He nodded. "I think so. I believe that we are in agreement that Jeremy and George need to grow up. If they're to be men, they need a man to show them how."

"I cannot afford a tutor."

"No, not a tutor; I was thinking of myself."

"You!"

"Is it so surprising? I *am* a man, you know."

Warmth flowed to her cheeks. Oh, but she was well aware of that! "I can think of no better influence for the boys, but, my lord, have you the time?"

"I'll make the time. Nothing I'm doing is of greater importance."

"If the way they have been behaving is any indication, they'll need much supervision, more than both of us together have been giving them."

"I'll do it, and furthermore, you won't often be troubled. I want Jeremy to move to my house. There are only a few things which I will need your assistance in accomplishing."

"Well . . ."

"You will give me a chance?" he urged.

She nodded doubtfully.

"Good! I promise you, you won't be sorry."

"I hope not, but I can't help but think you're taking on a very large order. What is your plan?" she asked curiously.

"I'd like to begin by taking Jeremy and George to the country for the weekend. They can expend some of their high spirits and it will orient them to me."

"All right."

"Then I would like to introduce them to Gentleman Jackson's and to horse races and cockfights."

"What!"

"Would you rather they did these things on their own for the first time? Sneaking around behind our backs? Getting in with the wrong people?"

"No, my lord, most certainly not."

"Brough."

She looked at him questioningly. "I beg your pardon?"

"Won't you call me 'Brough' if we are to continue our endeavor together? I am weary of your 'my lording' me, and I rather dislike calling you 'Mrs. James.' It doesn't suit you."

"I don't care for it either," she admitted.

"Then we are agreed." He went on. "I thought about the situation last night, Clarissa. I believe we should drop their academic education for now. They'll have enough of that when they return to school. Can't we concentrate on what a young man in society should know?"

"Boxing, horse races, and cockfights?"

His eyes twinkled.

"Very well!" she smiled. "I must trust you."

"Excellent, and if you could find time in your schedule, I wish you and Julia to teach them to dance. I'd ask Marie, but . . ." He sighed. "You do it so well."

"I shall try. I doubt that Julia could be cajoled into dancing with those two, but I imagine I can prevail in requesting her to play the pianoforte."

"Done! I intend to keep those boys so busy being young gentlemen that they'll forget all about their childish pranks."

"It sounds as though it just might work," Clarissa mused. "They're lucky that you have more sympathy for them at present than I do. Tell me, my lord ... ah ... Brough, were you ever guilty of the same type of thing?"

He grinned boyishly. "The truth?"

She nodded, laughing.

"Bran Rackthall and I ran some of the most famous rigs in the history of the school, but don't let Jeremy and George find that out. It would undermine my authority."

She shook her head. "I can't picture either of you being anything but perfect gentlemen."

"A not-so-simple matter of growing up. It's what put this idea in my head. I remembered what it was like when I was George's age."

"I'm glad you did." She took a deep breath of relief. "I wasn't very happy with banishing Jeremy to the country, but I was at wits' end."

"I am glad to be of assistance." He rose. "I've taken enough of your time, Clarissa, so I'll be on my way. Have Jeremy's things packed and I'll send a carriage by this afternoon." He bowed over her hand. "Wish me luck?"

"Wholeheartedly!" She walked with him to the front door. As Simmons opened it, he once again took her hand and brought it to his lips. "I shall drop by next week to report on my progress. Until then."

She watched him descend the stoop and enter his phaeton. Her hand still tingled from his feathery kiss. Oh, how wonderful it would be to marry him! But that was a dream for someone else, for some young lady like Julia who had never known another man. It wasn't for used goods like Mrs. Clarissa James.

Jeremy was amazed at what was happening to him. Instead of punishment, he seemed to be receiving a reward. Living with Brough and going to exciting places and events with him was almost more than he could comprehend. Clarissa, however, was quick to burst his bubble.

"One misstep, young man, and off you go to Essex," she warned over luncheon. "Lord Abingdon is going to a great deal of trouble for you. He won't take kindly to misbehavior. I intend to give him complete control of you, including the use of whatever discipline he feels is necessary."

Jeremy thought of Brough's crop descending smartly onto Georgie's backside, and sobered. "I'll be good."

"You had better be. This is your last chance."

"I understand." Uncomfortably he moved the food around on his plate, forgetting for the moment his youthful appetite. "I'll make you proud of me."

Julia harrumphed. "I cannot understand why Lord Abingdon is interested in a hair on your head. You're a bad little boy, Jeremy. You always have been and you always will be."

"That's enough of that," their sister chided gently.

"Well, it isn't fair!"

"Why, Julia? Why do you feel that way?" Clarissa asked. "You should be happy for your brother's good fortune."

"He is being rewarded for misbehavior."

"That was not Lord Abingdon's intent. He is trying to assist Jeremy and Georgie to become young gentlemen. This is not a reward. It is a form of education."

"Receiving vouchers for Almack's would have been an education, too."

"Jealous, Julia?" Jeremy said smoothly.

She ignored him and turned her attention to her elder sister. "Couldn't you ask Lord Abingdon for assistance in obtaining the vouchers, Clarissa? If you asked him, I'm sure he'd come up with them."

"We've been over this ground before," she said wearily.

"But I would so much like to go! Everyone goes to Almack's."

"Not you," her brother snorted.

"Jeremy," Clarissa reminded, "you would do well to mind your manners. You aren't at Lord Abingdon's yet. You can still be sent home to the country, you know. And, Julia, you must realize by now that I would never put myself forward like that, and neither must you. There will be no more discussion of the matter."

"But the vouchers would mean so much to my future!"

"If your future is dependent upon the patronesses of Almack's, I hesitate to think what it might bring. Forget Almack's! I know as a fact that you've met and are meeting many young men who don't care a fig whether you attend that assembly or not. Be yourself, Julia. It never pays to try to be someone you are not."

"Wise advice," Jeremy stated with a lordly intonation.

Julia pinched her lips together in a tight line. "I shall be glad when you are gone, little brat.

Clarissa, may I be excused? He has quite ruined my lunch."

"Very well." She shook her head. "I wish you two could get along together."

"He is so childish."

"*She* is such an antidote."

"Enough of that. There will be no more bickering today!"

Julia nodded pertly. "I shall remain in my room until he has gone." With a flounce, she left the dining room.

Jeremy quickly cleaned his plate and also asked to be excused. He had to make certain that Simmons had finished with his packing so that he would be ready to leave as soon as Brough's carriage arrived. Besides, Clarissa's weariness disturbed him. He wished there was something that Brough could do for her, too. Vouchers from Almack's weren't the answer. Clarissa needed something else. She needed a husband. He wondered if the earl would be interested in being the lucky man.

11

"I CAN SCARCELY believe my good fortune!"
Julia twirled happily around the entrance
hall, a creamy white envelope held aloft. "Simmons, do you know what this means?"

"No, miss, I do not," he said calmly, watching
the young lady's antics as though it were an everyday occurrence. "I assume you have had good
news of some sort."

"Good news? Simmons! This is my entrée! Now
... oh, now ... my Season can be considered a
success!"

Clarissa paused on the stairs, her heart tripling
its beat. Surely Lord Arlen could not have proposed by mail? Now that they were receiving
guests and going into Society once more, he could
have asked in person. But if it wasn't that, what
else could have flown her sister into the boughs?

Julia looked upward, catching sight of her.
"Clarissa! You won't believe what has happened!
We've vouchers. Vouchers from Almack's! We can
go there tomorrow night. Oh, isn't it famous?"

"Almack's?" She descended slowly, but her
mind raced. How could it have happened? Neither
of them had ever been introduced to a single pa-

troness of that august assembly. Nor had they seemed to have been noticed by any one of them.

Almack's was the epitome of all *ton* snobbishness. No one but the elite were permitted within its doors on Wednesday nights, and even these very fashionable people were governed by a strict set of rules. The doors were closed at eleven, and no one, even the Prince himself, was permitted to enter after that hour. Knee breeches and white cravats were the required dress for the gentlemen, who were encouraged to dance and flirt with the ladies and were only allowed to play cards for very low stakes. The young belles themselves were the cream of society, chosen for their social aplomb by those formidable patronesses: Lady Sarah Jersey, the high-nosed heiress; Lady Emily Castlereagh, the arrogant wife of a political genius; Princess Therese Esterhazy, niece of Queen Charlotte and wife of the Austrian ambassador; Countess Dorothea Lieven, beautiful aristocrat and wife of the Russian ambassador; Mrs. Drummond Burwell, haughty and intimidating; Lady Emily Cowper, lovely, discreet mistress of Lord Palmerston; and Lady Maria Sefton, the easiest and sweetest of the group, who was nevertheless very fine and sophisticated. No one was guaranteed acceptance to Almack's. Neither money nor birth afforded certain entry. One must be . . . *special.*

Julia waved the missive aloft. "Don't you see, Clarissa? We have been accepted!"

"I cannot imagine how this came about." She took the letter from her sister's hand and studied it. It was true. Not that she doubted Julia's word, but she had to see it in print before the news sank in. "This is strange," she mused. "Why would any of them suddenly single us out for their favor?"

"Oh, what difference does it make? It has happened! Let us cancel our engagements for Wednesday evening. We cannot miss going to Almack's. It would be beyond all reason! Please say that we may attend."

"All right." She nodded, stunned. "I just don't understand ..."

"What is there to understand? We are invited, and that's that. Let us not question our good luck!" Julia laughed. "Instead, let us consider what we are to wear. I wish to be absolutely perfect! Don't be so dour, Clarissa. Can you not show any enthusiasm?"

"The whole matter seems highly unusual."

"Don't question it," her sister repeated smugly.

A light dawned. Clarissa looked at her closely. "Julia, did you have anything to do with this?"

"Whatever gave you that idea?" Julia laid the precious vouchers on the hall table and turned to the mirror to adjust her jaunty blue bonnet.

Clarissa would have questioned her further, but a knock on the door interrupted them. Simmons opened it to reveal Vincent Arlen. The young marquess, dressed to the height of fashion in immaculate canary trousers and brown kerseymere coat, his elaborate cravat tied exceptionally high on his neck, entered and bowed deeply.

"Miss Julia." He flicked cool blue eyes toward Clarissa. "Ma'am."

"How do you do, my lord?"

"Well enough. I hope I am not late."

"Oh no, my lord." Julia looked pointedly toward the clock. "You are exactly on time."

"Then I am well rewarded in finding a lady who is ready and waiting. My horses, Miss Julia, will appreciate your punctuality, for they are much ready to go. And so am I."

She dropped him a saucy curtsy.

"You are going somewhere?" Clarissa asked.

"Lord Arlen has invited me to go driving. Didn't I tell you?"

"No, you did not."

"You don't mind, of course."

"No, Julia, but you must have a chaperon. I wish you had mentioned this earlier. I am not prepared . . ."

"I'm sure we do not require your company, Mrs. James," Lord Arlen intoned in haughty accents. "My groom will be present."

Clarissa wished that she could slap away his supercilious smile. "Simmons, please fetch Alice. She will accompany her mistress."

"I said, Mrs. James, that a chaperon is not necessary."

"And I said, Lord Arlen, that Alice will accompany her mistress."

Julia set her jaw stubbornly. "How perfectly *gauche*," she murmured under her breath. "Perhaps you should have brought a larger carriage, my lord. Then the entire household could have joined us. Perhaps that would better suit my sister's antiquated notions of propriety."

Clarissa fixed her with a warning glance. "We shall discuss this later."

Alice arrived in the hall and trailed out of the house behind the couple. Clarissa watched them enter the phaeton and set off down the street at a spanking trot, with Julia laughing and holding her bonnet. She sighed. She couldn't like Lord Arlen, but she wished indeed he'd marry the girl. She was getting nowhere with Julia. Twice more she had tried to warn her against him, and each time the young lady had contrived to escape the conversation. If he knew, Brough would not be very proud of her.

As she turned away, her eyes fell on the vouchers. Her sister was hiding something from her. Somehow Julia's hand was behind these invitations. Perhaps Lord Arlen had obtained them or . . . Her heart leaped to her throat. Surely the girl hadn't found some way to approach the earl for the favor! She had certainly tried it before.

Anger flaring, she nearly took up the papers and ripped them in two. She would get to the bottom of this. If it was as she suspected, she would see that Julia received a very hard lesson.

"Simmons, please summon Gibson. I wish him to deliver a message for me."

Having sent the boys for a driving lesson from John Coachman, Brough was going out the door on his way to his club when Gibson arrived with the missive and placed it directly into his hands. "Does she wish an immediate reply?" He gave the man a coin and opened the letter.

"Miss Clarissa was very o'erset, my lord. That's all I know."

She wished to speak with him. That was all she'd written. There seemed to be no turmoil, no urgency, but if Clarissa had gone to such lengths as to summon him, there was something very wrong.

"I'll go to see her now. Are you on foot, Gibson?"

"Yes, my lord."

"Then you may ride with me."

Gibson climbed up on the box beside the driver while Brough settled himself into the landau's comfortable seat. What had happened now? The past few days had been quiet ones for him, but of course, he'd been out of town. He'd had a good time with the boys, riding and fishing on the estate, teaching them to play a fair hand of cards, and talking to them about manly subjects. In fact, they'd stayed longer than he had originally intended. It seemed that he was making progress with the two.

Evidently it hadn't been the same for Clarissa. Julia must be kicking up her heels again. But why would she call for him? He wasn't the one to handle the foibles of a young lady.

Perhaps there was some mischief from George and Jeremy that he wasn't aware of. He rather doubted it, though. He and his entire staff of servants, both here in London and in the country, kept a close eye on them. Short of their sneaking out in the middle of the night, they could have done nothing out of line. No, whatever it was, they were innocent of it.

The carriage pulled up in front of the Dunstans' rented house. Brough slipped the letter into his pocket and stepped out. He would soon know.

Simmons must have been watching the street, for he opened the door before he raised his cane to knock. "Good afternoon, my lord."

"To you also, Simmons. Is Mrs. James available?"

"Indeed she is, sir." The butler showed him into the salon, where the flustered Clarissa made a hasty curtsy.

"I didn't realize that you would come so soon, Lord Abingdon."

"Brough," he reminded her.

"Yes, I won't forget again. Will you take tea, my ... Brough?"

She may have not expected callers, but she was attired very prettily just the same. Her willow green muslin was not of the first stare of fashion, but it was flatteringly cut and served to underline her brilliant beauty. Once again he wished that she hadn't spoiled the effect with the prim lace cap. She hadn't worn it at their last meeting.

"I have a better idea," he suggested. "May I take you for a drive in the park? It's such a nice day, and I think you would enjoy the outing."

"Oh . . . are you sure?" She looked surprised, as though she would never expect anyone to ask her to go anywhere.

"Yes I am." That was one way of ridding her of the unbecoming cap.

"Very well. I shall fetch my bonnet."

He waited for her in the hall. It wasn't long before she appeared, her face handsomely revealed under a fetching straw hat. "Very becoming."

"Thank you, sir." A tinge of blush colored her cheeks as she took his arm and walked from the house.

He handed her into the carriage and sat down beside her. "Now, isn't this better than being cooped up in the house?"

"It is. I'm glad you asked me." She turned up her face to smile at him.

His gaze locked with hers. A rush of desire spread through his body. He wanted to touch her, caress her, make love to her. Brough caught himself bending his head toward her lips and straightened up abruptly. Ye gods, had he been going to kiss her right there on the streets of London?

Clarissa, too, stiffened, heat flooding her cheeks. Something had happened, something that shouldn't happen, couldn't happen ever again. He had looked as though he'd been about to kiss her, and she would have willingly accepted it. Merciful heavens, what could he think of her? Was she such a hussy that she had overtly invited his embrace? She must watch herself very closely from now on or he would get the wrong idea of her. She might be used goods, but she was a proper lady, a chaperon, for God's sake! So where was her own chaperon? She had tripped right out to accompany Lord Abingdon with only his driver to lend propriety. She hoped that Julia didn't see her.

He noticed the tension in her shoulders. "Are you all right?"

"I just realized that I have no chaperon." She tried to laugh lightly.

"At our age I doubt it's necessary, especially with my driver present." He watched her lips draw a fine line, and could have kicked himself in the teeth. A chaperon was never necessary for a man, but for a lady it was mandatory, unless she was wed, or a lightskirt, or too old to be of any interest. Why did he always say the wrong things to this woman? Dammit, where was his smoothness, his sophistication, when she was around? He acted like a schoolboy with her.

"I can take you home if you prefer," he said quietly.

"No, you're right. It doesn't matter."

"Clarissa, I didn't mean . . ."

"Lord Abingdon, please . . . be quiet."

He looked at her with surprise, but his jolt was less than what she was feeling about her blatant command. Who was she to tell a fine peer of the realm to button his lip? Now he must indeed have a very low opinion of her. Suddenly she didn't care. She was heartily sick of London, of Julia, of the *ton*, of everything she could think of in her life. The handsome earl was just another part of it.

"My lord," she demanded, "did you procure those vouchers for Almack's?"

He looked at the fire dancing in her eyes. Clarissa was angry. At him.

"I would like to explain."

"Did you?"

No matter how much wrath was going to fall on his head, he wouldn't lie to her. Vaguely he watched the portals of Hyde Park glide past his vision. They were joining the fashionable promenade, and he was right in the midst of a quarrel with a very incensed lady. What grist for the gossip mill! But he'd tell her the truth.

"I asked Allesandra to do it."

"Why? Did Julia have something to do with this?"

He sighed. "Before I left for the country, I received a note from Julia begging me to assist in obtaining the vouchers."

"I see," she said tightly. "Why didn't you let me know what she was doing?"

"I didn't wish to overset you further. Please, Clarissa, won't you let me help you?"

"I don't want charity from anyone! I thought I made that clear."

Clarissa sighed with exasperation. Why couldn't he understand? She didn't want people to feel sorry for her, least of all the earl. It was absolutely humiliating.

"It isn't charity," he said anxiously. People's heads were suddenly beginning to turn. Every eye in the park seemed to be latched curiously on him and her.

With a haughty air, she lifted her chin. "I wish to be taken home immediately."

"Look around you, madam. If you can find a way to turn this carriage, I shall be happy to give the order."

Clarissa stared. In her anger she hadn't noticed

that they had joined the parade of the *ton*. At this important time of the afternoon it was impossible to move more than a crawling few feet at a time. Hyde Park was overflowing with vehicles. And the attention of every occupant was fixed on her.

"Merciful heavens." She looked at Lord Abingdon. "Everyone is staring! What are we going to do?"

"I suggest that we give the appearance of enjoying ourselves." He bit away a grin. "I know that I am a disagreeable lout, but really, Clarissa, can't you forget that for just an hour or so? I promise to . . . What did you say? Be quiet?"

Her sense of the ridiculous overcame her anger. She burst into laughter. "I'm sorry, Brough. I didn't mean to rip up at you. Everything is just so overwhelming at times." She laid her hand on his sleeve. "Forgive me?"

"Of course." He briefly covered her hand with his and squeezed. "May I give you a piece of advice?"

"Please do."

"Ease up on Julia. You can't control her every moment. To try to do so may even make her worse. You've done all that you can already, and you can guide her up to a certain point. Beyond that, she must be responsible for her own actions."

"For every action, there is a reaction. In this case, she will not be attending Almack's, because of her reprehensible behavior in obtaining the vouchers," she said firmly.

His hands lingered on hers. "Clarissa, do you consider me to be a friend?"

"Yes, of course."

"So does Jeremy. Perhaps Julia does, too. It is only natural that one might ask a friend for a favor. Take her to Almack's."

"I cannot agree."

"Don't be so strict with her that you'll drive her away."

"It's just so very difficult to stand by and watch her foolhardiness."

"I know, but try it and see. She'll be all right."

She sighed. "I hope so. Thank you for letting me cry on your shoulder."

"Any time. I do care for you, you know."

Clarissa lowered her head, casting him a thoughtful gaze from the corners of her eyes. His caring, of course, took the form of friendship. The Earl of Abingdon would never look upon her as his potential countess. He wouldn't want a widow. He was far too noble to be satisfied with another man's leavings.

She knew this, yet she couldn't help her heart's tripling its beat whenever he appeared. She couldn't stop her breathlessness when he touched her. She couldn't keep from dreaming.

She must cease this nonsense. She was in London for a purpose. She must not deviate from it. Julia would never have another chance at finding happiness. Her own was gone already.

"Ellen, do you see?" The Duchess of Rackthall nudged her companion.

Lady Singleton peered into the throngs. "What?"

"Brough has brought Mrs. James driving with him."

"It looks as though they're having a slight spat."

"Yes, it does, doesn't it?" Allesandra smiled. "I think that at last, Brough has met his lady."

Ellen's blue eyes glittered. "I do believe you're right. There has been something brewing in that quarter. He has been so watchful of her. It goes beyond their common interest in the boys. Yes, it's something more."

"What is your opinion of her?"

"She is so capable, it almost frightens me! The proficient way she has raised her brother and sister is beyond belief. She must have been very young when she was thrust into the situation. I think of what a muddle I would make in a similar circumstance."

"She is very attractive, too."

"Very."

"She seems sweet and pleasant."

"Indeed."

"She would make Brough a fine wife." Allesandra thoughtfully nibbled the inside of her lower lip. "He can be so wooden-headed at times, perhaps he needs an extra nudge. I believe I'll hold a dinner party, just a small one, and invite our circle of friends."

"Including Clarissa James?"

"Exactly. You and Harry will come, of course?"

"Certainly."

"Mrs. James was rather formal in the ballroom settings. This should loosen her up so that Brough will see how well she fits in with our group, and it will allow us an opportunity to befriend her. An intimate gathering will be just the thing. I shall also ask Brough to escort her."

"Will Brandon approve?"

Allesandra laughed brightly. "Why shouldn't he?"

"He'll accuse you of matchmaking. Like he did with Harry and me."

"That was different. In this context, it will never cross his mind."

* * *

She was wrong. When Allesandra outlined her plans to her husband, he eyed her warily.

"Meddling in Brough's affairs, love?"

She leaped to her guard, fluttering her lashes at him. "My goodness, such a thing has never occurred to me! Shall I fetch you a glass of brandy, dear?"

"Don't change the subject."

She brought him a drink whether he wished it or not, and sat down beside him on the love seat. "I'm not at all sure what the subject is."

"Shall I enlighten you?"

"Yes, Brandon, please do."

"The subject is Brough and Mrs. James. The subject is matchmaking!"

She favored him with innocent green eyes. "Oh, is that the way it appears?"

"Minx!" He tumbled her against his chest and kissed her thoroughly. "Don't think to fool me. I know you too well."

"It isn't really matchmaking," she protested. "I'm merely providing them an opportunity to be together."

He smoothed her dark hair. "Don't you think that Brough can provide that, if he wants to?"

"I suppose so." Her eyes widened. "Do you think that he doesn't want to?"

"I don't know. He hasn't spoken to me about her."

"Brandon, do you like Mrs. James?"

"She's lovely."

"Then you've no objection to including her on our guest list?"

"No, invite whomever you wish." He settled her onto his lap. "Just don't become involved in Brough's matrimonial future."

"I won't." She tilted her chin to be kissed. "I'm

just giving him a further opportunity to be in her company. She would be absolutely perfect for him, you know. Just like Ellen and Harry. Didn't I assist a bit in their case?"

He groaned.

"I was right in doing it, too. They are so in love. Just like we are." She combed her fingers through his guinea gold hair and drew his face toward hers. "Wouldn't you like the same for your very best friend?"

12

"WELL, JULIA." CLARISSA paused in her straightening of the drawing room to confront her sister. "Sit down. I have something to say to you."

The girl groaned. "I know what it is. I saw you driving with Lord Abingdon last afternoon. He told you, didn't he? He told you that I asked him to procure the vouchers. I should have known!"

"Do not be harsh on him, Julia. He would not have volunteered the information on his own. I asked him. And he is too honorable a gentleman to tell a falsehood."

"What are you going to do to me?"

"Nothing."

Julia looked at her with surprise.

Clarissa sank down in a chair. "I am weary of punishments. I cannot force you to behave like a lady. Nor can I train you further, for I believe that you already are well aware of the proper decorum. If you engage in improprieties and are caught at it, do not come crying to me. There will be nothing I can do to restore your reputation."

"I know there are social dangers, but I used my best judgment. I knew Lord Abingdon wouldn't tattle on me. You said yourself that he is a very honorable gentleman. And I did so want those vouchers!"

"Lord Abingdon would not willingly set out to start tongues wagging, but, Julia, he did have to ask for those vouchers. He didn't produce them from thin air."

She cringed. "I didn't think of that. I wonder whom he asked."

"The Duchess Rackthall."

"Surely she would not tell!"

"Let us hope not, but I must thank her, and it will be very embarrassing. Do you see from this that you must consider your actions very thoroughly? You cannot simply get an idea into your head and pounce upon it. There could be many unforeseen repercussions."

"I wonder how carefully you consider your own actions. Such as your driving with Lord Abingdon in the park without a chaperon," the girl asked slyly. "Lord Arlen himself remarked upon it."

Warmth flowed into Clarissa's cheeks. "I am of an age where something like that makes little difference."

"You shall not make me believe that!"

"Very well, Julia. I made a mistake."

"And what about the inordinate amount of time you spent alone in the Singletons' garden with Lord Abingdon?"

"There was a very good reason for it! If you recall, I was quite overset at your immodest behavior. I had to compose myself."

Her younger sister raised an eyebrow. "Did the earl assist you?"

"Yes, he did!" Clarissa snapped. "You may be thankful to him for that. I was all for marching you home, but he dissuaded me. Now, there's an end to it!"

"It is always difficult when the pot is found as black as the kettle," Julia mused.

Further discussion was halted by a tap at the door. Simmons entered with the morning mail, which Julia grabbed at once and began to sort. Clarissa, sighing, returned to her chores. Her sister was right. Her own behavior had not been exemplary of late. She must take care that nothing went amiss from now on. In Julia, certain slips could be blamed on her youthful high spirits. For Clarissa, there could be no excuses.

"Oh, here is one for you!" the girl cried. "Shall I open it?"

"Please do." She flicked her feather duster across the mantel.

"It's from the Duchess of Rackthall. She desires your company at a dinner party next week." Julia's lips formed a pout. "I am also invited, but it is the evening of Mary's ball. I cannot think why the duchess would schedule an event on the same night."

"Obviously the Rackthalls and their other friends do not plan to attend."

"But we do! Clarissa, I have to go to Mary's ball! She's my friend!"

"Of course you must. You shall." She thoughtfully laid down her duster. She wanted very much to go to the Rackthalls' dinner party, especially because Brough would probably be in attendance. Try as she might, she couldn't dismiss him from her mind. What harm would come from seeing him occasionally during the time she had left in London? Wasn't she mature enough and controlled enough to keep herself from blowing their visits all out of proportion? They were friends, and that was that. Besides, she must keep in touch with him on the matter of Jeremy. It was only natural that they should meet.

"Perhaps you could stay at Mary's," she suggested. "I'm sure that her parents wouldn't mind, and you'd have ever so much fun discussing the ball afterwards. I do feel that one of us should accept the Rackthalls' invitation, especially after the duchess was so kind in procuring those vouchers."

"Yes, you are right. It wouldn't do to insult her. I'll send a note to Mary to make sure that it will be all right, although I'm sure it will."

"You may take Alice with you."

"Oh, thank you, Clarissa! I shall have my own personal maid. What fun!"

"Just be certain that you behave like a proper young lady."

"I shall. I promise!"

While Julia went off to compose her missive, Clarissa picked up the heavy, crested Rackthall invitation. How kind it was of the duchess to include them in her entertainment. She hoped that Julia's absence would not discommode Her Grace's numbers, but she herself was glad that her sister would not be attending. She couldn't help but admit that an evening away from the girl would be very pleasant. In the small house and the London social atmosphere, they were too much in each other's pockets. It was good to be separated now and then. Of course, Mary's mother was not the ideal chaperon, but she must take her chances. She would once again admonish Julia to mind her p's and q's. As Brough had said, she could not watch her every moment.

Brough. Heart fluttering, she took a deep breath. Certainly he would be there. The duke was his best friend. It was inevitable.

* * *

The smart-stepping team of horses pulling the glossy black Singleton carriage drew up in front of Rackthall House and came to a natty halt. A footman leaped off, let down the steps, and assisted his marchioness to the brick pavement. With a preoccupied nod to him, Lady Ellen Singleton, forgetting her dignity, darted up the stoop and through the opened door.

"I must see the duchess immediately," she firmly told the butler.

"Certainly, my lady. She and the duke are in the library."

Ellen sped past him, rapped perfunctorily, and entered the room. "Allesandra, Brandon, I have heard such news that you must be made aware of it."

The duchess dropped her sewing, but the duke, ever the sophisticate, observed Ellen with only mild curiosity.

"It's about Clarissa James and her sister. Oh, it's just awful! I truly can scarcely believe it."

Brandon looked from his friend's wife's agitated blue eyes to his own wife's wide green ones. What a pair of beauties they were, especially when they were excited. But this wasn't the time to think of the ladies' attributes. Something had stirred the scandalmongers. Whatever it was, since it concerned Mrs. James, it might effect Brough.

"What is it, Ellen?" he asked.

"Yes." Allesandra recovered. "Sit down and tell us all."

She sat on the edge of a chair. "My goodness! As I said, I actually don't think it can be true. Clarissa seems to be such an estimable lady. But the gossip is making its rounds."

"Gossip is frequently exaggerated." Brandon handed her a glass of sherry.

"Thank you." She sipped daintily. "This morning I had a visit from Harry's aunt, who is aware of every piece of rumor that is going round. She informed me that Miss Dunstan is quite a wealthy heiress, but that her fortune is ironhandedly controlled, usurped really, by her elder sister. She said that Clarissa is saving it for the boy."

Allesandra gasped. "It can't be true! Mrs. James seems so conscientious."

"That is what I said, but nevertheless, the story is being circulated."

"Where did Harry's aunt hear of this?" Brandon probed.

"From the Duchess of Tarkingham."

"Arlen's mother."

"Yes. She heard it from her son, who heard it from Julia Dunstan herself. Lord Arlen has been courting her, you know."

"Then that explains it," said the duke with finality. "The little minx created the story herself. She's trying to ensnare him, and she's found out that that family always marries for money."

"Must you be so plainspoken?" his wife admonished.

"It's the truth, darling. I'd wager any amount on it."

"I cannot believe that such a very young lady could be that calculating."

"I can. I've had the experience of it." He grinned. "Oh, not from Miss Julia Dunstan, but from others. Before your time, of course."

Ellen giggled, but Allesandra rolled her eyes heavenward. "She seems like a nicely brought up young lady."

"She's a flirt," he countered. "Just ask Brough."

At that moment the butler, his knock unnoticed, opened the door and ushered Lord Abingdon into the room. Once again, as in the park, all eyes silently turned toward the earl. He stared at the inquisitive faces.

"What have I done now?" Brough asked.

Poor Clarissa. When Brough's friends had finished relating the news they had heard, he could think of nothing else. Didn't she have enough to worry her without adding the poisonous gossip of the *ton?* The lady was already at her wits' end when he had assumed the dilemma of Jeremy. Helping her had seemed perfectly reasonable. After all, he had to deal with George, so what difference could one more young man make? He was doing well with the boys, too. What with cockfights and horse races and visits to Gentleman Jackson's boxing establishment, they were too busy with manly pursuits to engage in juvenile mischief. Lately he had tried to offer a bit of advice about Julia. Clarissa needed someone. She had done so well raising her brother and sister, and now it was becoming too much for her. He would be glad to have her lean on him. She deserved a friend.

He poured himself a glass of brandy and turned to face Allesandra, Ellen, and Bran. "The story cannot be true. Clarissa wouldn't do such a thing. Julia must have fabricated it. She is quite smitten with Arlen."

There was a short silence, broken by the duke. "You are sure, Brough."

"I am well enough acquainted with Clarissa to know that if Julia had any money whatsoever, it would be spent to the girl's benefit. She has always sought the very best for her sister and brother. In my opinion she does it to her own detriment, but that is neither here nor there. It merely serves to indicate the kind of person she is. She doesn't deserve what's happened to her in the past or in the present. I hope to hell that somebody sets the slate clean."

"I like her," Ellen murmured, "although she intimidates me somewhat. She seems so very capable."

"At first she seemed that way to me," he said, "but now . . . she's becoming overwhelmed. She is a wonderful woman and she needs all the friends she can muster. Of course, she'd never admit to it."

"How may we help?" Allesandra implored.

"Mainly by ignoring the gossip. By refuting it, if you will. I know I am right. The Dunstans are not well-to-do."

"I doubt that my social prestige is that great, but our supper party should be a step in the right direction." She smiled. "You won't mind escorting Mrs. James, will you, Brough?"

"Not at all. Your dinner invitation," he remarked cynically, "is the reason I dropped by. I intended to convey my acceptance personally."

"My influence is certainly unimportant, but I will call on her," Ellen offered. "Perhaps we may go shopping or driving together."

Brough exchanged significant looks with Brandon.

"When," demanded the duke gently, "will the two of you realize that you are almost as great style-setters as the patronesses of Almack's?"

"Not me!" Ellen laughed.

"I am merely a wife and a mama," Allesandra maintained.

"They don't know," Brandon said.

His wife ignored him, piquantly eyeing Brough. "What shall you do?"

"I shall escort her to your party."

"Shouldn't she be told of the gossip?" Ellen asked.

He clenched his jaw. "Yes, she should."

"You'll do it?"

"I suppose I'll have to. I'd rather do anything else, but Clarissa must be warned." He shook his head. "This will disturb her deeply."

He finished his drink and bade good-bye to the ladies. Brandon accompanied him to the door.

"If there's anything I can do, Brough, please let me know. Somehow I feel that she means a great deal to you."

"Yes," he answered quietly, "I do believe that she does. Unfortunately there was another man in her life, and I don't think she's ready to let him go. I can't play rival to a memory."

"He's dead."

"Physically, yes, but I can't help but think that he's alive in her mind. He must be. My God, Bran, it doesn't matter if they were wed for only a short period of time! He made love to her ... He held her in his arms ..."

"I see that the first husband bothers you, too."

"Dammit, wouldn't it concern you? How would you feel if you were the second man for Allesandra?"

"I'd make her forget the first."

"You always were conceited." He allowed himself a smile. "Time will tell, I suppose."

"It usually does. Just make sure you don't let too much of it pass."

Brough nodded and strode down the steps to his curricle. He'd said more to his friend than he'd intended. In fact, he'd admitted much more than he'd realized himself. He did care for Clarissa James. It had become more than a matter of friendship. He was in love with her. He had finally found a woman with whom he wished to spend the rest of his life. But there was something wrong. There was another man, a man he couldn't challenge. Despite Jeremy's adverse description of Captain James, the man had been Clarissa's husband. He would give anything if he could erase his memory from the face of the earth.

He set the horses into the traffic and drove toward Clarissa's house. His feelings for her could not take precedence over the potential scandal associated with Julia's rumor. He must warn her of what was being said and must help her find a solution. If he didn't tell her, someone else eventually would. It was going to distress her terribly.

Morning calling hours had ended. Julia's face had grown more troubled with each minute that Lord Arlen did not appear. She had looked anxiously toward the door at each new arrival, only to be disappointed.

Clarissa sensed the girl's poignant disappointment and was sorry for her. Yet she couldn't keep from hoping that the marquess had found other game to chase. He just wasn't the man for her. Julia would be brokenhearted for a while, then she would recover her attractive vivaciousness. All would be well, and Clarissa would be saved from further warning her sister away from the young man.

When the last visitor departed, Julia flung her hands in her lap. "He didn't come. He told me he would!"

"I'm sorry," Clarissa sympathized.

"I doubt it," she said dryly. "You never did approve of him!"

"I merely thought that you would be better

suited to an older, more mature man. Lord Arlen is young. Perhaps he isn't ready to settle down to a wife and family."

"I loved him!" she cried, lips quivering. "It would have been so wonderful. Money . . . a noble title . . ."

She was interrupted by Simmons's scratch at the door. "Miss Clarissa, Lord Arlen is waiting in the hall. He asked to see you privately."

"Not me?" Julia entreated.

"He asked for Miss Clarissa."

"Oh, Clarissa, do you suppose he has come to ask you the question? It could be the reason he waited until the others left."

"It is nearly time for luncheon." She hesitated.

She must get her thoughts together. What if that was indeed the case? It must be! Lord Arlen would not otherwise ask to see her alone. What would she say? She looked at Julia's eager eyes and knew that the answer must be yes.

"Clarissa, please!"

"Very well."

Julia leaped to her feet and hugged her. "I shall have all my hopes up!"

"Don't count on . . ." The girl had skipped from the room.

Clarissa resolved herself to the interview. Perhaps Brough was wrong. Perhaps Lord Arlen had fallen so head over heels in love that he and his family wouldn't care about the small dowry. After all, Julia was a very pretty and pleasing young lady. In time, she would make an appropriate wife, mother, and hostess.

The marquess entered, bowed, and fixed her with a cool, blue-eyed stare. "Mrs. James."

"Good morning, my lord. Please sit down."

He did so, lounging gracefully. "What I have to say will only take a moment of your time."

"I am in no rush, Lord Arlen."

He nodded abruptly. "As you might have guessed, I have come to ask your permission to pay my addresses to Miss Julia. I have not mentioned this to her as yet, but I have no doubt that she will accept my suit. I trust that you also will approve."

"You have taken me somewhat by surprise," Clarissa murmured.

"For that I apologize."

His eyes. How cold they were when they looked at her! Was it the same way when he looked at Julia?

"Mrs. James, I promise you that I will do my utmost to make Miss Julia the happiest of ladies. She will have the best of everything."

Would she have love? Clarissa couldn't help contrasting Arlen's chilliness with Brough's warmth. She hoped that he was different with Julia, for there was nothing else she could do. She must give them her blessing. Anything less would alienate her sister beyond all redemption.

"You have my permission, Lord Arlen," she breathed, "but you must ask Julia yourself. Her word shall be the final one."

"Thank you, madam." He rose, affording her a thin, humorless smile. "May I see Miss Julia at once?"

"Of course." She, too, stood. "There is the matter of the dowry."

He airily waved a hand. "It is of no matter at present. My father shall be in contact with you concerning that. I suppose that it might be best if the engagement was not made official until after the settlement is agreed upon."

"All right. I shall fetch Julia. Perhaps the two of you would like to stroll in the garden out back."

He inclined his head.

Clarissa preceded him out of the room, caught Alice in the hall, and sent her for her mistress. She saw the couple into the garden, and as she returned, the front door knocker fell. Simmons opened it to reveal Lord Abingdon.

She drew him quickly to the salon. "Brough, you won't believe what has just happened! Arlen has asked me for Julia's hand, and he doesn't seem to care about the dowry!"

13

BROUGH LEFT THE Dunstan residence and turned his horses toward White's Club. Furious with himself, he drove quickly and almost dangerously through the city streets until he pulled up in front of the splendid establishment on St. James's Street. Arranging his expression to one of composure, he ignored the sophisticated curiosity seekers seated in the famous bow window and went inside. In the vestibule he paused, allowing his eyes to adjust from the bright noon sunlight to the richly paneled, darkened atmosphere. He handed his hat and gloves to the footman.

"Tell me," he asked, "is the Duke of Rackthall present?"

"Yes, my lord. I believe His Grace is taking luncheon."

"Thank you." He proceeded onward and found Brandon cutting into a thick, tender beefsteak. He dropped into a chair opposite. "I've been to see Clarissa," he said without preamble, "and I've failed miserably."

The duke laid down his knife and fork, wiping his mouth on the snowy white napkin. "You angered her?"

"No. At least I didn't do that." He nodded to

174

the waiter. "I'll have the same as His Grace."
When the man disappeared he returned to the
subject. "I didn't apprise her of the gossip."

"Why not? What happened?"

"When I arrived, Arlen was there. He had just
asked Clarissa for permission to pay his addresses
to Julia. He seemed to indicate that the dowry
didn't matter to him." He shrugged. "She was so
relieved that I couldn't repeat what is being said.
I suppose I'm hen-hearted, Bran. I just couldn't do
it."

"Perhaps nothing will come it it. Ellen may have
been wrong."

"I doubt it. Telling a story like that is exactly
what Julia might do if she heard the history of
Arlen's family's penchant for wealthy brides."

"A distasteful young lady."

"Not really. She's very young and foolish. Her
featherheadedness is equal to her determination to
snare a prize catch. I do believe that she's sweet at
heart. She just needs a strong, guiding hand."

"Mrs. James can't control her?"

"She probably did until they came to London.
The Season is causing Julia to mature, however little it may show. Their age difference is seeming
less and less, so she doesn't listen as much to
Clarissa as she did before. Furthermore, I believe
that the girl is jealous of her."

"Remarkable insight for a bachelor. Rather more
like a father."

"Dammit, Bran, I'm trying to understand all
this!"

They fell silent as the waiter served the earl's
luncheon. Brough glanced at his juicy steak and
felt his appetite wane. How could he enjoy his
meal when Clarissa was going about blithely igno-
rant of the rubbish that was being told about her?

The duke cleared his throat. "I'm sorry, Brough. I did not intend to make light of the situation. We have digressed into territory which really has nothing to do with the situation. Julia's personality or her actions have no bearing on the issue. What you must decide is whether or not Mrs. James should be informed of the rumor."

"I'd like to spare her any and all unpleasantries." He took a long sip of his port.

"Perhaps the news of the engagement will overshadow the thing."

"If it's done up hastily. I failed to tell you that Arlen himself didn't negotiate the settlement. His father is to see Clarissa about that point. The engagement will not become official until then."

Brandon's eyes narrowed. "The gossip stemmed from Harry's aunt's conversation with the Duchess of Tarkingham. If Arlen's parents believe the story, Tarkingham may accuse Mrs. James of withholding the major portion of the dowry."

"Good God!" Brough's stomach dropped to his feet. "Why didn't I think of that? I've really bungled this, haven't I?"

"Not really. No one makes calls at luncheon time, even on matters of this import. Besides, Arlen will need time to notify his father of his success. At the very earliest, I can't see Tarkingham putting in an appearance until late afternoon. You've plenty of time to set the record straight."

"You're right." He sighed. "I'll have to do it. Clarissa must be warned."

"Let us finish our luncheon. You can go to her house right after that. You'll be there long before Tarkingham." The duke chuckled. "The man probably won't call until tomorrow. He wouldn't consider it good *ton* to appear hasty."

Brough grinned with relief. "He wouldn't,

would he? Thank you, friend. I'm not looking forward to telling Clarissa, but you've made me see the necessity of it. I just don't understand why I couldn't reason myself into doing it before."

"Simple. You were trying to spare her worry. I'd do the same with Allesandra." He returned the smile. "The question now is when you are going to pay your own addresses. Perhaps you should do that this afternoon, too. Mrs. James's engagement to the Earl of Abingdon would go a long way to silence any adverse rumor."

"Rushing your fences, Bran." He took a deep breath. "But I'll think about it."

Clarissa curtsied. "How do you do, Your Grace?"

The Duke of Tarkingham bent over her hand. "I am well; and you, madam?"

"Tolerably, sir. Won't you be seated?"

He did so with a flaring of coattails. "Of course, you are aware of the reason that I am here. My son is quite taken with Miss Julia."

"Yes. And she, with him."

"That is how it should be, isn't it? The two of them should concentrate upon their feelings for each other and not upon the business side of things. That is for us to do, for I understand that the male of this family is far too young to dispense of such issues."

"That is true." She felt herself warming to the duke. He was assuming a remarkably modern outlook on the match. It was amazing that a man of his age and stature should acknowledge such romantical notions.

"There is the matter of the settlement which we must deal with."

Clarissa smiled. "Yes, we must tie up the official

knots. It scarcely seems worth your time, Your Grace, for you must know that Julia's dowry is very small. It is negligible, in fact, to a man of your distinction."

The duke's pleasant expression faded. "Let us not play games, Mrs. James. We are not at Tattersall's, bartering over a horse."

Her smile withered. "I do not know what you mean."

"It's very simple, madam. I shall not permit you to withhold any funds which rightfully belong to Miss Julia."

She stared at him with bewilderment. In the recesses of her consciousness she heard the door knocker fall, announcing another caller. It didn't matter. Simmons knew the import of Tarkingham's visit and would never interrupt it.

"I realize, Mrs. James, that you and the young viscount will have to live in straightened circumstances, but surely you do not believe that this family will leave you destitute," he continued pedantically. "I will even assist you in managing the estate, in making it more productive. But you cannot retain Julia's inheritance. I won't permit it. Furthermore, it isn't honest."

"Inheritance?" Clarissa regained her senses. "Oh, Your Grace, you are mistaken! Julia is not an heiress. I have only managed to set aside two hundred pounds for her dowry."

The duke straightened his shoulders and glared at her with cold blue eyes. "Have you spent it all? Or hidden it in a secret fund?"

Her heart pounded in her throat. How could he accuse her of cheating Julia? She, who had worked so hard and scrimped so arduously to provide even that small amount!

"Come now, Mrs. James, let us not practice intrigue. My son cares for the young lady and has asked for her hand. To me, that affords her the protection of being a member of my family, even if that sanctuary includes being safeguarded against the intrigues of her own sister. I will not stand for this subterfuge!"

"Julia is not an heiress," Clarissa repeated. "I do not know how you came under such a misapprehension."

"I have it on the best authority. Your sister told my son."

"Oh, surely not." She shook her head slowly. "How can she have done such a thing?"

"Because it was true?" He smiled with satisfaction. "You are quite the actress, Mrs. James. Most convincing! But your deception has ended."

"Deception?" Clarissa sprang to her feet. "How dare you accuse me of lying!"

He laughed cynically. "I accuse you of lying, young woman, because you indeed are a liar. You are a liar of the worst sort, and you are a swindler."

The drawing room door burst open. "Carry on your present course, Tarkingham, and I shall meet you at ten paces," Brough said glacially.

"Abingdon?" The duke, calm for a man just threatened with a duel, raised a sarcastic eyebrow. "Eavesdropping? What is your interest in this?"

"I am a friend of the family."

"Of the whole family?" the duke asked knowingly, casting an eye toward Clarissa.

She missed the underlying sexual connotations of his statement. "Yes, he is."

Thank God that Brough was here! He could clear up the misunderstanding. Despite his threat of pistols at dawn, he was an even-tempered man.

He could make the duke comprehend the error. Perhaps he could even save the engagement.

The duke laughed coldly. "I have no wish to meet you, Abingdon. I set no great store with settling one's differences at gunpoint, especially such conflicts as those brought about by a woman."

"I would gain no pleasure in meeting you either," the earl mandated. "Therefore the incident will be concluded with your apology to Mrs. James."

The elder man stood. "You'll whistle against the wind for that, my lord."

"Then you may name your seconds."

Clarissa's stomach twisted in knots. Merciful Heavens! Her being called a liar wasn't worth the risk of lives! How had the awful situation degenerated into this melee? It was only a misunderstanding, for God's sake! It could be rectified.

"Both of you must listen to reason!" she cried. "It is all a misunderstanding that can be cleared up by my man of business!"

"Clarissa," Brough said quietly, "be still."

"I will not! My being called names is not worth someone's life!"

The Duke of Tarkingham, staring at the composed, collected younger man, faltered. "Perhaps I was mistaken." He barely inclined his head toward Clarissa. "You will accept my apologies, Mrs. James?"

"Gladly," she breathed.

"Then I bid you both good day." He made his way to the door and, opening it, paused. "Of course, you realize that the engagement is terminated."

"But if—"

"Surely you can grasp, madam, why I have no

wish to ally my family with yours." He snapped the door shut behind him.

"Oh, God." Clarissa collapsed onto the love seat. "What now? How shall I tell Julia?"

"Do you blame me?" Brough asked.

"No. There was little you could do about it. No matter what transpired here, the man would not have agreed to the match without a sizable dowry. You were right all along."

He exhaled a sigh of relief.

"I only wish that there was a simple way of explaining it to Julia."

"Perhaps you'd best begin by confronting her with her deception. Julia herself caused this predicament, Clarissa. She finally went too far."

"What do you mean?" she demanded.

"Julia proclaimed herself an heiress to Arlen and accused you of treachery," he said wearily. "Ellen heard it this morning. The gossip is spreading. I meant to tell you earlier, but . . ."

"You knew it and you didn't tell me? Oh, how very bad of you, Brough!"

"I wanted to save you distress."

"Save me distress! What do you think I have been going through? If I had known . . . Dammit, Brough! Why can't you cease meddling in my life!"

"My dear." He hurriedly sat down beside her, hands on her shoulders. "I've no intention of interfering. I'm merely trying to help."

"I've told you! I will accept no one's charity!" She shook herself free and wrenched to her feet. "Get out."

"Clarissa . . ."

"Get out! I never want to see you again. Never! Not for the rest of my life!"

"All right." His voice was husky. "But if you reconsider—"

"I shall not."

He rose and bowed. "I will always wish you well."

"Keep your wishes to yourself!" she snapped. She watched through a haze as he crossed the room. "Lord Abingdon?"

He whirled.

"Jeremy will not remain in your house. Please send him home immediately."

"None of this is necessary, Clarissa. If you would let me explain . . ."

She turned her back to him.

"Very well. I shall send him."

She heard the door close softly behind him and burst into tears. Brough was gone. He was gone forever. She had banished him from her life. A terrible ache of loneliness throbbed in her breast. Slowly she sank to her knees, burying her face in her hands.

Her private mourning lasted only a few minutes.

"Clarissa, what has happened?" Julia cried. "I heard raised voices. Then Vincent's father, and then Lord Abingdon, left. You're crying! What is the matter?"

Clarissa rose, wiping her eyes. She blew her nose and turned, rapidly trying to regain her control. "Close the door."

The girl sprang to obey. "Why are you so overset?"

"There is no easy way to tell you this, Julia," she said soberly. "The engagement is off."

"What?"

"There will be no marriage between you and Lord Arlen. His family will not settle for the modest dowry I have put aside for you. If you had not led them to believe that you were an heiress, the affair would not have continued to this length."

"It's not true. Vincent loves me! We will elope!"

"No, Julia. Lord Arlen will do as his father directs. It's over."

The girl's face flamed. "You never cared for Vincent. You have brought this about!"

"I have not!" Clarissa shouted, surprising her sister and even herself with the magnitude of her shriek. "You caused it with your frauds and falsehoods! I have done nothing but suffer the scorn created by your deception! My God, I even had to stop a duel because of it!"

Julia's ears pricked up. Her color faded to a delicate pink. "A duel? Over me? Perhaps Lord Abingdon has developed a regard we were unaware of."

"So much for your love of Lord Arlen," Clarissa muttered. So much for the weeping hysteria she had expected. Had her sister grown so cold and calculating that she could toss one man aside for another as easily as she changed bonnets?

"Well, Vincent *was* rather childish at times. Lord Abingdon is handsome for an older man. He is wealthy and has a title. Perhaps seeing me with the marquess sparked his interest."

"You stupid girl." Clarissa collapsed into a chair. "You stupid, stupid girl!"

"I am not! I merely made a small mistake."

"Small? The entire town is talking about it!"

She shrugged. "If Lord Abingdon has defended me once, he will do so again."

Clarissa eyed her sister with disgust. "Ninny-hammer! Lord Abingdon was defending *me* against that awful Tarkingham's abhorrent accusations, allegations brought forth by *your* pernicious tongue. He considers you to be nothing but a child, and a very foolish one at that."

"How do you know that?"

"Because he told me so."

"Can I believe you?"

"You had better!"

Tears formed in Julia's eyes. Two large drops slid down her cheeks. "So I have nothing."

"You have brought it all upon yourself," Clarissa stated harshly. "You have no one else to blame."

"What shall we do?" the young lady wailed, beginning to weep in earnest. "What if everyone laughs at me?"

"That should be the least of your worries." Clarissa's vision blurred. Lights danced in front of her eyes. Her head commenced a painful throb. "We shall be lucky if we are not ruined."

"Oh, Clarissa!" The young lady threw herself into her lap. "You must help me!"

"I have tried to do that for so very, very long." She brought her hands to her pulsating temples. "Go to your room, Julia. I want to be alone."

"I need your advice!"

"I'm sorry," she murmured. "Right now I have none left to give."

Julia clung to her knees. "You must! You always think of something we can do! Perhaps Lord Abingdon can help."

"Not this time. I have sent him away. Forever!" She leaped up, sending her sister careening to her bottom. "Can't you see that I have problems enough of my own?"

With a wrenching sob, Clarissa dashed from the room.

Morosely Brough entered his library and sat down behind the desk. He seemed to ache all over.

When she had told him to get out, it had felt as if the entire contents of his chest had been ripped out. Oh Lord, how he had botched this dilemma! He had blundered so badly that there would be no repairing the error. Clarissa was lost to him. Forever.

"Brandy, my lord?" the footman asked.

"Thank you." He watched broodingly as the amber liquid filled the glass. "Leave the bottle on the desk. And, Palmer, please fetch young Lord Dunstan. I don't care where he is. Find him and bring him here."

"Yes, sir."

The boys must have been nearby, for it wasn't long before they entered. "You asked for us, Brough?"

"I sent for you, Jeremy. Have George's valet pack your belongings. Your sister wishes you to return home."

"But I didn't do anything wrong!"

The earl smiled cynically. "No, I'm afraid that I was the one who did."

"What did you do, Brough?" his brother asked. "Did you try to take liberties. . .?"

"It is none of your affair, George!" he roared.

"Damn." The two young men exchanged glances.

Brough took a deep breath, exhaled slowly, and lowered his voice. "I meddled in her concerns, and she didn't take kindly to it. Now, be off with you."

Jeremy and George withdrew solemnly. When the door was closed, the earl drained his glass and refilled it quickly. He was going to spend the rest of the day and the evening alone in his library. He was going to get gloriously drunk. By tomorrow things might seem brighter, and losing her would not hurt so much.

14

"WHERE IS MY sister?" Jeremy demanded of Simmons as Lord Abingdon's coachman set down his bags in the vestibule.

"Miss Clarissa is in her room; Miss Julia is in the salon, my lord."

Jeremy started up the stairs.

"Master Jeremy," the butler intoned. "It wouldn't do to disturb Miss Clarissa. She is quite overset at present."

"Why?"

"I wouldn't know, sir." Simmons set his face into a blank expression.

"Like hell." Jeremy turned and made his way toward the salon. "Servants know everything."

He burst through the door to confront a red-eyed, anguished Julia. "Ju! What's the matter?"

"Oh, it's terrible," she whimpered. "The most odious, loathsome thing has happened!" She dabbed her cheeks with a lace handkerchief.

"You'd better tell me all." He took her by the hand and led her to the love seat. "What's wrong with Kissy?"

She sank to the pillows, leaned back her head, and shaded her forehead with a limp hand. "My engagement is off."

"I didn't know you were engaged."

"I was this morning. To Lord Arlen."

"That fribble."

"He isn't a fribble! Vincent is wealthy and he has a title."

"That's no criterion. He's a coxcomb."

She sat up straight. "I happen to think that he would have made an absolutely perfect husband."

"All right, all right. What happened?"

"His father put a period to it because of my lack of dowry."

"That old court card!" Jeremy flared. "You're good enough for his simpleton son, dowry or no!"

"Thank you, dear brother." Julia resumed her declining posture.

"Is that what is wrong with Kissy?"

"Not entirely."

"Tell me!"

She took a deep breath. "I did something wrong. At the time I didn't realize that the consequences would be so serious. I only thought to attract Lord Arlen long enough to affix his affection."

"Good God, Julia, you didn't allow him liberties?"

"Certainly not!" she snapped. "How can you think that I would do such a thing as that? I could box your ears!"

Jeremy casually moved some distance away. "Please go on."

"Not if you continue to interrupt me! This is difficult enough as it is."

"I'm sorry, Julia. I promise to remain silent."

"Very well then." She sighed. "I told Vincent that I was an heiress and that Clarissa refused to allow me my fortune."

"Oh, what a corker!" Jeremy bit the inside of his

lip to hide a smile. "Why did you trump up something like that?"

"I overheard Lord Abingdon tell Clarissa that Vincent's family always married wealth, so I thought the story would keep him attracted to me long enough for him to fall in love. Well, it worked for a while. Unfortunately," she sniffled, "the tale has spread. We are probably ruined."

"You can overcome it," he stated confidently. "Everyone knows you're a shallow pate to begin with, but you're a pretty little baggage. So you lost Arlen! Another fool will come along. But I can't think that's why Kissy is so overset. She always finds ways to set our errors right. Besides, Arlen didn't seem to be a favorite of hers."

"She had a most unpleasant interview with Vincent's father. He so much as called her a liar and a cheat, then Lord Abingdon called him out. Clarissa stopped that, but she and the earl had a terrible quarrel. She sent him away."

"So."

Julia removed her hand from her eyes long enough to search her brother's face. "So?"

"So that's what's upset Kissy."

"It has been a most ghastly day."

He shook his head. "The business with you, Ju, would make her angry, not precisely overset. It's the fracas with Brough." He grinned. "She's in love with him."

"With Lord Abingdon? Don't be ridiculous!"

"Why couldn't she be?"

"Clarissa isn't interested in being in love."

"I don't see why not. She's a woman, and all women are interested in being in love."

"Not Clarissa," Julia mandated. "She didn't even cry when Captain James was killed."

"She wasn't in love with *him*, stupid! She married him for what she thought was necessity. I'll wager my next quarter's allowance that she's in love with Brough!"

"Surely not. My goodness, Jeremy, she's a penniless widow! Clarissa is smart enough to know that he is ineligible for her. Lord Abingdon is a friend, and that is all."

"Tell *him* that," Jeremy said smugly.

Julia eyed him suspiciously. "You know something, don't you?"

He hastened to her side. "Ju, you should see Brough right now. He looks as if he's lost everything he ever had. Blue-deviled isn't even the word for it. The man is positively morose!"

"You think he's in love with her."

"I am certain of it!" He grasped her hands. "Think of it, Julia. Brough and Clarissa. They're perfect for each other!"

"But she sent him away."

"Deplorable, isn't it? We'll just have to think of a way to get them back together again."

Julia gazed into her brother's sparkling eyes and drew back. "Oh no, Jeremy, I refuse to become involved in one of your rigs. I'm in enough trouble as it is."

"Think of the kind of future you would have with Brough as a brother-in-law." He grinned slyly. "Arlen would return to your side in an instant. His father would have no objections then!"

"That is true," she murmured, "though the duke would remember Lord Abingdon's calling him out."

"Then the devil take Arlen! You'll lure others just like him. Handsome. Titled. Wealthy."

"It's possible . . ."

"Of course it is! That's not all. If Clarissa is a countess, she won't spend her time making dresses. She'll have the finest modiste in London! And so will you."

"Probably."

"You should see Brough's town house and his estate. They have ballrooms, Ju, and huge staffs of servants. You'll have your own lady's maid."

"It seems like heaven."

"Well? Will you help?"

"What do you wish me to do?"

"That's the problem. I don't know just yet." He settled back, satisfied. "Let's put our heads together on this. I'm sure we can come up with something."

"I hope so." Her tears began to flow once more. "I want Clarissa to be happy, too! I love her, Jeremy, but I keep doing things to hurt her!"

"So do I." Spontaneously he gathered her into his arms. "We'll set aside our differences and work as one. We'll make her happy. I know we will!"

"I don't understand this at all," Allesandra mused, studying the three letters before her.

Her husband looked up from his business papers. "Understand what, my dear?"

"Oh, I'm sorry. I was merely thinking out loud. I didn't mean to interrupt you."

He grinned fondly at her. "Since you already have, perhaps you'd best explain."

"Thank you." Her green eyes glistened with mischievous guilt. "These are replies from our dinner party invitation. Two are from Clarissa James. One contains her acceptance; the other, her regrets. The third is from Miss Julia Dunstan. She accepts for both of them."

"Which one was the last to arrive?"

"I don't know. I was out when all of them arrived, so they were mixed in with other correspondence."

"Then you had best be prepared for both ladies to attend."

"I suppose so," she pondered. "But don't you think it seems strange"

He nodded, sensing that he hadn't heard the last of it.

"Perhaps you could go round to Brough's house, Brandon. Something isn't right here. Perhaps he should be made aware of it."

"Allesandra, I will not allow you to involve me in your matchmaking schemes, and that's final."

"Ah well, then I shall have to do it myself." She rose and glided across the room to the bellpull.

"What are you doing?"

"I'm ordering my carriage, of course. You don't expect me to walk?"

He quickly stood up. "You can't go to Brough's house alone!"

"I shall take my maid."

"You still can't! It isn't proper."

"Why not? He is your best friend." She pulled the cord.

"It will create a scandal!"

"Perhaps no one will see me enter."

"Allesandra! Listen to reason!" He was distracted from his lecture by the entrance of a footman.

His wife smiled sweetly.

"Timmons," the duke said wearily. "Please bring my carriage round immediately. I'm going out." When the servant departed he turned on his duchess. "Minx! If you think to twist me around your finger every time you wish, you are sadly mistaken."

"Why, Brandon! That would be the farthest

thing from my mind." She leaned across the desk to kiss his cheek.

"Save your kisses until later, madam. You now owe me a debt, which I intend to collect."

"As usual, I shall be happy to pay."

"You could have gone to Mrs. James's house and found out firsthand what was going on."

"That would be rather forward of me, wouldn't it?"

"And going to Brough's would not be?" He strode around the desk. "Well, here I go off on your fool's errand. After this episode, Allesandra, you will cease this matchmaking. Now, there's an end to it!"

"It adds spice to my life."

"*I'll* put spice to it!" He left the room and waited in the front hall for his coachman. What a meddlesome little beauty he had married! But he couldn't resist her, and unfortunately, she knew it as well as he did. It would serve her right if he were tossed out on his ear.

That was almost what happened. When Brough's butler informed him that the earl was unavailable to callers, he'd practically had to push his way past the man. Without introduction and with a collection of footmen on his heels, he thrust open the library door.

"Can't a man even get drunk in peace?" his friend asked.

"You don't look foxed yet."

"I'm on my way." He shrugged. "You might as well join me."

"Trouble?" Brandon closed the door.

"Of the worst sort. How did you know?"

"Allesandra received conflicting replies to her invitation." He helped himself to the liquor.

"Well, Clarissa won't be there if she expects me

to attend." He quickly briefed him on the events of the afternoon. "There's nothing I can do, Bran. She hates me."

"Coming it a bit too strong, aren't you?"

"I don't think so."

"In time, things will smooth out. It was all too much for her right then. You'll find a chance to explain matters."

"Time is what I don't have. That damn scandal, remember? She'll probably return to the country," he said moodily.

"If she does, you'll just have to follow her there. Dammit, Brough, where's your determination? You've never had trouble attracting ladies."

"There's that Captain James. Don't forget him."

"He's dead!" Brandon cried.

"Physically."

"Clarissa James doesn't seem like a mourning widow to me. She doesn't wear black or lavender."

"She wears his damned old wedding ring," Brough lisped.

"To prove her status."

"True."

"So don't give him another minute's thought. Unless, of course, you've decided that a widow isn't good enough for you."

Brough's eyes blazed. "Clarissa is good enough for any man! Most men would be lucky to find a lady of her quality!"

"I agree." Brandon finished his drink and rose. He had done as much as he could do here. The next move would be up to his friend. "We'll see you at our party."

"I can't come. What if Clarissa would appear?"

"What if she does?"

"It would be awkward!"

Brandon shrugged. "Surely you don't intend to avoid her? How can you make things right between you if you never see her again?"

"I suppose you're right. I'll come, but I doubt very seriously that she'll be there."

"Who knows? If she decides to weather out the scandal, she will attend."

"I wouldn't even know how to act around her."

"I'm sure you'll think of something."

He left his friend refilling his glass. He hoped that Allesandra would be pleased with his day's work. He had found out what had happened and he had secured Brough's presence at the dinner party. There was nothing more that either of them could do, and he intended to make certain that his impertinent wife kept her nose out of it from this point forward.

Clarissa's head was throbbing dully, but she forced herself to dress for supper. She must put her own heartbreak behind her and concentrate on her brother and sister. Jeremy would have returned home by now and be demanding to know what had happened. Julia would still be distraught, and she would be trying to discover a way to avert the gossip. Both of them needed her now, probably more than they ever did.

She was surprised to find them calmly seated at the dining table. Julia's eyes were dry and, while still red, did not threaten to spill over with tears. Jeremy's expression was so benign that no one would ever guess his certain disappointment. Wonderingly she sat down and took up her napkin.

The meal continued peacefully. The two youths did not bicker with each other, nor did they bring up the subject of the day's happenings. Clarissa grew vigilant. Why hadn't the storm broke? She felt as though she were feeling the breezeless, dead quiet of a summer day before the wind and lightning and thunder swooped down. Her nerves grew taut. At last she brought up the subject herself.

"It appears that you have discussed with each other what has happened today."

They nodded solemnly.

"Have you come to a conclusion?" she asked.

"We have some ideas," Jeremy ventured. "Have you?"

"No. Nothing." She laid down her fork. "Let us have our dessert in the salon. With our tea. We can talk more freely."

In unison they retired from the room. Julia poured the coffee while Jeremy helped himself to several jam tarts. After consuming one of them, it was he who began the conversation.

"When there is trouble, a family must pull together," he said wisely. "It doesn't matter whose fault it was."

Julia shot him a glance of irritation. Here we go, thought Clarissa. But the young lady did not voice her annoyance.

"Jeremy is right," she said. "We know, however, that this disaster is all my fault. I did not look far enough ahead to visualize the consequences. I am willing to shoulder the blame, and I will assure you both that nothing like this will ever happen again."

"Don't be so hard on yourself, Ju," Jeremy directed. "I haven't made things easy either. We're sorry that we've put you through all this, Clarissa. We know you've only strived to have the best for us."

"Goodness!" She sensed her headache diminishing. If only the two would always be so genial! She could face anything if she had this peace at home.

"We're willing to return to Essex if it will make you happy," they said at once.

Clarissa gazed thoughtfully at Julia. "If there was any way that we could overcome this gossip . . ."

"We've thought of the only thing that can be done," Jeremy said triumphantly. "We'll brazen it out."

"I don't know if it's possible," she murmured. "If people cut us, there is nothing we can do about it."

"We have already been invited to a number of parties," Julia reminded her, "beginning with the invitation from the Duchess of Rackthall."

Clarissa shook her head. "I declined it . . . after what happened."

Younger sister and brother exchanged peeks.

"I reaccepted then," Julia blurted.

"What!"

"Jeremy and I had discussed matters. The time was growing short for replying to Her Grace's request, so I accepted for us both. Oh dear, I have done it again! What will the duchess think of us?"

Stunned briefly, Clarissa couldn't help but laugh. Once she had started, she could scarcely stop. "Merciful heavens! The Season has never seen such a family as ours!"

"What shall we do!" Julia cried. "You, Jeremy. This is your fault! You said I should make haste to accept!"

Tears of laughter streamed down Clarissa's face. "Do not start in on each other. The problem is simple. I shall write to the duchess to explain and hope that she understands."

"Then we will attend?" she asked anxiously.

Clarissa sobered. "I think not. You wanted to go to Mary's ball, didn't you?"

"You cannot slight the duchess!"

"I will be your chaperon at the ball. When I enlighten the sweet duchess on how much you had your heart set on attending your friend's ball, I am sure that she will understand. Probably she will be just as pleased that I am not her guest."

"But you must go, Clarissa," Julia urged. "You were looking forward to it."

"Yes," Jeremy seconded. "You'll have a much more enjoyable time there than you would at a debutante ball."

"I shall accompany Julia."

"No, you won't," the young lady decreed, "for I won't go."

"This is your Season," Clarissa began. "There will be people your own age at Mary's ball. It is a good opportunity for you to commence making amends."

"Then I'll do it myself. While you are at the Rackthalls' dinner party."

"That's right," her brother agreed. "Julia caused this tangle. Let her grope her way through on her own."

"I shall do it!" Julia shrilled. "You will not be disappointed!"

"Neither of you understand! I *can't* go to the Rackthalls'!"

"Why not?"

"He might be there," she whispered.

"Who?"

She stared at a point over their heads. "Lord Abingdon."

"So?"

"I was horrible to him. No, I cannot face him again."

"I never knew you to be chickenhearted." Jeremy shook his head.

"I'm not!"

"Then don't run from him. If Julia is brave enough to stand up alone at Mary's ball, it looks as if you could look one man in the eye."

"But I was awful to him!"

"Then apologize."

"It isn't that easy, Jeremy."

"Then we had best go home to Essex."

Clarissa stared at her brother. How had the shoe been removed from one foot and placed on another? Why was she listening to Jeremy's advice? He was a little boy. He hadn't been under Brough's care long enough to grow up that much. Yet she knew he was right. Someday, if they remained in London, she would meet Brough.

"All right." She nodded. "I'll do it. If it will help alleviate this gossip, I'll do it. Maybe I'll be lucky and he won't even attend."

15

CLARISSA STOOD TRANSFIXED in front of the mirror and wished that her sister could see her now. Over her protestations, Julia had unequivocally decreed that she have a new gown for the Rackthalls' dinner party. The girl had even assisted in its construction. So it was that Clarissa was now attired in what must be the most beautiful dress she had ever owned. It was of rich satin, a dark capucine orange, which brought out the bronze highlights in her hair. It had a small train, which amazingly made an ordinary walk into a graceful glide, and its neckline was cut as low as any proper lady could wear. Gazing once again at her soft, very exposed bosoms, Clarissa was slightly horrified and wondered why she had allowed her younger sister to talk her into it.

"And now the shoes, ma'am." Grinning broadly, Alice held up Julia's flimsy cream-on-cream brocade slippers.

"My sister's pumps? I don't think I can get into them."

"Let's try. Be a shame to wear your old pair with that dress." The maid lifted the back of Clarissa's gown so that she could sit down without wrinkling it. Kneeling, she wedged a slipper onto her mistress's foot.

"It's awfully tight."

Alice fitted the other one. "They're prettier," she announced. "Just wear 'em, Miss Clarissa, while I do your hair, and then decide." She whisked a dressing cape around Clarissa's shoulders and set to work.

"Just a simple bun, Alice. I fear that your talents are wasted on me." Clarissa smiled into the mirror at her. "I thought you would attend Miss Julia, but she insisted that you stay here."

"Her friend's maid'll help her."

"Not as expertly, I'm sure. You should be a regular lady's maid, Alice."

"I'd like that, ma'am."

The simple bun became an elaborate knot as Alice loosely gathered Clarissa's hair to the back of her head and applied the curling tongs. Wavy tendrils drifted from it down the back and along the sides of her face. Thin interwoven ribbon that matched the dress completed the coiffure.

"Mercy," Clarissa breathed. "I look so elegant."

The maid quickly touched her cheeks and lips with rouge and removed the cape. "You're perfect. Now, which jewelry will you wear?"

"You make it sound as though I have a large selection," she laughed.

"I wish you had diamonds."

"So do I, but if I had, I would have probably sold them by now. Mama's amber, it shall be."

Alice fastened the necklace and hung the drops in her earlobes. "What about the shoes?"

Clarissa winced. "I'll wear them. Perhaps I can slip out of the heels during dinner and ease my feet. I suppose that I should have listened to my sister and bought myself a new pair of slippers, but this fabric was so terribly expensive." She stood and couldn't help going to the cheval mirror once more to admire herself. "If you will fetch my shawl, Alice, I suppose I'll be ready."

Chuckling, the maid brought out a creamy satin cape. "Miss Julia insisted."

"Goodness! I should be going to a ball."

"I've never seen you more beautiful, ma'am. Never!"

"Thank you, Alice. You have a magical touch." With a final smile, she left the room and descended the stairway to enter the salon.

"Gibson's waiting." Her brother turned, his mouth dropping open. "Damnation!"

"Don't swear, Jeremy."

"But ... but ... Clarissa, you're magnificent! I always knew you were pretty, but this!" He swallowed. "Brough won't have a chance."

"I wish you would not mention Lord Abingdon," she murmured. "If he knows that I am coming, I doubt that he will attend."

Jeremy knew better than to pursue the present course. "Let me remove your wrap so I may see you all over!"

Clarissa twirled coquettishly in front of him.

"Well, you don't look like a lady who acts as her own housekeeper." He grinned. "If Arlen had seen you like this, he wouldn't have given a second glance at Julia, and he'd have told his father to catch cold about the dowry!"

"Then I am glad that he didn't, for he would have been sorely disappointed by my answer."

Laughing, he returned the cape to her shoulders.

"So I'll do?"

"You'll do more than just 'do.' You'll outshine every lady present!"

"Not the duchess, nor Lady Singleton. You should see them, Jeremy. They are diamonds of the first water!"

"They also have husbands who can afford the accoutrements. You must marry a wealthy man, Clarissa, who can dress you like this all the time."

"Perhaps I should look among the ranks of the cits," she teased.

"Dammit."

"Jeremy!"

"Well! I know you're joking, but if you would have more dresses like this, you'd have just as good a chance as Julia to find a suitable match. Let's mortgage the estate and take a flyer on it."

"We'll do no such thing. I am well enough attired." She kissed his cheek. "Thank you for wanting the best for me, but I am satisfied just as I am. I have two very pretty gowns that I didn't expect to have. After all, this is—"

"Julia's Season," he finished.

She nodded unbendingly. "Now wish me well."

"I do." He escorted her out of the house and settled her into the carriage. "Take care of her, Gibson," he admonished. "She's an absolute gem tonight!"

"I shall, m'lord. I shall!" Proudly he set off the horses at a spanking trot down the street.

Nervously Clarissa entered Rackthall House. The solemn butler took her cape and escorted her majestically through the entrance hall. She scarcely had time to admire her superb surroundings before he opened the door to the drawing room.

"Mrs. Clarissa James," he intoned.

"Mrs. James." The duchess was beside her in an instant. "How nice of you to come!"

"It is an honor, Your Grace." Clarissa curtsied.

Her hostess smiled. "Please do not stand on ceremony. We are a rather informal group, so you must call me 'Allesandra,' for I intend to address you as 'Clarissa' from now on." She took her elbow and led her first to greet the handsome duke, who gallantly placed a glass of champagne in her hand, and then to meet the other guests.

He was there. Clarissa had glimpsed him standing by the hearth as soon as she had entered the room. He had looked at her, too, and had made his bow. Now she could feel his eyes upon her as Allesandra led her around the room. Her heart pounded so hard that she feared it would burst through her throat.

"You are already acquainted with Brough, of course," the duchess said.

"Clarissa." His lips brushed her hand, setting it afire.

Her mouth moved to speak, but words would not come.

"Clarissa!" Ellen Singleton beckoned. "Come sit with me. I have been deserted."

Gratefully she joined the marchioness on the love seat while Allesandra sat in a chair beside. The two ladies began a spirited discussion of the latest *on-dits* of the ton. The conversation, for the most part, flowed over Clarissa's head. She was far too absorbed by Brough's presence to care about what Lady This or Lord That had done. She chanced a hurried glance at him. He was studying her, his eyes shadowed and thoughtful. She quickly looked away and sipped her champagne, murmuring a response to Ellen's polite inquiry into the health of Julia and Jeremy. This promised to be an exceedingly difficult evening. Why on earth had she allowed her brother and sister to talk her into attending? She was going to be perfectly miserable.

"The Duke and Duchess of Sommerfield," the butler announced. "Lady Christina."

With a quick pat of Clarissa's hand, Allesandra rose to tend her hostess duty.

"I'd hoped that your Julia might become acquainted with Christina," Ellen said. "I believe that they would get along famously, although Tina can be rather a handful at times. Perhaps we can arrange for them to meet."

Clarissa assented.

"Tomorrow for tea at my house?"

"That would be very kind of you." She smiled. "I'm sure that Julia would enjoy it. She has made a number of friends, but . . ." She knew that Julia's friendship with a duke's granddaughter would go a long way towards furthering her chances, and it would most certainly help in laying the scandal to rest. Surely the marchioness had heard of it. Clarissa certainly did not wish to involve her in an embarrassing situation.

"My lady," she began in a lowered voice.

"Ellen."

"Yes . . . Ellen. There has been a most unpleasant matter. Julia put it about that she was a wealthy heiress, and then Lord Arlen—"

Lady Singleton silenced her with a wave of her hand. "A simple, youthful error."

"You may be unaware of all that is involved," Clarissa warned. "In fact, I probably should not have come here tonight. I have no wish to harm anyone's reputation by my presence."

"Allesandra is also familiar with what has happened. Think nothing of it."

"But it is far from simple," she persisted. "You

see, Lord Arlen offered for Julia. Then his father came to the house—"

"We know. Brough has told us."

Her eyes narrowed. How dare he go about telling people of what happened in her drawing room? This was much worse than his asking Allesandra to obtain the vouchers to Almack's.

"Do not think the less of him, Clarissa," the marchioness advised. "Brough and Harry and Brandon are very, very close friends. No one outside of our circle will know of what happened unless Tarkingham spills the news. We all wish to help."

"Thank you, Ellen, but I can handle matters," Clarissa said stiffly. "I should despise seeing your reputation besmirched."

"Oh, I am not concerned with that. The *ton* does not threaten me. I have my friends and I have Harry. What more could I want? We are trying to be your friends, too. We wish to help," she repeated. "At times like this, one needs one's friends. I know. All has not been easy for me either."

Clarissa studied her tightly folded hands. She had sent away the best friend she had ever had. She couldn't keep from glancing at Brough.

The pretty Lady Tina was flirting outrageously with him. Grinning, Brough bent to whisper something in her ear. The young lady burst into gales of laughter.

A stab of jealously pierced Clarissa's stomach. Oh no, she should not have come here tonight! It was just too awful.

"You should not judge Tina by her conduct here tonight." Ellen smiled. "She is a dear friend of us all. Outside this group I will assure you that she behaves with propriety. Well . . . most of the time."

"She's quite lovely," Clarissa said against the lump in her throat, "and most suitable for Lord Abingdon."

"My goodness! That would never be a match. The two of them would drive each other lunatic in no time at all. And they both know it!" She looked questioningly at Clarissa. "You and Julia will come for tea tomorrow?"

"If you still wish it, but I must insist that neither you nor the duchess will go out of your way for us, nor jeopardize your good names."

"Clarissa," the marchioness sighed, "you may despise me for saying this, but you are being entirely too independent. I realize that you have been forced to assume much more responsibility than a young woman should have to bear, but you must learn to accept assistance from others. You are not alone in this world. You have friends. Think on it."

She nodded tensely. "I simply do not wish to inflict my troubles on others."

"I know, but when others are willing to help shoulder them, it can be a great relief."

"You are probably right."

"I know I am." She dimpled. "Now let us leave off serious topics and enjoy the evening. I hope you will like our little group. We find a great deal of amusement together."

The Rackthalls' butler immediately announced the supper. The duchess smoothly paired her guests. "Brough, you will take Clarissa in?"

He nodded his consent and approached her, bowing elegantly and extending his hand.

Clarissa's heart tripped into a gallop. How could Allesandra have arranged this! Didn't she envision how awkward this would be? If she knew all, as Ellen claimed, she would know that

Clarissa had perfunctorily dismissed the earl. To place them together was absolutely maladroit! Oh, this evening was beyond all belief.

"Clarissa?" the earl prompted.

Avoiding his eyes, she placed trembling fingers on his and stood.

Brough warmly clasped her hand and laid it on his arm. "I don't bite, you know."

"No," she stammered. Her emotions were in tatters. On the one hand, she wished she could tear free and run as fast as she could out the front door. On the other, she felt perilously close to bursting into sobs and throwing herself into his arms. What on earth would people think if she did either one? Well, she wouldn't have to worry about friends! None of these people would ever wish to see her again.

"You look very beautiful tonight."

"Thank you, my lord."

"It used to be 'Brough.' "

They entered the dining room. He held the chair, and Clarissa collapsed gratefully, if ungracefully, onto it. He seated himself beside her.

The duchess had arranged her guests informally at the table. With the exception of the Duke of Sommerfield, who was positioned on her right, and his duchess on Lord Rackthall's right, the diners were placed with disregard to rank. With Brough on her right, Clarissa found Lord Singleton on her left.

As the interminable meal progressed, she attempted to direct most of her small conversation toward the charming marquess. Ellen's husband seemed to sense her distress and afforded her his full attention. If this was what Ellen meant by friendship, then thank God for it. She didn't know what she would have done if she had had to carry on a lengthy discourse with Brough. Even his casual overtures left her tongue-tied.

At last the dessert course was finished and Allesandra rose to lead the ladies to the drawing room for tea. If it had gone on for another moment, Clarissa thought that she would surely burst. Now she need only stay a reasonable time before she took her thankful leave.

"Thank you, Harry," Brough said irritably under his breath. "I do appreciate your monopolizing the conversation."

"I? It wasn't my fault! Clarissa monopolized *me*."

"It's very easy to be taken in by a handsome rake."

"Dammit, Brough. I'm not a rake. I'm a happily married man, and you know it."

"Old habits are hard to break."

Lord Singleton set his jaw. "Keep your voice down. We don't want Tina's grandpa to hear this ridiculous interchange."

"Feeling guilty?"

"No, I am not. Why must all of you take out your little jealousies on me?"

"Why, Harry, I'm not jealous of you." But he was. He was jealous of the marquess's perfect marriage, but mostly of the way that Clarissa had seemed to hang on the man's every word. Harry Singleton, and Brandon, too, for that matter, had a way with women that he could only envy. He took a long drink of port.

"The lady is terrified of you, Brough. Why don't you straighten it out?"

"I haven't had an opportunity."

"Then make one, man!" Harry moved to the

head of the table and joined the political discussion there.

Brough stared into his bloodred wine. That was easier said than done. Clarissa wished to avoid him. She couldn't have made it more plain than she had at the supper table. But terrified? Surely she couldn't be that! They had had a petty quarrel, and that was all. The matter could be rectified, and this gathering provided him with the best possible opening. He would talk with her tonight whether she wished it or not. This strain must come to an end. Then they could proceed to things that mattered.

He was glad when the men rejoined the ladies. Declining Allesandra's offer of a cup of tea, he went straight to Clarissa. Taking her hand, he nearly pulled her up out of her chair.

"Come, I wish to talk with you."

Her eyes widened. "Where?"

"Out here." He propelled her to the balcony and away from the opened French doors.

"Brough, what will people think?"

"I don't care."

"Well, I do! I am already caught up in one scandal!"

"Allesandra will explain." He didn't know what the duchess would say, but he assumed that she would think of something reasonable. "It's time that we settled this difference between us."

Speechless, she shivered.

As he had in the Singletons' garden, he stripped off his coat and put it around her shoulders. "Now, my dear, may we talk?"

Snuggling into the garment, she nodded soberly.

"Clarissa," he began slowly, "I am heartily sorry that I interfered in your affairs. I shouldn't have arranged for those vouchers without discussing it with you first. I shouldn't have intruded in your matters with Julia. Perhaps I have also meddled too much with Jeremy. Above all, I should have warned you of the scandal. I can only plead that my ineptitude was the result of my good intentions, however misguided they were."

Her lower lip quivered.

He shrugged. "I can't think of anything else to say to you. Can't you forgive me?"

"I have been wrong, too," she whispered. "I knew all along that you wished no harm. I don't know why I have been such a shrew."

"Then we shall forgive each other?"

She nodded, lifting her chin to smile tremulously at him.

Brough looked at her lips, so soft and tempting, and at the plunging neckline of her delectable dress. He repressed his urge to plunder her mouth very thoroughly and very arousingly. Instead he brushed his lips against her forehead and drew her gently into his arms.

"May I escort you home?"

"I would like that," she said a little breathlessly. "Brough? I . . . I think I am ready to go home now. The evening has been exhausting. Do you think that the duchess would feel insulted?"

"I am sure that she would not." He freed her from his embrace and walked toward the door.

"Oh my goodness!" Clarissa stopped.

"Yes?"

"Your coat. Really, Brough! Scandal on top of scandal after more scandal!"

He let her help him into it and grinned at her little smoothing gestures.

"There now." She smiled. "We shall make our farewells."

As she preceded him into the drawing room,

Brough threw a glance of satisfaction over her
head toward his friends and watched Harry feign
a sigh of relief. It was enough. They realized that
all was well once again.

"Thank you for such a lovely evening," Clarissa
effused to Allesandra. "I can't remember when I
have had a more enjoyable time."

"We shall do it again." The duchess kissed her
cheek and squeezed Brough's hand. "It gives me
great pleasure to think that I have been a successful hostess."

"Indeed you are, Alli," he acclaimed. "As usual,
of course."

He conducted Clarissa to the vestibule, helped
her into her cloak, and took her arm in his. "I'm
glad that this is over with."

"The evening?"

"No, our quarrel."

"I am, too," she said with relief. "I have been so
... so *uncomfortable!*"

"I, too."

Beaming broadly, Gibson came off the box and
opened the carriage door.

Brough settled Clarissa inside and drew back for
a moment. "The lady wishes to go home." He
pressed a guinea into the man's hand. "Take the
long way."

"Yes, m'lord! As long a way as I can make it!"

16

As the carriage rolled through the dark London streets, Clarissa felt as though her heart were light as a feather. How happy, how relieved, she was that the quarrel had ended. Knowing that the animosity was gone between herself and Brough made everything else seem so much easier to bear.

Lowering her chin, she glanced through her thick lashes at his profile, his finely chiseled, noble cheekbones, his firm, straight nose. He was so handsome. And even more wonderful than that was the strength that emanated from him. She could almost visualize the potent muscles that rippled along his arms and across his chest. When he had stripped off his coat on the balcony, his thin silk shirt had barely hidden them. A frisson of strange excitement swept over her. She blushed and shifted in her seat. Such a thought! Truly she must set her mind to something else, difficult though it might be with the powerfully masculine earl sitting so close beside her. She wondered if her sister had ever had such ridiculous thoughts about Lord Arlen.

Julia! In the glow of her own successful evening, she had nearly forgotten the girl. It would have been very difficult for Julia to face the eyes of the *ton* tonight, but the worst of it would be over by now. She was just too pretty and too vivacious to remain in contempt very long. It was a youthful mistake. Surely everyone would realize that, and would see how rigorously she was trying to make up for it. Some of the old sticklers might hold on to their prejudices, but most of the *ton* would forgive. They must!

At least Julia had Mary and her parents to ease her way. She would also find her other friends among the guests. Friends. Ellen had been right. One must depend on one's friends. She couldn't help turning to smile at Brough.

He returned it. "Thinking serious thoughts?"

Clarissa laughed lightly. "I haven't been very good company, have I?"

"I find you excellent company. Conversation is overrated by the *ton*." He picked up her hand, squeezed it gently, and retained it companionably in his. "Silence can be just as congenial."

"I agree, though I must admit that my silence was not a particularly comfortable one. I was thinking of Julia." She lifted her shoulders in a guilty shrug. "I know. The next thing you will say is that I worry too much about her. I know I do, but this evening must be extremely difficult for her."

"Indeed?"

"Yes. She is staying the night with Mary Grantham and attending her come-out ball. She insisted on facing the *ton* alone, so to speak, without hiding behind my skirt tails! So yes, I am concerned about her. Surely everything has gone smoothly, but . . . well . . ."

"Would you like to stop by the ball to check up on her?"

"Could we?"

"Why not? We were both invited. All I need do is to give Gibson the direction."

"It isn't that." She studied his fingers laced through hers. "It's that I am unchaperoned."

"Clarissa, you are a widow, albeit a young one, and I am known to be a friend of the family. The *ton* will allow you a certain latitude."

"Are you sure? This family cannot withstand another impropriety."

"If it disturbs you, we can return to the Rackthalls' and fetch Ellen or Allesandra to accompany us."

"Oh no, I do not wish to drag the marchioness away from the party, and the duchess is the hostess. She couldn't leave." She nodded. "If you think it's all right, Brough, we will go."

He tapped on the carriage roof and, when Gibson halted, leaned out to give him the direction.

"I'm sure we will find her happy and enjoying herself," Clarissa mused. "I just can't help playing the role of the mother hen!"

He laughed. "Then while you are thinking about your chicks, I'd like to bring up the subject of Jeremy. Shall we resume our previous arrangement concerning him? I don't mind it, you know."

"You're sure?"

"Yes, I am. I feel as though I'm getting through to the boys. At least I've been keeping them so busy that they've stayed out of mischief."

"It has been wonderful having him off my hands."

"Then plan on him returning to my house tomorrow."

"Thank you." She smiled wistfully. "I owe you so many debts."

"Think nothing of it."

"I'm trying, but I am unaccustomed to having others' support and assistance. I don't wish to be a burden to anyone."

"You couldn't be."

"Well, if I become so, you must tell me. Tonight Ellen told me, quite firmly, that one must depend on one's friends. It also must work the other way. If one becomes a trial, one's friends must mention it."

"Very well." He grinned. "I'll tell you if you become an annoyance."

The coach halted before the brightly lit Grantham residence. Soft music drifted from the open windows. In the dim light from the side portico, couples could be seen standing together and walking in the garden.

"This will provide an added pleasure to the evening," Brough said. "I'll be able to dance with you. You will save me a waltz, won't you, madam?"

"I would be honored, my lord," she laughed as he assisted her to the pavement and tucked her arm through his.

They relinquished their outerwear to the footmen and proceeded up the stairs to the ballroom. The receiving line had long since broken up. There was only the butler to greet them.

"Mrs. Clarissa James. The Earl of Abingdon," he grandly intoned.

Clarissa thought of how lofty his name sounded when spoken formally and how she was so acutely aware of this well-bred peer at her side. Brough probably thought nothing of his title. He would be too used to hearing it.

In the din of the crowd, the music, and the dancing, few seemed to notice their arrival. The hostess was nowhere to be seen. Sir Richard Grantham stood across the room, but he was deep in conversation and oblivious to everything around him.

Clarissa searched the dancers for a glimpse of Julia, but the girl was not on the dance floor. Surely she couldn't have committed a further faux pas by going to the terrace or the garden? She clutched Brough's arm a little tighter and surveyed the room more closely until she spotted her.

Julia was sitting alone on one of the little gilt chairs that ringed the dance floor. Her pretty face was frozen in a fixed expression of demure composure. Only her hands, clenching her dance card, revealed her inner turmoil.

"Oh dear," Clarissa gasped. "Brough? She's not dancing."

He followed her gaze, his lips tightening.

"I don't understand . . ."

The earl propelled her toward her sister. Julia saw them and leaped to her feet. Hurriedly she skirted the floor, a heartbeat away from breaking into a run.

"Clarissa! Lord Abingdon! It has been so awful!" she wailed, her blue eyes filling with tears. She made a move to throw herself into her sister's arms.

Brough forestalled her, catching her arm with his other hand and escorting both ladies toward a row of chairs. "Don't break now, Julia," he said severely. "You've come too far."

"But they hate me!" she cried.

"Then hate them back. Pretend as though they are not worthy to kiss the hem of your gown."

She looked up at him doubtfully.

"Pretend you are a princess. Come, Julia, did you never play 'pretend'?"

"Yes . . ."

"Then do so now."

"I just want to go home."

"So you shall. Just a little while longer." He seated the ladies.

The dance ended and people began shuffling to the sidelines to find their next set's partners. Clarissa reached for Julia's dance card. "Have you any more dances promised?"

"Any more? I haven't had one! Everyone avoids me!" She threw the card and its dainty gold pencil to the floor. "Even Mary will not sit beside me! She acts as though she doesn't even know me!"

Brough bent over her hand. "Julia, may I have this dance?"

"But wouldn't you rather dance with Clarissa?" she cried.

Clarissa briefly met his eyes. "Dance with the gentleman, Julia."

"You don't mind?"

"Dance!" she ordered.

"I . . . I . . . would be . . ."

Brough whisked her away to the dance floor.

Clarissa drew a deep breath. Thank God for Brough and for his quick thinking. Her first impulse had been to grasp Julia's hand and run for the door, but Brough knew how to handle the *ton*. He understood how to manipulate them. And he was confident enough in his own social position to fling a bit of their own into their faces. She watched him expertly lead Julia in the quadrille and actually manage to coax a smile from her. If anyone could save the evening, he could. She should take lessons from him.

"Mrs. James, I am surprised to see you here, but truly I am grateful." Lady Grantham loomed over her. "I assume that you will be taking Julia home?"

"Yes," Clarissa said carefully, "I thought I would."

"I knew that you would understand." The baronet's wife sat down, leaving an empty chair between them as if she did not wish to sit too close.

"Understand what?"

"I refer to the scandal!" she whispered. "I know that Mary and Julia have been friends, but there is a time when friendship can interfere with matters of importance. My daughter cannot jeopardize her future by remaining in close contact with your sister. It is unfortunate, but true. If Lord Arlen had not spilled the truth of the rumor, it might have been a different story, but as it is . . . I hope that you will leave as soon as possible. Where is Julia? Is she seeing to her packing?"

"Julia is dancing," Clarissa said coldly, "but we shall leave as soon as it is finished."

"Dancing?" Lady Grantham peered toward the dancers. "With whom?"

The quadrille ended at that moment and Brough escorted Julia to Clarissa.

"Lord Abingdon," the lady preened. "How nice of you to come to dear Mary's ball! I shall locate her in just a moment and—"

Clarissa lifted her chin, caught Brough's eye, and prayed she was doing the right thing. "My lord, Lady Grantham has asked us to leave," she interrupted sweetly.

"Indeed?" He looked the woman up and down as though he were examining a not very desirable piece of horseflesh.

"Oh no, my lord," she shuttered, her face quickly draining its color. "Mrs. James, you mistook me!"

"I think I did not. Come, Julia. We'll send Gibson tomorrow for your things. Good evening,

Lady Grantham. I am certain that Mary's ball has been a memorable one."

Brough bowed coolly to the woman, offered Clarissa one arm and Julia the other, and conducted them toward the door.

"But, Lord Abingdon ... Mrs. James!" Lady Grantham shrieked.

Clarissa was glad to leave the confines of that house. How horrid the Granthams had been to Julia! What terrible people made up their guest list! But they were the *ton*. They were not perhaps the highest, most desirable members of that haughty class, but *ton* nonetheless. At that moment she knew that neither she nor Julia could bear another evening in society, no matter what the efforts of Brough and Allesandra and Ellen. Enough was enough. They would return to Essex.

She leaned against the musty squabs of the carriage, smiling slightly as Brough seated Julia on the seat with the broken spring and sat down beside her himself. Thank God he had stood by her through this unpleasantness, but no matter what Ellen said, she couldn't bring herself to ask for further sacrifice. It would be best for all of them if the Dunstan family quietly disappeared.

In the hall of the rented house, Julia threw her arms around Brough's neck as a young lady would do with an older male relative. "Thank you, thank you! I could not have borne another minute!"

"Of course you could have," he said confidently, hugging her.

"And you, Clarissa." She fondly eyed her sister. "That setdown you gave Lady Grantham!"

"I? I did no such thing!"

"No? 'I think I did not,'" she mimicked in a

wintry voice. " 'I am certain that Mary's ball has been a memorable one.' It was priceless! I believe that you set her up for the whole thing!"

"I most certainly did not," Clarissa said briskly, seeing the twinkle in Brough's eyes.

"Perhaps you were pretending, too. Were you a princess?" She looked back and forth between the two of them. "Or a countess, perhaps?"

Clarissa flushed. "Julia, it is your bedtime. Go upstairs now, and I shall be along to help you with your dress." She turned to Brough as the girl fled up the stairs. "I cannot thank you enough."

"May I wait until you tuck your 'chick' into bed, Mrs. Mother Hen? I would like to talk with you."

"Very well," she said quietly, and turned to the butler, who was hovering nearby. "Simmons, please serve Lord Abingdon a glass of wine and . . . whatever else he may wish."

"At once, Miss Clarissa."

"Thank you." She followed her sister upstairs and into her room.

Julia's momentary elation in the entrance hall had turned to despair. She sank down at her dressing table and stared sightlessly into the mirror. "I have failed."

"That is not entirely true." Clarissa moved to unbutton the pretty pink gown. "Were all of your beaux present?"

"No, but what does it matter? I am certain that they would have ignored me, too. There was not one friendly face, Clarissa. There can be no doubt about it. I have been rejected. I am cast beyond the pale."

"Anytime one learns a lesson, it cannot be counted as total failure."

"Well, I have indeed learned a lesson!" she said

bitterly. "We should go home, shouldn't we? To Essex."

"I fear that is the only thing we can do."

"May we come again? Next year perhaps the scandal will have faded from people's minds."

Clarissa bit the inside of her lip. "I do not think we can afford to do so, Julia," she said honestly, "but perhaps, if we are very careful in our spending, we might manage a short trip to Bath."

"Then we shall have to make do with that." The girl clenched her teeth. "I'm sorry, Clarissa. I did so want to find a wealthy husband so that none of us need worry about money again!"

"In time you will find a husband." She embraced her sister's shoulders. "But make your decision on the man himself, not on his wealth or title. My only wish is for you to be happy. That's all I've ever wanted."

"But I felt a responsibility to you and Jeremy!"

"We shall be just fine, like we always have. I made that mistake with Captain James. Please don't make the same one. Promise me?"

She nodded, then cheered. "In all the confusion I did not comment that you and Lord Abingdon seem to have patched up your quarrel."

"Yes." Clarissa smiled.

"What will happen to the two of you if we return to Essex?"

"Why, we shall go on as before, I suppose," she murmured, trying to ignore the sudden stabbing pain in her heart. "Perhaps I shall see him again sometime."

"Do you love him?"

"I . . ." She couldn't trust herself to answer. Not right now. Not when the truth was so hard to accept. "Good night, dear." She kissed the top of her curly blond head. "I must see him out. He's still

waiting downstairs. We shall talk of everything tomorrow."

"Clarissa?"

She paused at the door.

"Tell him that you love him," Julia said quietly.

"Don't be ridiculous. It would only serve to
make us both very uncomfortable. Good night,
Julia!" She hurried down the hall.

Brough swirled the wine in his glass and gazed
idly at its rich color. He wished it were brandy. After the events of the evening, he could have used
something more fortifying than sherry. So could
Clarissa, for that matter. He grinned, thinking of
how the effects of the liquor would alter her. She
would let down her rigid control and ... and ...
He took a deep drink. This was not the time to envision Clarissa melting into his embrace. He
tugged at his cravat to loosen it slightly.

Simmons entered with a tray of refreshments
and set it down on the tea table. Unprompted, he
refilled Brough's glass. "Shall you be wishing else,
m'lord?"

"No. Thank you." He glanced at the clock on
the mantel. What was taking her so long? Or was
he only imagining it?

She hastened into the room as Simmons left it.
"I'm sorry you had to wait, but I am glad you
did." She sat down, her cheeks still a becoming
rose from her earlier blush.

"So am I." God, she was beautiful! With the
color in her face and the vivid orange dress, she
was overwhelming so. He felt an aching urge and
swallowed hard. "Will you have some sherry?" he
asked faintly.

"Thank you."

He was grateful for the opportunity for action.

He stood and walked to the sideboard, where Simmons had left the bottle and glasses. Pouring her drink, he returned and made the mistake of bending over her shoulder to hand it to her. At that angle he could see down the enticing cleavage of her gown. He was mesmerized.

"Brough?" she inquired.

His hand was still on the glass, and she was trying to take it from him. He straightened quickly. "I'm sorry. I was wool-gathering."

"It has been a most oversetting evening."

"Yes." He took a deep breath and strode to his chair, quickly helping himself to a small ham sandwich.

"Julia and I have made a decision that concerns Jeremy, too," she said sadly. "We are returning to Essex."

"What!" She couldn't go home yet. He hadn't had time to make his proposal in a proper manner or . . . to ascertain her feelings for her late husband.

"You must agree that we have no other choice."

"No, I don't see," he stated flatly. "Give it a little longer and—"

"We cannot continue to expose ourselves to this censure."

"But I can—"

"No. Brough, I don't think that even you or Allesandra and Ellen can hasten matters. The gossip will take time to fade. There is no point in our remaining here, paying London prices." She firmly shook her head. "It is out of the question. We shall leave as soon as possible."

His mind raced. "Will you grant me a favor before you leave?"

"Of course I will!" She dimpled. "How could I refuse after all you have done for me?"

"Give me a day of your time. I wish you to have an enjoyable interval, without Julia and Jeremy, before you return to your everyday concerns."

"What did you have in mind?"

"A picnic?"

Clarissa's heart soared at the idea, but was soon brought down to earth. "If we're to leave for Essex, I can only spare tomorrow for a picnic, but I was to take Julia to call at the Singletons' then. Ellen was arranging for her to meet Lady Christina."

"Allesandra can chaperon Julia. Bran and Harry can take care of the boys."

"I should hate to impose."

"They won't mind. They'll enjoy it."

"If you are sure," she murmured doubtfully.

"I am. I shall make all the arrangements."

"All right," she said slowly. "What shall I bring?"

"Only yourself. I'll take care of everything." He rose. If he left now, he stood a good chance of catching his friends still together at Rackthall House. He hadn't a moment to waste in making his plans.

"I shall look forward to it." She accompanied him to the door.

He wished he could have kissed her good night, even on the forehead or cheek, but Simmons was standing by. He bent over her hand, brushing his lips against her warm skin. "Until tomorrow then."

"Yes." She smiled pensively. "Until tomorrow."

17

THE DAY COULD not have been more perfect for a picnic. The morning sun and brilliant blue sky promised fair weather for some time to come. If it rained at all, it could not amount to more than a quick, light shower.

Clarissa was glad to be going to the country for the day. In fact, she wouldn't have minded leaving for Essex on the morrow if it were not for two factors. Julia had not found a husband, and she herself would deeply miss Brough.

Beyond a doubt, Julia's dilemma was a temporary one. If she would truly remove from her head all the thoughts of lofty, rich, and titled gentlemen, there would be many options available to her. In time she would find a man she could love and who would love her. He might not have the glitter of a Lord Arlen, but he would care for her, provide for her, and perhaps even spoil her a bit. It would all work out in time.

For Clarissa, though, there could be no others. No one could take the place in her heart of the man beside her now. According to Julia's ideas, gleaned from romantical novels, love was a most wonderful thing. They were wrong. Love hurt.

After today, she would probably never see

Brough again. Coming with him on this picnic was a ghastly idea. The day would bring nothing but sweet torture. She had lost all sense of actuality where he was concerned and had made a fatal error. She had allowed herself to fall irrevocably in love with him. Now she must pay. She must say good-bye.

Accompanied by Brough's silent groom, they left London far behind and trotted through the countryside. The sun bore down on Clarissa's shoulders. Little caring that she might become unfashionably tanned, she removed her shawl. The brownness wouldn't matter at home, and the cool breeze raised her spirits. She was glad, however, when they reached a coppice of shady trees and Brough slowed to a walk.

"It is so pretty here." She smiled.

"I'm glad that you like it. I know of a nice picnic spot up ahead. A nice cool spot." He had unbuttoned his coat, and she noted a trace of dampness on his shirt.

"It is rather warm for the season. If you wish to remove your coat, please do so, Brough. There is no one here to cause gossip."

"Thank you. I shall probably do so, but are you uncomfortable?" he asked anxiously.

"Not at all! It is so pleasant having time away from Julia and Jeremy that it would take more than the sun to discomfort me!"

"You must continue to make time away from them." He hesitated. "Clarissa, how do you feel about having children of your own?"

"What?" she asked, startled.

"You've spent such a large part of your life bringing up your brother and sister. I wondered if you might . . . look forward to the day when you had no responsibility for that type of thing."

Clarissa smiled. "Children are wonderful. Exasperating at times, as you well know, but wonderful. I wish . . ."

"Yes?" he prompted.

Her dream nearly overwhelmed her. She couldn't tell him that she wanted children very much, provided that they were his children. He would push her from the phaeton and drive away at a gallop.

"Clarissa?"

"I'm sorry! I wasn't attending," she said meekly. "What were we saying?"

He eyed her curiously. "You were saying that you thought that children were wonderful and you wished . . ."

"I wished? Oh, I can't remember what I wished!" She turned a bright face to him. "My nanny always said that wishing was impractical, for wishes seldom come true unless one is wealthy enough to make them happen."

"May I disagree with your nanny and say that some wishes cannot be bought but may perhaps come true?"

"Of course you may," she laughed. "That is your prerogative!"

"And furthermore, may I venture to guess that you were going to say that you wished for children of your own?"

Clarissa shook her head. "A wish like that must also include a wish for a husband. I doubt that I shall ever marry again."

During their strange and altogether too personal conversation, he had driven off on a little traveled lane. Still under the shade of the trees, he drew up.

"Did you love your husband so much, Clarissa, that you could never consider marrying again?" he asked bluntly.

She gripped the side of the phaeton as if they were careening along at great speed. It wasn't like Brough to pry, and yet he was asking the most impossibly personal questions. She should remind him of propriety, but she hadn't the heart for it. He was her friend. After all, weren't friends supposed to be free with each other?

"I didn't love my husband at all," she answered quietly. "In the end, I did not even respect him."

Brough laced the reins back and forth through his fingers, thoughtfully staring off into the distance.

"Did I surprise you in saying that?" Clarissa asked.

"No, Jeremy hinted at much the same."

She bristled. "Jeremy knows nothing about it! I cannot believe that he would go about discussing my personal life. Oh, just wait until I get my hands on that scamp!"

"In a sense, I suppose I rather asked him about it."

"And then he blabbed nonsense to you! If you wished to know about my marriage, you should have asked me!"

"That's what I am doing—" he grinned repentantly "—even if it is impertinent."

"Very well, Brough; if you must know, I will tell you myself!"

"Not *must* know, Clarissa, *wish* to know. And that, my dear, is a wish that cannot be bought!"

Suddenly remembering that they were not alone, she looked over her shoulder at the earl's groom. The man sat stonily in his seat in the rear, his expression the epitome of deafness. Surely the servant must be the soul of discretion or Brough would not talk so in front of him.

"Would you like to walk?" Brough asked. "We have reached our picnic spot."

She nodded with relief.

He hopped lithely from the phaeton and reached up for her while the groom moved to take the reins. Clarissa's heart skipped a beat as Brough's hands circled her waist. Laying hers on his broad shoulders, she let him lift her, slightly breathlessly, to the ground. She took his arm and followed him off the road onto a footpath.

"I wonder whose land this is," she mused.

"It's mine. We're on the back side of Abingdon Hall."

"Oh, I didn't realize that your country seat was so close to the city." She looked around the pretty woodland. "It's lovely here."

"Thank you. I have always liked this spot. Perhaps you would like to see the house as well. It has a view of the Thames."

"I would like that above everything! If we have the time . . ."

"We have all the time we wish."

"But Julia—"

"Don't concern yourself with your little sister. By now, Allesandra will have her well in hand. Bran and Harry are taking the boys to a horse race. Tonight all will go to the theater."

"But—"

He silenced her. "You promised me that we would neglect our duties today."

"But this evening as well? I hate to impose!"

"Nonsense. They don't mind at all. They're happy to do it! Won't you put 'our children' out of your mind?"

Clarissa felt a strange sensation in the pit of her stomach when he referred to the young people in such a fashion. If only it were true and they were, indeed, discussing their mutual children! It would be a dream made in Heaven.

"Now, madam," he reminded, suddenly serious, "you were to ignore my impertinence and tell me of your marriage."

She sighed. Thinking of Mark James cast a shadow on the lovely day. Brough, however, seemed so particularly persistent that she might as well get it over with.

"I shouldn't have married him," she began weakly. "I hadn't known him long enough and I didn't love him." She glanced through her eyelashes at the earl. "I am convinced that no one should marry for convenience' sake. It creates . . . difficulties."

He nodded encouragingly.

"I didn't realize that at the time. Mark offered security for me, and for Julia and Jeremy. I didn't like it when he touched me . . ." She broke off in confusion.

"Please do not continue, Clarissa," he said kindly, "if it is too painful to remember."

"No." She plowed on. Telling him was almost like a cathartic. "In the short time Mark and I were together, I began to see that he had been untruthful to me. He didn't care for Julia and Jeremy the way he said he did. He was often so impatient with them! You know, of course, that they can be a trial, but they are simply children growing up!" She shook her head. "Mark didn't understand them and had no wish to try.

"Later, when he died, I learned the full extent of his misrepresentation. He had little money and no property at all. He had deliberately lied to me. So that is the story of my unfortunate marriage. Perhaps it was all my fault. Maybe I received my just due because I wed for all the wrong reasons."

Her hand, which had been on his arm, was now entwined securely in his. He squeezed it comfortingly. She smiled.

"Are you afraid to wed again?" he asked. "Marriage doesn't have to be like that."

"I know. One only has to look at Brandon and Allesandra and Harry and Ellen! They are so very perfect for each other."

"Yes, they're very special people. And so are you."

She laughed outright. She felt so much better, now that she had told the truth of her terrible mistake. It was as if a great weight had been lifted from her shoulders. But there was one more thing that needed to be said.

"Brough? Do you think I was cold and mercenary to do as I did?"

"No," he said thoughtfully, "I think you needed someone very much, and that you were doing what you felt best for Julia and Jeremy."

"I was so wrong!" She burst into tears.

He drew her into his arms and held her close. "It might have worked out. You mustn't blame yourself."

"But I do!"

"It's over now," he said softly. "You need never think of it again."

He held her until the sobs subsided, then produced a handkerchief, wiped her eyes and cheeks, and held it to her nose. She took it from him and blew.

"My goodness," she sniffled, "I have made your clothes a sodden mess."

"I don't mind. Better now?"

She nodded. "You do not think that I am a terrible person?"

"As always, I think you are wonderful." He grinned.

"As always, you are too kind." She straightened, absently smoothing his mussed attire. "You didn't bargain on bringing a watering pot on this expedition."

"If being a watering pot has made you feel better, I could never object."

She smiled. "Telling someone has made me feel much better about everything. I should have done so long ago, but there was no one ... who I felt would understand. I promise you, I have no more dark secrets."

"I would always be willing to listen if you did."

"Thank you, my dear friend." She flushed, realizing that she was still within his light embrace. "And now, perhaps we should have our picnic. After baring my soul, I find myself quite famished!"

Brough reclined on the blanket and watched Clarissa removing their luncheon from the hamper. His thoughts were occupied with what she had told him. He found that he wasn't surprised by any of it. She hadn't seemed like a grieving widow, and Jeremy had, more or less, expressed the same view. Only his own conjuring had made him wary of the late Captain James.

Clarissa had disliked the man's touch. No doubt she had been terrified by the intimacies of marriage. Yet he didn't think that the unpleasant experience had ruined her desire. She had accepted his embraces and willingly touched him in return. No, her distaste for her husband did not extend to other men. Nor did she express a weariness of children. In fact, he had thought her close to admitting that she wished for children of her own.

So why did she doubt that she would ever marry again? She had admitted that she thought that marriage could be wonderful.

Brough was acutely conscious of the beautiful Abingdon betrothal ring in his pocket. Clarissa Dunstan James was the only woman he had ever really wanted to make his wife, and he was running out of time. Tomorrow she would leave for Essex. Should he give her more time and pursue her there? No, he would ask her today. If she turned him down, he would simply continue to try. One day he would make her Lady Abingdon.

"Our luncheon is ready," she said smiling, "and it looks ever so delicious."

Lord, how beautiful she was! Especially with her chip straw hat slightly askew and her thick, rich tresses threatening to tumble down. Someday he would bury his face in that luscious hair.

She sensed the cause of his distraction. "Do I look a fright?"

"You are adorable."

"Flatterer." She removed the hat and set about repinning her hair. "You must be honest, Brough. I do not wish my appearance to shame you in front of your servants. Now how do I look?" She returned her hat to her head.

"You look just as before. Adorable."

"Cease flirting with me and have your lunch." She handed him a plate. "Just look at this array! We could stay right here in this spot for days and not be hungry."

No? He was famished right now, and it was not for food. He was ravenous to touch her, to hold her, to make love to her. Dammit, he must take control of himself. Should Clarissa guess his thoughts, she would take to her heels and run.

If she agreed to marry him, there would be no

waiting. He would obtain a special license and wed her as quickly as humanly possible. He had lost his heart and was fast losing his head as well.

While his lordship dined with the lady, the groom Felix dashed cross-country to the mansion to warn the occupants of their impending arrival. He threw himself through the kitchen door and collapsed at the scrubbed-oak table. "Ale."

"Ale be damned!" the housekeeper cried, coming through the door to the main hall. "Are they coming?"

"Yes," he panted. "They're picnicking right now and then they'll come."

"Mercy me. A lady!" she marveled. "Finally."

"I don't think he's asked her. At least she's not wearing the ring."

"Give him time. Give him time!" She wrung her hands. "Cook! Is all well?"

"I'm doin' me best."

"Then do better!" She sighed. "A lady."

Other servants crowded around Felix. "What does she look like? Is she pretty?"

He drew himself up and observed them with disdain. "My ale."

Someone shoved a frothy mug into his hands.

"Well now." He took a deep drink. "She's not bad."

"Tell us."

"Aw, you'll see for yourselves."

"Tell us now!"

"Her eyes are brown. And her hair . . ."

They leaned forward.

"Brown, with lots of gold sparklies when the sun shines on it. And the rest of her . . ." he chuckled. "As for the rest of her . . . Well, no man wed to her'll be gettin' up early in the morning!"

18

"**O**H, IT IS perfectly lovely!" Clarissa exclaimed as they trotted down the avenue of oaks to the beautiful mansion.

The house at Abingdon Park was not an old one, but it gave the appearance of strength and permanence. Built in the Georgian style, it was a stately, three-storied brick with elongated windows and steeply pitched mansard roof. A cupola, circled by a narrow balcony, crowned the top.

"I wonder that you can bear to leave it to come to London," Clarissa sighed. "I'm sure that your house there is fine, too, but this . . . It's like a fairy tale, Brough!"

"I'm glad you like it." He grinned.

"I adore it! My, isn't it big? It could hold two of Dunstan Hall within its walls! It must take a very large staff to care for it properly."

"Yes, I am a great provider of employment."

"I hope that our arrival shall not discommode them."

"They are always prepared for me to pop in at any moment, but I did send word of the possibility that we would come by. I'm glad we didn't disappoint them. They will enjoy the change of pace."

As they approached the immediate foreground of the building, the shaded avenue gave way to an immaculate brick-paved courtyard. Flawlessly trimmed boxwoods lined the edges. A brick walkway, also flanked with box, led to a charming pool on the lawn below. Clarissa couldn't help comparing the setting with the rather untidy front lawn of her own home. She knew from bleak experience that it would take an army of gardeners to keep up such a place as this. She had realized that Brough was well-to-do, but this went beyond her wildest imagination. She felt a slight discomfort in these surroundings. She and he were so far apart. He could not have the smallest concept of what it was like to struggle to pay the monthly bills.

She looked up at the lofty facade now looming above her. "Do you entertain a great deal?"

"Scarcely at all. My sister and her family visit now and then, and my closest friends."

"Being so close to London, I would think you would be flooded by visitors."

"I don't encourage it. Are you disappointed?"

She shook her head. "I have never learned to enjoy a great crush. Even if I had the means to entertain, my guests would be small in number. I fear I would never be a society hostess."

Once again she revolved her head to admire the surroundings. "If I had this house, I would be quite selfish and keep it all to myself."

"Then you and I are in agreement," he said quietly.

Her eyes fell on a thicket of tall boxwood at the side of the domicile. "Can that be a maze?"

"It is. A folly of my grandmother's."

"Oh, how splendid! May I try to find my way to the center?"

"You may do whatever you please." He drew up to a halt in front of the gleaming front door.

A liveried servant hastened to assist Clarissa, but Brough lifted her down himself. Taking his arm, she walked up the short flight of steps, past a very dignified butler and into a spacious entrance hall, where a beaming older woman stood. The butler moved solemnly to the matron's side.

"Mrs. James," Brough said formally, "I would like you to meet Burnley—" he nodded to the butler "—and Mrs. Horner, my housekeeper."

"How do you do?" She smiled genially. "You must be very proud of this beautiful home."

They returned the pleasantry, both unable to keep from looking at her with curious gazes.

"Burnley and Mrs. Horner have lived here longer than I," Brough said fondly.

"Then I am sure they have many a tale to tell of you, my lord!" She laughed teasingly.

But scanning the hall, she felt her smile fading to wistfulness. The opulence, the beauty of it, once again served to remind her of the huge chasm that lay between them. Which daughter of a high-ranking peer would become the mistress here? Would she love the house and, more important, love its master as he should be loved? A lump rose in her throat, and it was all she could do to keep from crying again.

Brough must have noticed her expression. "Clarissa, are you all right?"

"Perhaps Mrs. James would like to freshen up a bit from the trip," Mrs. Horner interceded.

"Yes, I would," Clarissa answered gratefully.

"Then please come with me," she ordered, "and don't you fret, m'lord. I'll have her back in two shakes of a sheep's tail!"

Clarissa followed Mrs. Horner's broad back up

the stairs and into a lovely mint green bedchamber, where a maid waited with washcloth and basin of water. They sat her down, removed her hat, and began to wash her face.

"Oh, I can do this. Please don't bother." Their solicitous pampering unsettled her further. She took the cloth and smiled. "You will spoil me."

"Do allow us to see to your comfort, madam," the housekeeper said, slightly hurt.

"Very well." She submitted, but she did finish washing her own face and hands, accepting a thick, fluffy towel from the maid.

Under the housekeeper's watchful eye, the servant continued with Clarissa's hair, releasing it from the pins and brushing it until it shone.

"I've known Lord Abingdon all his life," Mrs. Horner chatted. "No one could ask for a finer man. He is the best master and the kindest friend."

Clarissa smiled.

"Never out of sorts, never moody . . . And he is a handsome man as well! There are none better-looking nor more amiable than Lord Abingdon."

"Indeed so," she agreed. Brough certainly had the love and loyalty of his housekeeper and probably of the rest of the staff. It didn't surprise her. Who could fail to adore him?

"Lord Abingdon is very particular as to whom he invites as a guest. He has never brought here a young, unmarried woman."

The statement gave her a jolt. What on earth was the staff thinking of? Surely they didn't misconstrue the situation!

"The earl and I have become good *friends*," she explained, "through the companionship of our younger brothers."

"Friends . . ."

"Yes." She was thankful when the maid put the last pin in her hair and she could escape the inquisitive servants. "Thank you so much for your kindness," she said, standing. "Mrs. Horner, will you kindly place me in the right direction? The house is so large, and I don't wish to keep his lordship waiting."

"It shall be my pleasure, Mrs. James. While you are here, please consider this room to be your own and Frances to be your abigail."

"Thank you so much."

When she joined Brough on the terrace she saw that he, too, had freshened up. He bore no signs of the dampening she had given him, and his cravat lay in pristine orderliness. Of course, he would have clean clothes here. She hoped that she did not look too rumpled in comparison.

He rose to seat her. "I hope that you were well cared for, Clarissa."

"Quite so."

"Tea or sherry?"

"Nothing for me, please. I am yet full to bursting from our picnic." She looked over the vast back lawn that rolled in manicured stateliness to the riverside. "It's so lovely and peaceful here. Do you have a boat?"

" 'Yacht,' Clarissa, and yes, I have a small one."

She colored. "As you can see, I've no knowledge of things nautical."

He grinned. "The *Lady Abingdon* is still in winter harbor or we could have had our picnic on her today, but perhaps you will allow me to take you out in it sometime and introduce you to sailing."

"I wish it were possible."

"Your wish is my wish, so it is indeed possible. There are a great many wishes floating around this afternoon, Clarissa. Your old nanny would be appalled!"

"She probably would," she murmured.

He dragged his chair over next to hers and took her hand. "Why do I keep feeling that something is wrong? Did I overstep my bounds with my inquiries today?"

"Oh no. Don't give a thought to it! It isn't that."

He carried her hand to his lips. "Tell me?"

"It's this house, Brough," she said, shaking her head. "It's far too grand for me. I don't feel as though I belong here."

"The house? Good God, Clarissa, it's just an ordinary—"

"It's a palace and you know it!"

"Well, I am sorry." His eyes sparkled. "Shall I have the servants chop up some of the furniture for firewood? Perhaps if you put your foot through a painting or two . . ."

She giggled.

"Good! I've made you laugh. Now I hope you'll rid yourself of that nonsensical attitude. I wanted you to like it."

"I do!"

Her hand still caught in his, he stared at the river and absently began kissing each slender finger.

"Brough!" She snatched her hand away. "You forget yourself."

"I'm sorry," he said contritely. "You have such lovely hands."

She folded them into her lap to hide their quivering. How different it was with Brough than it had been with Captain James. She wanted him to touch her, and she wanted to touch him. But it was too dangerous and would only make her that much more unhappy.

"Perhaps you would show me the maze now?"

"All right." He stood and once again enclosed her hand securely in his.

Brough was still grinning to himself when he came down the stairs to the library to await Clarissa. She'd had fun in the maze, and he had enjoyed watching her. After many blind alleys and turns that had taken her back to the place that she had started from, she finally found the center. Then, of course, she couldn't find her way out, and the process repeated itself while she determinedly refused any help from him. It had all played into his hands, for she squandered so much time that she had readily accepted his invitation for dinner.

The maze had given him a glimpse of her that he'd rarely seen before. She'd giggled like a schoolgirl and had even skipped along some of the paths. She had been enchanting, and he was even more fascinated with her.

It had been a wonderful day, with the exception of his oversetting her by asking about her marriage, her intimidation by the house, and his kissing her fingers. He was sorry that he'd caused her to cry, but he had to settle his nagging doubts concerning Captain James. Now he was sure that the man would never come between them. As soon as he could obliterate her unhappy marital experiences, he had no doubt that he himself would seem to be the first man in her life. The shadow of Mark James would disappear altogether.

Abingdon Park was a different story. Perceiving it through Clarissa's eyes, he could see that it was an outright statement of wealth. With her years of difficulty in making ends meet, it would naturally overawe her. It would simply take time for her to get used to it and to become accustomed to having enough money to do with as she pleased.

The kisses? He grinned. Before the evening was out, he was resolved to kiss her mouth very lingeringly and very thoroughly.

Shaking his head, he poured himself a glass of brandy. He was thinking as though she had already accepted him. He still had that hurdle to cross.

A footman opened the door, and Clarissa entered. "Am I late? I was certain that I could find my own way, but I made a wrong turn."

"Of course you're not late." He set down his glass and came forward to take her hands, refraining from telling her that neither she nor he had to worry about that since the household revolved around them.

"I did see some lovely portraits in a long gallery, and I'll admit that I took a little time to study them."

"Then you've met my family, most of them at least. Here's Papa hanging over the mantel." While she moved forward to gaze at the portrait, he poured her a glass of sherry.

"He looks like a kind man."

"He was. And he was well liked by all."

"And your mama?"

"Her portrait is in the drawing room. You'll see it after supper."

She turned away from the mantel and sat down in a big leather chair. "This is a comfortable room. Am I correct in thinking that this is your special place?"

"You are. Especially so. It's one of the few rooms I've had redecorated since I became the earl."

"It suits you." Smiling, she took a sip of her sherry. "This has been a splendid day, Brough. I thank you for it. However," she said ruefully, pointing to a smudge of dirt on her gown, "had I known what was to take place, I would have brought a change of clothes."

He laughed. "You are perfect just as you are!"

"And you, my lord, are a flatterer."

"Clarissa, if you have had an enjoyable time, I wouldn't care if you were streaked with mud from head to toe!"

"That's a hum! Well, I *have* had an enjoyable time. I shall never forget it, nor your kindness all Season. You've made things so much easier for me."

"It has been my pleasure, but you sound as though you are saying good-bye."

"I ... I suppose I am."

"Clarissa ..." He set down his empty glass and leaned forward.

With a polite scratch on the door, Burnley entered, bowing. "The dinner is ready, my lord."

"Thank you," Brough replied weakly.

Damn! Why was his staff so well trained? They knew to the second how long it took for a predinner drink. Why couldn't they have been a bit tardy?

He stood and offered her his arm. Perhaps it was just as well. He really hadn't had time to ask her properly. He would have to wait until after dinner.

Candlelight glowed on the vast table with its complement of fine china, glittering silverplate, and the huge epergne of springtime flowers. It would be Clarissa's first and only dinner in a great country house, for despite Julia's beauty, the girl probably would never marry into such luxury. She wished that her sister could have been here tonight to see how it was to live without a care for expense. But most likely that was not a good idea. It would make her dissatisfied with everyday reality at Dunstan Hall.

She consumed a bite of her tender, succulent sirloin and smiled at her host. "This is a beautiful room. Do you take all of your meals here?"

"Lord, no. I usually dine in the breakfast room."

"Oh, I wouldn't have minded doing that! It really wasn't necessary to put your staff to extra trouble on account of me!"

"I wanted this evening to be special."

"It is indeed, and the food is so delicious. You must convey my appreciation to your staff for taking such good care of me."

"They are happy to do it."

By the time they had finished the dessert course, Clarissa was becoming concerned with the time. "I dislike ending the evening, but it is growing late and—"

"Our friends have matters well in hand in London."

"You know I don't like to take advantage."

"Promise me you won't even think about that 'Terrible Threesome' until we reach the city. Let us have tea in the drawing room. You haven't met Mama yet."

"Very well, but I really do not wish to be late."

"Another wish granted."

She smiled, laying her napkin on the table and bidding a silent farewell to the magnificent dining room.

The tea tray awaited them, but Clarissa was drawn instead to the portrait of the lady, hanging over the mantel. "She is beautiful," she breathed.

He came up behind her. "I always thought so."

"How well the painting accents the rest of the room!"

"It was decorated around her. The portrait of the mistress of the house always hangs in this position." He slipped his arms around her waist. "I wish your portrait to hang here, Clarissa."

Her heart leaped to a gallop. What was he saying? As she began to tremble madly, he tightened his hold.

"You will make me the happiest man in the world if you will grant me my wish," he said softly. "Will you marry me, my precious dear?"

"I ... I ..."

He turned her in his arms. "I love you very much."

Clarissa looked into his earnest hazel eyes and burst into tears.

"My darling, I didn't meant to overset you. Please ... don't ..."

"I'm not overset. I'm happy!" she gasped, trying desperately to regain her control. "I love you so!"

"Then?"

She managed to nod before pressing her face against his chest and proceeding to dampen his coat again.

Brough piloted her to the sofa and sat down, drawing her onto his lap and cradling her head against his shoulder. He produced a clean handkerchief.

Clarissa wiped her face and blew her nose. "My goodness, how can you love such a watering pot? I don't know what's come over me!"

"Happiness, I hope."

"Oh yes! I never thought it possible that you could love me, too!"

"How could I help myself? You are such an exquisite woman."

"You cannot think that."

In answer his lips came down to meet hers,

gently at first and then fiercely possessive. Clarissa gave herself up to his endearments, basking in his caresses and in the warmth of his security. How different marriage would be with Brough as her husband! She felt as though she had never been wed and that he was the only perfect man ever to enter her life. She would never feel again the way she had felt with Captain James. She wanted Brough Abingdon. She wanted him to make love to her.

"You are so very perfect for me," she whispered.

He unpinned her hair and sent it tumbling over her shoulders, burying his face in the silky mass. "I've wanted to do that for the longest time," he said huskily. "If you ever wear another lace cap, I'll divorce you."

"So that is the extent of your love?" she laughed pertly. "Well, my lord, I suppose I must throw them all away!"

He lifted his head and drew her closer. "You know I would love you if you had every lace cap in England sitting on your head at one time. You shall always be the most cherished thing in my life."

"And so shall you be in mine."

He took her hand and slipped the shining betrothal ring onto her finger. "It seems that you and Mama wore close to the same size."

"It's beautiful!" She admired the ring and then gazed up at the portrait. "I hate to banish her."

"She would be happy to join the others in the gallery. We'll send Papa to accompany her, and I'll have my portrait done as well. The house will be truly ours then, my darling."

"The house! My goodness, I shall be the mistress of this palace!"

"Indeed," he said, slightly anxiously.

"Well!" She nodded firmly. "I won't let it daunt me."

"I thought you'd come around to the idea."

"Come around? Within a few hours I am already becoming very comfortable and spoiled, but . . ." She looked toward the mantel clock.

He sighed. "We must return to our trio in London."

"They are our responsibility."

"Not for long," Brough grumbled. "I'm planning to take you to Paris for our honeymoon, and there will be no children accompanying us."

"Yes, dear."

"Then the boys will be returning to school, and I'm going to find the perfect husband for Julia."

"It all sounds marvelous, but—"

"No 'buts,' Clarissa."

She smiled, stroking his cheek. "We may have children of our own before we are entirely finished with Julia and Jeremy and Georgie."

He grinned. "I was away from home during much of George's younger life, but I am sure that babies and small children cannot be as great a problem as those three."

Clarissa remembered little Julia and Jeremy romping through the house, fussing with each other and bringing general confusion to Dunstan Hall. Poor Brough did not realize what would be coming his way. He was not the type of man to banish their children to the care of servants. This beautiful house would ring with laughter, squabbles, and running feet. The two of them would have no peace whatsoever; nor would they care. They would be a happy family. She let her head drift once more to his shoulder.

"Yes, dear," she whispered, "I know that everything shall be absolutely perfect!"

Epilogue

"WHAT SHALL YOU wear this morning, my lady?" inquired Ella, Clarissa's new lady's maid.

Clarissa stared uncertainly at her lovely, large wardrobe. There was attire for every occasion, all of it designed and constructed by London's and Paris's most stylish modistes. The morning and afternoon dresses, walking and traveling ensembles, riding habits, ball gowns, and all their accessories nearly filled her entire dressing room. The choice was staggering and had become one of her happiest daily dilemmas.

"My lady?"

"The autumn gold morning dress," she decided, "although there is scarcely any part of the morning left. I must stop sleeping so late."

The maid eyed her knowingly, bringing a flush to Clarissa's cheeks.

"Please let us hurry, Ella. There is much I wish to accomplish today."

A tap sounded on the interconnecting door between her dressing room and the earl's. Brough entered, looking impeccably attired and fully alert. He kissed her forehead as the abigail laid the gown across a chair and discreetly withdrew through the hall passageway.

"Well, madam, you are certainly behind times this morning."

"I wonder why," she countered.

He grinned wickedly. "Did I keep you up too late last night?"

"Really, Brough."

"Should I apologize?"

Clarissa giggled. "No, you should not. Now, if you will allow me a few moments with Ella, I shall dress and—"

"I want to show you something." He took her hand and led her to the window. "We have a visitor this morning."

"A visitor! Oh, I must get dressed immediately!" She broke away. "Whatever will our guest think of me?"

"I believe he has only one thought on his mind." He drew her back. "Look down there."

Below them Julia and Sir Howard Milsom strolled hand in hand down the front lawn. By the tilt of her sister's head, Clarissa could picture the dreamy expression on the young lady's face. The couple reached a stone bench and Sir Howard seated her, then fell to one knee.

"He's proposing!" Clarissa cried.

"Yes." He slipped his arms around her, cradling her against his chest. "He asked my permission to make his addresses. He had already traveled to Jeremy's school to beg his permission, but your brother popped the decision back to me. Did I make the right one?"

"Yes indeed." She watched Julia's slow nod. Sir Howard leaped to his feet and took her in his arms. "He was my favorite choice for her."

"He'll take good care of her."

"He'll spoil her rotten." She laid back her head against his shoulder. "It will be strange to have Julia off my hands."

"I'll be more than glad. Now you'll have some time for me."

She burst into laughter. "How dare you say that when you know that I spend almost every hour of every day with you!"

"But I want every minute. Just think of it! No more Julia. No more boys! We'll have the house to ourselves." He bent his head to kiss her throat.

A movement in the avenue caught her eye. A hired chaise trotted slowly toward the house. Within it were two young gentlemen, their shoulders sagging.

"Brough darling, I wouldn't be too sure of it."

"What?" He followed her gaze. "Jeremy and George! Dammit, not again! This time, I can promise you, they'll receive a good, sound thrashing!"

"Brough ..." She turned to him, slipping her arms around his neck and lifting her lips to be kissed. "Can't we just forget about them for a while?"

"Are you bent on distracting me, Kissy?"

"Exactly so."

"In broad daylight?"

She smiled mischievously. "Do you object?"

He studied her with mock solemnity. "I think not." Holding her closely, he lowered his mouth to hers.